AIN'T MISBEHAVIN'

A Roaring Twenties Novel

———❦———

You're the cat's whiskers!

By Jennifer Lamont Leo

Jennifer Lamont Leo

SMITTEN
HISTORICAL ROMANCE
LIGHTHOUSE PUBLISHING of the CAROLINAS

AIN'T MISBEHAVIN' BY JENNIFER LAMONT LEO
Published by Smitten Historical Romance
an imprint of Lighthouse Publishing of the Carolinas
2333 Barton Oaks Dr., Raleigh, NC 27614

ISBN: 978-1-946016-42-3
Copyright © 2018 by Jennifer Lamont Leo
Cover design by Elaina Lee
Interior design by Karthick Srinivasan

Available in print from your local bookstore, online, or from the publisher at: ShopLPC.com

For more information on this book and the author visit:
http://jenniferlamontleo.com/

All rights reserved. Noncommercial interests may reproduce portions of this book without the express written permission of Lighthouse Publishing of the Carolinas, provided the text does not exceed 500 words. When reproducing text from this book, include the following credit line: *"Ain't Misbehavin'* by Jennifer Lamont Leo published by Lighthouse Publishing of the Carolinas. Used by permission."

Commercial interests: No part of this publication may be reproduced in any form, stored in a retrieval system, or transmitted in any form by any means—electronic, photocopy, recording, or otherwise—without prior written permission of the publisher, except as provided by the United States of America copyright law.

This is a work of fiction. Names, characters, and incidents are all products of the author's imagination or are used for fictional purposes. Any mentioned brand names, places, and trademarks remain the property of their respective owners, bear no association with the author or the publisher, and are used for fictional purposes only.

All scripture quotations, unless otherwise indicated, are taken from the Holy Bible, New International Version®, NIV®. Copyright ©1973, 1978, 1984, 2011 by Biblica, Inc.™. Used by permission of Zondervan. All rights reserved worldwide. www.zondervan.com. "NIV" and "New International Version" are trademarks registered in the United States Patent and Trademark Office by Biblica, Inc.™.

Brought to you by the creative team at Lighthouse Publishing of the Carolinas (LPCBooks.com): Robin Patchen, Pegg Thomas, Eddie Jones, Shonda Savage, Brian Cross, Judah Raine, and Lucie Winborne

Library of Congress Cataloging-in-Publication Data
Leo, Jennifer Lamont
Ain't Misbehavin' / Jennifer Lamont Leo

Printed in the United States of America

More Roaring Twenties books
by Jennifer Lamont Leo

You're the Cream in My Coffee

Praise for *Ain't Misbehavin'*

Opening this follow-up to *You're the Cream in My Coffee* was like returning home after a time away. In *Ain't Misbehavin'* Jennifer Lamont Leo has brought us characters who are at once flawed and endearing. Dot and Charlie's story is one of ups and downs, twists and turns that keep the reader guessing what might be next. While the ending is altogether satisfying I still find myself craving more from this author.

~**Susie Finkbeiner**
Author of *A Cup of Dust, A Trail of Crumbs,* and *A Song of Home*

I always love reading novels that have characters who seem like real people. The characters in *Ain't Misbehavin'* are so much so, you'll find yourself engaging in what they're feeling, and relating to their failures. I enjoyed the ups and downs, twists and turns of this delightful story, as well as the Roaring Twenties setting, so expertly re-created.

~**Jan Cline**
Author of *Emancipated Heart, Finding Christmas and You, The Greatest of These is Love,* and *A Heart Out of Hiding*

Jennifer Lamont Leo's characters, Charlie and Dot, are as flawed and real as they are charming and endearing. *Ain't Misbehavin'* has you rooting for them both as they traverse the changing societal landscape and overcome obstacles in this skillfully crafted story set in the Roaring Twenties. Get ready to be transported to a time with smoky speakeasies and cunning mobsters, where department store customer service is paramount, faith and worship are a part of the daily fabric of country living, and the community pulls together when tragedy strikes. Once you start reading, you won't be able to stop! Rich and beautiful writing, a must-read.

~**April McGowan**
Award-winning author of *Jasmine, Macy,* and *Hold the Light*

Ain't Misbehavin' is an absolute delight; a jazzy romp through 1920s Chicago. Jennifer Lamont Leo draws readers in from the first page with snappy dialogue, intriguing characters, and a heartfelt journey. I can't wait to read more from this author. She's the cat's meow!

~**Karen Barnett**
Award-winning author of *The Road to Paradise*

For Thomas

CHAPTER ONE

Dot Rodgers slid the lacy, peppermint-pink dress over her head and tied the satin sash around her slim hips. She looked at her reflection in the bedroom mirror.

"Ugh!" It would be just the thing if she were attending a holiday hop at her old high school instead of a sophisticated soirée at her friend Veronica's Chicago apartment. But this was New Year's Eve, 1928. At twenty-four, Dot was long past high school.

Charlie would probably like the frothy frock. He'd say she looked sweet.

Which was one of the things she loved about him.

But tonight she wanted to wear something dazzling. Eye-catching and fun. A dress like she used to wear, back before she met Charlie. Tonight, she'd be reintroducing him to all her city friends. He'd met them once, briefly, when he'd come to the cabaret to hear her sing. But that episode had been awkward and uncomfortable, as she'd still been seeing Louie Braccio at the time. Her friends had barely paid attention to Charlie. This time would be different, now that he was her man. And she knew he would grow to love the glamour and excitement of city life, if he'd give it half a chance.

Furthermore, Veronica had mentioned that some members of the Northside Eskimos dance orchestra might be coming to the party. If Dot could meet them and charm her way into an audition, maybe she could stop selling hats and revive her fledgling singing career. She needed to make a good impression.

But she wouldn't impress anyone dressed like Little Nell.

She flung the offending garment onto the pile of discarded clothing strewn across her brass bed. Demure things, all of them, with ribbon and lace. She had only herself to blame. She'd bought every garment over the last couple of months, trying to transform Dot Rodgers into someone she was not. Someone who would make a good wife for an upstanding straight-arrow like Charlie Corrigan.

That was, if he ever popped the question.

If Marjorie had been there, Dot would have given her the pink dress. She would have been delighted to watch her eyes light up. But her friend, roommate, and possible future sister-in-law was several hundred miles away with the rest of the Corrigans, neck-deep in preparations for her Valentine's Day wedding. Trust a romantic soul like Marjorie to choose a wedding day that was already laden with hearts and flowers, not to mention cherubs aiming poison darts at unsuspecting people.

Not that love was poison, exactly. But it did complicate a girl's life.

Hands on hips, Dot surveyed the wreckage. Not one outfit would do. She wanted something spectacular. But also the sort of dress Charlie would approve of. No need to shock the fellow. Not that he ever complained about what she wore. He never complained about anything she did, which was part of the problem. He treated her as if she were some ideal specimen of womanhood.

How very wrong he was.

She loved Charlie, truly she did. But she was tired of clipping her wings. He'd have to understand that this was how things were done in the city. And now it was New Year's Eve, a night to shine if there ever was one.

Frankly, she deserved to have a good time after her disastrous Christmas. She should have known better than to show up unannounced on her family's Indiana doorstep on Christmas Day, bearing new hats for her mother and sisters and a fine fedora for her father. He'd grudgingly let her come in, but now his angry voice still rang in her head.

"You come here with fancy gifts that you bought with dirty money, earned by parading yourself on the stage. You think you can buy your way back into this family? Well, you can't. You're an ungrateful, selfish girl. No decent man will ever want you."

That ringing declaration had come after she'd described how she'd been supporting herself, that in addition to selling hats in a department store, she'd been trying to launch her singing career. She'd described her part-time job singing at a cabaret, described how the place had closed, and how she was sure to get another job singing. She'd wanted to show them—to show *him*—she was making it on her own. She wanted to ease old wounds, forget the past, relate to her father as an adult.

It hadn't worked.

It was partly Charlie's fault, of course. She would never have gone, would never have attempted a reconciliation after all this time, if Charlie hadn't encouraged her. *Make peace with your mother and sisters*, he'd said. *Don't let your father bully you.* Well, *that* had gone well, hadn't it? Maybe all that forgiveness and reconciliation stuff worked well in a picture-perfect family like the Corrigans, but not in the Reverend Oliver Barker household.

She marched to her jam-packed closet and reached to the back for a sparkly silver dress, last worn to a shindig at Louie's Villa Italiana. She slipped it over her head and surveyed herself. Perfect. Metallic beads and silky fringe caught the light with every move she made. From the top drawer of the dresser, she selected a headband encrusted with jet beads and rhinestones and slid it over her smooth dark bangs. She clipped on a pair of ornate chandelier earrings, the cool metal grazing her jawline, and added a long rope of beads, knotting them at the breastbone. A quick swipe of red lip rouge and a sweep of kohl around her eyes, and she was ready just as the buzzer sounded.

Charlie Corrigan stood on the cement porch of the small brick two-story building and reflexively patted the left pocket of his overcoat, a gesture he'd repeatedly performed over the course of the day. Through the thick black wool, his gloved hand could just make out the outline of the tiny square box that held his future. Reassured that the precious diamond ring hadn't fallen out and gotten lost somewhere between Kerryville and Chicago, he straightened his shoulders and adjusted the brim of his fedora. In the crook of his elbow lay a dozen red roses wrapped in green paper. All was ready. Tonight, he was going to ask Miss Dorothy Rodgers to do him the honor of becoming his wife. During the drive, he'd rehearsed his lines and pictured exactly how the moment would go. In an atmosphere of softly crooning clarinets and candlelight, he'd produce the little velvet box, and her dark eyes would grow enormous, and he'd say, "Dot, will you marry me?" and she'd say—

Buzzzz!

The alarming rasp and click of the door's lock startled him. He pulled open the heavy, glass-paneled portal and crossed the tiled floor of the slightly musty-smelling vestibule just as the door to the first-floor apartment cracked open. A woman's face peered out.

"Oh, Charlie, it's you." The door opened wider to reveal a sixtyish woman wrapped in a blue chenille bathrobe and wearing scuffed slippers. Her iron-gray hair was curled in soft white rags all over her head, and she wore a gleeful grin on her broad face. "I thought I heard someone come in."

With strained patience, Charlie stopped and touched the brim of his hat. "Just me, Mrs. Moran, and a happy New Year to you."

No army sentinel kept a closer watch on his post than the landlady did on the comings and goings from her building. On previous visits, Charlie had found out how nearly impossible it was to make it from the front door to the staircase unobserved. Which was probably a good thing, he reflected, if inconvenient at times. Chicago wasn't a safe and peaceful place like Kerryville. With only ladies living in the two-flat, the landlady downstairs and Dot and Marjorie upstairs, they couldn't be too cautious about opening the door to strangers.

"The same to you, young man." The landlady's grin turned girlish as she patted her rag-rolled head. "I must look a fright."

"Look at you, getting all dolled up for a date," he teased. "Who's the lucky fellow?"

"Oh, go on with you." Mrs. Moran scoffed, but her green eyes twinkled. "I'll be having a date with that handsome young bandleader, Guy Lombardo. Did you know he's doing a special New Year's Eve broadcast on the wireless?"

"You don't say." Charlie shifted his weight and glanced toward the staircase. For a brief, awkward moment, he feared she was going to invite him in to listen with her. On impulse, he drew a rose from the bunch in his arm and handed it to the woman. "For you. You can't meet a man like Mr. Lombardo without a corsage."

She took the bloom and lifted it to her nose, her face beaming as she sniffed deeply. "Why, Charlie Corrigan, aren't you a charmer. You're so much nicer than that fella she used to go with, with his flashy suits and jeweled stickpins. Used to drive up here in his fancy automobile and bring her costly presents—earrings and what have you. But he didn't treat her very nice, if you ask me." She leaned in close and lowered her voice, even though they were the only two in the vestibule. "They said he owned an Italian restaurant, but you don't make that kind of money from spaghetti, if you know what I mean."

Charlie did know. "Is that so? Well, I need to be going …" The last thing he felt like doing was discussing Dot's wealthy former beau, who had indeed owned a restaurant that fronted a speakeasy. And now the man was locked up in jail. She was well rid of the crumb. But all at once, Charlie felt tinges of doubt shadow the edges of his mind. What would she think of the ring in his coat pocket if she was used to expensive baubles? His family's dry-goods store was doing well these days, but he didn't have a bootlegger's budget to spend on jewelry.

"Now go on, shoo." Mrs. Moran waved the flower as if he were the one detaining them both. "You young people enjoy yourselves tonight."

"Thank you. We will."

As the landlady retreated and closed her door, he took the carpeted stairs, bounding up them two at a time in his heart but constrained to a dignified pace by his bum leg, a souvenir from his scrape with the Kaiser's army.

All he had to do now was talk his girl out of this crazy party she'd mentioned. The last thing he wanted was to share tonight with anyone else but her.

Dot swung open the door to her apartment before he could knock, and he stood dazzled by glints of silver dancing off her dress like a thousand shooting stars. For a moment, he couldn't speak.

How did an ordinary fellow like him end up with an extraordinary creature like her?

"Well," she said with a smile. "Aren't you going to come in?"

He cleared his throat.

This was going to be one heck of a night.

CHAPTER TWO

Dot's heart fluttered as Charlie stepped over the threshold looking uncharacteristically dapper in evening clothes and a charcoal-gray Chesterfield that she hadn't seen before. He cast a slow, appreciative glance at her and gave a long, low whistle.

"You look like a million bucks."

"Do I?" She'd half expected him to think the sparkly, low-cut dress was too outrageous, but his expression clearly said otherwise. "So do you. New duds?"

Embarrassment reddened his angular cheekbones, and he shrugged, but she could tell he was pleased. "Peter clued me in to some bargains at Field's."

"You mean to tell me you two came to Marshall Field's, and you didn't pay me a visit?" She placed her hands on her hips in mock offense, secretly pleased that he'd finally purchased some up-to-date apparel. She'd make a city boy out of him yet.

He coughed. "I believe you were in Indiana at the time."

"Oh." A brief bubble of tension rose between them, then burst. They'd have to talk about Indiana sooner or later, but now was not the time. "Well, anyway, you look mighty spiffy."

"Thanks. Needless to say, that's some dress." He ran a hand over his sandy-brown hair, center-parted and smoothed to patent-leather perfection.

"These roses are lovely. I'll go find a vase."

He followed her into the cramped kitchen. "There are only eleven," he confessed. "I gave one to Mrs. Moran."

Dot laughed as she set the bouquet on the small oilcloth-covered table. "On sentry duty, was she?" She tilted her head and smiled at him. "That was awfully sweet of you."

She pulled a vase from a cabinet, filled it with water from the tap, then carefully slid the roses from the green paper and arranged them with deft fingers.

When she'd finished, he took a step forward, drew her in his arms, and kissed her soundly. "Happy New Year to you, a few hours early."

Her heart raced as she returned his kiss. She breathed in the clean, soapy scent of Burma-Shave—a new product he'd received for Christmas from his stepmother. Dot liked it. It made him seem modern and sophisticated and not like an old granddad stuck in his bay-rum ways. He was still not quite thirty years old, after all, even if he often acted older.

"Say," he said, holding her close, his breath hot against her hair. "What do you say we skip this shindig and have a quiet supper, just the two of us? I made us a reservation at the Blackhawk for ten thirty. We can ring in the New Year in peace."

"The Blackhawk." She sighed, pulling back slightly to look at his face. "Oh, I love that place. Although I doubt that any spot will be peaceful on New Year's Eve." She jutted out her lower lip. "But I promised Veronica we'd put in an appearance at her party. I so rarely see the old gang, now that the Villa Italiana's been shut down." She ran a finger along his lapel. "Besides, they're all eager to meet the man who's stolen my heart."

His back stiffened, and he pulled away slightly. "Speaking of stealing, I'm surprised you still want to see the 'old gang,' as you call them. Especially since some of them have been in hot water lately—like, say, jail. Haven't they caused enough trouble for you?"

She cringed at the mention of jail, where at that moment her former boyfriend, Louie Braccio, sat serving time for trafficking in booze. He'd gotten away with a hand-slap for running a popular speakeasy in the basement of the Villa Italiana, thanks to regular payoffs to crooked law enforcement, persuaded by hush-hush gifts of cash and fine Canadian whiskey to look the other way as they strolled their beat. But he wasn't able to escape jail for the more serious crime of running a citywide liquor-trafficking ring. This time, he'd gone too far. Too much dough and too many people were involved. Charlie knew all about it. After all, it had been his sister Marjorie who'd innocently stumbled upon the clue that broke open the case. But just because Louie turned out to be a bad egg didn't mean that *everyone* who'd frequented the Villa Italiana was a criminal.

She lifted her chin. "I know they're not perfect, Charlie, but they're still my friends. And Veronica in particular. Why, she was one of the very first people I met when I came to the city. She took me under her wing and let me sleep on her sofa for several weeks until I got myself established. I owe her a lot. It's the least we can do to show up at her little party."

His jaw tensed and released. "If you say so."

"I know you don't agree with their—with the way they live their lives. But I'm sure you'll like them, once you get to know them. You'll see." She gave him a beseeching glance through her dark lashes. "We'll just stop in for a little while and say hello. It'll be more fun than a barrel of monkeys. And we'll leave in plenty of time to make the reservation. I promise."

Charlie lifted his hands in surrender. "I don't see the appeal, but if it means that much to you …"

She slipped her arms around his neck. "Oh, thank you. You're the bee's knees, you know that?" He kissed her again, then broke it off with a sigh.

"We'd better stop this now, or we'll never get there at all," he said. "Let's hit the road. Where's your coat?"

Dot retrieved her rabbit-fur-collared coat from the rack, and he helped her settle it around her narrow shoulders. He glanced at her feet. "Can you manage to walk in the snow with those fancy shoes? Shouldn't you be wearing boots?"

She lifted one dainty silver dancing pump and smiled. "Oh, Charlie," she said in mock exasperation as if a man couldn't possibly be expected to understand, "I'm not going to throw off my entire ensemble by wearing clunky boots. I'll be fine walking to and from the car." She winked at him. "And if I'm not, you'll just have to carry me."

She locked the door to the apartment. In the landing, he offered her his arm, and she slipped her hand around his biceps and held on while they walked down the slippery front steps and the sidewalk to where Betty, his old black jalopy, sat parked by the curb.

Always the gentleman, Charlie opened the car door, helped Dot get settled onto the passenger seat, and tucked a wool plaid lap robe around her knees. Then he moved around to the front of the vehicle, bent down, and gave the lever several good hearty cranks. The engine immediately sparked to life, still warm from the long drive from Kerryville. As he maneuvered the elderly Model T through snowy streets, Dot marveled, as she often did, at his remarkable ability to operate the machine despite his crippled leg and arm, injuries he'd sustained in the Great War. He'd modified the gear shift and the pedals so he could operate them with his stronger arm and leg. He was quite mechanically inclined, whereas she had never even driven an automobile. Perhaps he would give her driving lessons when the weather improved.

He interrupted her thoughts. "Honey? I need you to give me directions." He peered intently through the windshield.

"Oh, sorry. Go straight ahead for about three blocks."

He shifted gears. "Remind me which one is Veronica. The platinum blonde?"

"No, no, you're thinking of Charlotte. Veronica is the one with the short dark hair and the mole on her upper lip. Turn left at the next corner."

"Oh, yeah. The smoker." He extended his arm out the open window, signaled as best he could with his limited mobility, and navigated the turn.

Dot laughed. "They're all smokers."

"I know, but the dark-haired one never seems to let the cigarette leave her mouth, except to down a shot of liquor. She talks around it and everything. It's amazing to watch."

"I see." Dot teased. "Is that why you couldn't keep your eyes off her that night at the Villa Italiana? Don't think I didn't notice."

Charlie smirked. "Yeah, I guess so. It's like some crazy parlor trick. I don't know how she does it." He glanced sideways at Dot. "What's her story?"

"Story?" Dot snuggled more deeply under the wool blanket. "I don't know that much about her, really. She's single, works in the candy department at Field's. Used to be a waitress, I think. Goes out with Carlo Brunetti, off and on. Turn right at the stop sign."

When at last they reached Veronica's brown brick three-flat—practically a duplicate of Dot's, only with three stories instead of two—Charlie had to hunt for a parking space. At last he found one and wedged the battered black Ford between a showroom-new Nash coupe and a Model A that looked tricked out with all the latest gizmos. He cut the engine and turned to Dot, lacing his gloved fingers through hers.

"Honey, before we go inside, I just wanted to say how sorry I am that things went sour in Indiana. You sounded pretty upset on the telephone yesterday. Do you want to talk about it?"

"There isn't much to say." Dot looked down at the plaid lap blanket and toyed with a bit of fringe. "It was awful. He treated me like a pariah. Said he was ashamed of me for moving to Chicago on my own and singing in a speakeasy."

"He's a monster."

She shrugged. "The Reverend Oliver Barker is an ogre, and that's that. I don't know why I thought things might turn out differently this time." She glanced at Charlie. He shouldn't have expected anything out of her father after witnessing the so-called healing service a few months before. He'd seen firsthand the way Oliver had separated good people from their money by making false claims and empty promises. But Charlie was like that, always believing the best in people.

She wouldn't bring up the memory. Charlie'd hoped the renowned preacher would heal his war wounds and make him a healthy man. Instead, he'd reaped only disappointment.

"He's a charlatan all right," Charlie said, "but it's not him I'm worried about. It's you. You're carrying so much resentment. If you could just reconcile with your mother and sisters ..."

She pinched the bridge of her nose. "Believe me, I tried. I lurked in the alley like a stray cat until my mother came out to empty the ashcan." She fought to control the tremble in her voice. "We spoke hurriedly for a few minutes, and she gave me a hug, but she kept looking over her shoulder. She advised me to steer clear, to stay in the city and not try to come home again."

Charlie's eyes filled with sympathy. "Poor kid."

"But she did promise to write me letters, even if she has to do it on the sly. I tried to talk her into leaving him and moving here to Chicago with the girls. My place would be awfully crowded with that many people, but Marjorie will be moving out as soon as she and Peter are married. We could make it work. Maybe even get a bigger place, eventually."

"Sure you could." Charlie spoke calmly, but his mind whirled. When he'd decided to ask Dot to marry him, the prospect of sharing their home with a mother and two younger sisters hadn't been part of the equation. But if that's what Dot wanted, he'd figure out a way to make it work.

"But Mother wouldn't listen to me," Dot continued. "She's determined to honor her marriage vows, even if he tramples all over them." She swept the plaid blanket from her lap and folded it. "Anyway, soon we'll be celebrating a brand-new year. A clean start. And I don't intend to spoil it by thinking or talking about the illustrious Reverend Barker any more than I have to."

He sat up straighter and leaned forward. "But, see, I still think that if you'd just—"

"Charlie." She laid a gentle hand on his arm. "It's time for you to stop trying to fix things between my family and me. End of discussion."

He pressed his lips into a line. "Sounds like a nice way of telling me to butt out."

She leaned over and kissed his cheek, then rubbed off a tiny smudge of crimson lip rouge with her gloved finger. "I appreciate that you care about me."

"That I do." Charlie exhaled and glanced toward the apartment building. She followed his gaze. The top floor was aglow with light, and the animated shapes silhouetted against the golden window shades indicated a room crowded with revelers. "One last time—is your heart truly set on going to this party? Are you sure you wouldn't rather enjoy a quiet dinner, just the two of us?"

"Sure, I'm sure!" Dot pulled a compact from her purse and checked her makeup in the glow of a streetlamp. "Listen. Doesn't the music sound divine?"

"Divine." Setting his jaw, Charlie opened the car door. "Come on, then, let's get it over with."

CHAPTER THREE

With Charlie's arm around Dot's back, he steadied her as they made their way up the icy sidewalk. He glanced back at Betty, where she sat looking stodgy and forlorn among the stylish roadsters and sedans. He would like to have chauffeured Dot to the party in style. a glitzy girl like her deserved to be squired around in a classy car. If he had one, maybe Charlie wouldn't have felt so out of place among her glamorous crowd. The prospect of a new automobile cheered him up, at least momentarily. Business at Corrigan's Dry Goods and Sundries had been brisk for many months now. The Christmas season had been especially lucrative. On the advice of several men he trusted in the Kerryville Chamber of Commerce (with the notable exception of his own father), he'd invested considerable cash into the stock market, and his investments were paying off. Yes, he decided happily, he could afford a roadster. Maybe it was time to retire old Betty and purchase a sleek new car that would impress his girl, soon to be his fiancée.

But his cheerful demeanor dissolved when they reached the door. Every inch of the apartment was jam-packed with revelers. The women wore glittery gowns, fringe and beading—shimmer galore. They'd rimmed their eyes with kohl and painted their lips red with rouge. The men sported dinner jackets and bow ties and brogues, their hair slicked back with macassar oil. Loud jazz music poured from a Victrola. The air was thick with cigarette smoke coming from both women and men—a phenomenon one simply didn't see in Kerryville. People were practically yelling to be heard over the music. As Charlie and Dot wedged themselves into the crowded, overheated living room, Dot was almost immediately swept up in the revelry.

"Dottie, darling. How lovely to see you! I was afraid you wouldn't make it." Veronica slinked up wearing a skintight black dress covered with hot-pink sequins in swirling patterns that made Charlie dizzy. Her black hair was plastered to her head in a shingle bob with thin, fishhook curls pressed against each rouged cheek. She lifted the cigarette holder from her lips just long enough to give Dot a quick kiss on the cheek.

"Can't stay but a few minutes," Dot said in a voice filled with apology. "We have dinner reservations."

"Whatever for?" Veronica scoffed. "We've got plenty of eats. Charlotte practically cleared out her family's delicatessen and brought over the most divine stuff." She glanced at Charlie. Her sooty eyes gave him a cold, appraising look. "Oh, hello. Coats go in the bedroom."

Her cool greeting did nothing to ease his awkwardness. He took Dot's coat as well as his own to the bedroom but felt uneasy about leaving it there—a brand-new coat with a diamond ring hidden in the breast pocket. He didn't trust these people as far as he could throw, which, given his gimpy pitching arm, wasn't far. But he couldn't exactly stand there all evening with his coat slung over his arm as if waiting for a train. Besides, he and his girl wouldn't be staying long. At last, he placed both coats under a pile of wraps on the bed and vowed to keep an eye on the door.

A balding man with a prominent stomach and blustering demeanor sidled up to Dot. Charlie vaguely remembered his name was Spike. Or Spud. Or something equally juvenile.

"There you are, baby," the man drawled. "We were wondering when you'd get here. Come on and dance with me." To Charlie he said, "You don't mind, do you, pal?"

"Of course not," he lied, minding very much. Where did he get off calling her baby? But to Dot he said, "Go on and have a good time."

"Are you sure?"

"No reason you can't dance just because I can't."

She kissed his cheek and moved off with the portly fellow. Charlie sighed and looked around. Good manners dictated that he circulate, hobnob, shoot the breeze. Mingling wasn't in Charlie's nature. He much preferred a good conversation in the company of a few close friends. But he steeled himself and turned to a fellow standing nearby.

"Nice party," he ventured.

The man turned to him slowly. His glassy, red-rimmed gaze told Charlie that the cigarette he was smoking contained something other than tobacco.

"Ain't we got fun," the man drawled in a bored monotone.

The rest of his attempts at conversation convinced Charlie to give it up. He ate too many soda crackers and slices of prosciutto and sipped ginger ale from a teacup.

"Sure you don't want some gin in that, fella?" said the man tending bar, which was set into a recess in the wall. Charlie noted how a large painting—one of those nonsensical modern canvases covered in meaningless squiggles and shapes—sat to one side of the bottle-laden alcove and could easily slide in front of it, concealing it from view, should the police raid the party. Charlie had to admit it was a clever set-up, if disturbing. All the guests drank from teacups, as if that would keep the cops from knowing that the booze flowed freely. As if they couldn't smell it on everyone's breath. Charlie could smell it, and it made him long for something stronger than ginger ale. Something to take the edge off.

"No, thanks," he said to the bartender. "I'm laying off the stuff."

"You poor fish," the bartender muttered.

Charlie moved as far away as he could get from the bar.

In spite of his sour mood, his foot tapped in time to the music. He remembered dancing. Foxtrot, turkey trot—all those crazy dances his sister Marjorie had taught him, shuffling around the front parlor to scratchy records on the Victrola. He'd been pretty good at it, too. Could have given Vernon Castle a run for his money until a round of shrapnel in his knee had put an end to his dancing days.

He wanted nothing more than to get away from this overheated room and these silly painted half-drunken former comrades of Dot's with their jangling bracelets and beads. Where'd they get the dough to buy all that jewelry, anyway, and those fancy cars parked out front? From what Dot had told him, these were ordinary working-class people—factory workers, store clerks, waiters—hardly titans of industry. Perhaps they'd invested wisely in the stock market, as he had. From the looks of it, though, they made their money in less savory ways.

He stuck himself off in a corner, clutching his cup of ginger ale and finding the whole thing dreadful. He watched the partygoers as they flocked in and out, greeting each other boisterously, noisily. The women especially seemed coarse, brazen, and hard under their outward glamour. For all the supposed optimism of a brand-new year, the women here seemed as if they'd lost joy. Charlie sensed their deep unhappiness in their hollow laughter and cheap jokes. He thought wistfully of his friends in Kerryville, who were probably at that moment enjoying a rousing game of charades and a hearty country-style spread that filled a man's belly. Dot would enjoy that kind of wholesome small-town social life. Wouldn't she?

The music blared and made his ears ring, and the laughter rang false. He checked his watch. They'd have to leave soon if they wanted to make it to dinner on time, but he had trouble finding Dot in a crowd. Finally he saw her standing on the back porch talking to some man Charlie didn't know. He wished she weren't standing so close to him, looking at him as if he were the most fascinating person alive.

She used to look at you that way, whispered an inner voice, the voice that taunted him late at night. *When you first met, how you talked about your job at the dry goods store and your overhaul of the inventory system, she hung on your every word. Just like she is with that other fellow now.*

He was on the verge of storming out there, grabbing her arm, and pulling her back inside. But that inner voice stopped him.

Face it, pal, it said with a cruel mocking snarl. *If she wanted to be stuck inside with you, she would be.*

On the optimistically named back porch—a rattletrap wooden platform with rickety stairs leading to the frozen backyard far below—Dot shivered in the freezing night air and listened to Duke Palmer rattle on about some injustice that had been done to him at the shoe factory where he worked. At first she'd been grateful to step out of the crowded party for a breath of fresh, cold air, but Duke had followed her as if tied on a leash. It seemed like he always had some grievance against somebody or something and usually found a willing ear in Dot. Well, she wasn't so willing now, but it was hard to break away. Even so, she needed to find Charlie. Surely it was nearly time to leave for the restaurant. Maybe he'd been right. It had been a mistake to come to this party.

But it wasn't her fault that he wasn't having fun, she thought ruefully. Early in the evening, she'd attempted to introduce him to a number of people, but she'd had trouble making herself heard over the din. Finally she'd given up and decided to let him fend for himself. He could introduce himself and make conversation with people if he wanted to.

The screen door between the kitchen and the back porch swung open, and a blonde woman dressed in jet-black fringe leaned out.

"Dottie," Charlotte shouted, "come on and sing for us. The gang's waiting."

"Yeah, come on," said another standing behind her.

Dot seized the opportunity to leave the freezing porch and Duke's endless tale of injustice.

"Excuse me." She scurried into the warm kitchen.

Charlie intercepted her and murmured. "Think you'll be ready to leave soon?"

"They're asking me to sing," she said, gazing up into his eyes. "Just a song or two, for old times' sake."

Surely he'd understand the delay. He'd often said how much he loved to hear her sing.

His expression shifted into what she chose to interpret as a smile.

Charlotte grabbed her arm and dragged her through the crowded dining room and to a spinet piano that stood in a corner of the front room. Someone else shut off the Victrola. A good-looking, dark-haired man sat on the piano bench. He looked vaguely familiar. Dot thought she may have seen him once or twice at the Villa Italiana.

"Say, aren't you Louie Braccio's girl?" he said with a grin. His teeth glowed remarkably white against his olive skin.

Dot's palms grew clammy. Any mention of Louie's name invariably brought on a cascade of emotions. She'd been a number of things to Louie Braccio—his employee, his protégée, the object of his flirtation when he didn't have something more interesting going on. But not his girl. He'd mesmerized her with kohl-black eyes, kept her on the hook, never quite reeling her in, dangling romance like a lure then snatching it away. Cool, hot, cool. She'd swallowed the bait, thought she adored him, but now realized that what she'd felt for Louie wasn't love. Gratitude, maybe, at being given a job and a microphone. Relief at not wandering the streets. But not love. And now her mentor was serving six months for his involvement with a liquor-smuggling ring. Dot pretended she hadn't heard the man's question. Instead, she extended her hand and said, "Dot Rodgers."

"Eddie Valencio. Shame about what happened to the Villa Italiana. My band played there a few times. The Northside Eskimos."

The Eskimos! Dot's insides did a flip. All thoughts about finding Charlie and going to dinner slipped from her mind as Eddie grasped her hand. She'd forgotten Veronica's mentioning they might be here.

The Northside Eskimos were local musical royalty, playing warm-up sets for more famous acts as well as their own bookings. Any singer worth her torch would covet a chance to sing with the Eskimos. And she was getting to do so—well, with one of them—right here in Veronica's front room.

If he liked the way she sang, he might recommend her to the other band members for a steady gig. Her internal butterflies turned to bat wings. "How about 'That Old Gang of Mine?'" Eddie suggested. He turned to the piano and let his practiced fingers run swiftly up and down the keys.

"Oh. Oh, yeah. Sure." She cleared her throat.

He played the opening chords, and Dot sang the first line, with its poignant lyrics about old friends drifting apart. As she sang, partygoers gathered to listen. She glanced around the crowd. There were Veronica, Charlotte, Bobby, even Duke. *That old gang of mine.* Warmth and goodwill swirled through her chest. These were her friends, the people who had supported her youthful dream of making it in the city, of becoming a professional singer. When the song ended, everyone clapped. She and Eddie immediately swung into more upbeat numbers: "You're the Cream in My Coffee," and then "Ain't Misbehavin'" and "Yes, We Have No Bananas" and "Black Bottom," and several other numbers. Singing them gave her the same soaring, electrified feeling as she'd felt on a good night at the Villa Italiana, and she was having a blast.

Eddie must have been reading her mind. "It amazes me that we've never performed together at Louie's place," he said during a break. "I'm sure I would have remembered."

Charlie watched Dot sing, her voice flowing like caramel syrup over the crowd. Jazz wasn't really his kind of music—he was more of a gospel fan—but, boy, she could sure croon a tune. In spite of his black mood, he loved to hear her sing, as did many others, judging by the way they hushed and turned their lacquered heads toward the piano. He'd probably spark a riot if he went up there now and dragged her away. Besides, she looked so happy, her face aglow. He couldn't bring himself to make her stop. The hour of their dinner reservations came and went. He'd lost his appetite, anyway. He decided that the diamond ring would have to stay in his coat pocket until another opportunity presented itself. If it ever did.

She not only sounded sensational, she looked it, too. She was a peach, for sure. Her silver dress glittered in the lamplight, and long delicate earrings sparkled and swung as she moved her head. A burning sensation kindled in his chest. Had Louie given her those earrings?

His stomach roiled. Who was that piano guy? Was he flirting with her? Worse, was she flirting with him? Any fellow who looked at her like that was surely up to no good.

He threaded through the crowd to the bar, slid his cup to the bartender, and through gritted teeth said, "Fill 'er up with gin ... ger ale."

———

Between songs, Dot took a sip of water to moisten her throat. "Gosh, the Eskimos must meet a lot of famous people when they come to town."

Eddie nodded. "We opened last weekend for Bix Beiderbecke."

She gave a little gasp. "You know Bix Beiderbecke? He's a legend."

He grinned. "Sure, I know him. Say, maybe you and I could go listen sometime. I could introduce you."

She caught her breath. "No kidding?"

Eddie laughed. "Why would I lie?" His black eyes locked on hers. "Say, kid, the Eskimos are thinking about taking on a girl singer. You've got a strong set of pipes. You oughtta think about auditioning."

Her heart sang. "Do you really think so?" She hardly dared hope for such an opportunity. Was he just flattering her?

"Let me know where to get a hold of you, and I'll set something up." He ran his hands over the keys, playing a popular melody. "Unless you got some other deal going, something with Louie when he gets out of the slammer. You think he'll open another place?"

Dot shuddered. "I have no idea. But we definitely don't have any sort of deal."

Eddie glanced up at her. "You're not seein' him anymore?"

"No."

"I see." His dark gaze flitted across the room. "If you don't mind my sayin' so, he doesn't seem like your type, either."

"Louie?"

Eddie jerked his head. "That fellow over there in the corner, the one lookin' like he's waitin' for a bus. Figured he was with you."

Dot looked over to where Charlie stood holding his teacup, looking miserable, and her focus hitched on the clock behind him. Her hand flew to her cheek. A wave of remorse crashed through her. "Oh, no! I completely forgot. How could I ..."

Eddie had turned his attention back to the keyboard. "What do you say we do 'Honeysuckle Rose'?"

She grabbed the beaded evening bag she'd set on top of the piano. "I'm sorry. I have to leave now."

"Wait." Eddie lifted his voice. "Your telephone number."

Flustered, Dot called over her shoulder, "Ask Veronica." She shoved through the crowd to where Charlie stood. "I'm so, so sorry. I got caught up and lost track of time."

"We missed dinner," he said in a tight voice.

She tugged on his arm. "Come on, let's go. If we hurry, maybe we can still …"

"Did you hear me? Forget it. Our reservation came and went an hour ago."

"Why didn't you remind me?"

A muscle worked in his jaw. "I didn't want to spoil your fun."

She blinked away the moisture that threatened. How could she have been so thoughtless?

"You said we'd only stay a little while." Accusation colored his tone.

"I know, but … The music, and … You see, he's an Eskimo, and …" She heard herself rambling and started over. "Eddie's with the Northside Eskimos, and he thinks he can get me an audition. I'd be able to sing again, and with a real band, not just in a speakeasy. Wouldn't that be swell?"

"Swell," he said without inflection.

"Oh, Charlie, I *am* sorry."

"It's all right. Don't worry about it." But his flat voice and the way he avoided looking her in the eye said otherwise.

She closed her mouth, not knowing what to say. A mix of emotions tumbled through her heart. He was right. She should have let him talk her into skipping the party. Except, why shouldn't she have some fun? These people were her friends. More than that, they were her family. She felt more at home here than she ever had under the good reverend's roof. Was it so awful to want to spend New Year's with the people who made her feel loved? Why couldn't Charlie at least try to get to know them instead of standing in the corner like judge and jury? What did he know about them, anyway? At least they weren't the nosy biddies in Kerryville, those holier-than-thou women so bent on criticizing her every move. Here, Dot felt accepted and loved. But Charlie wouldn't even try. He'd already made up his mind.

Words stuck in Charlie's throat. She had every right to want to be with the people she loved. And now here she was, at his side, moist-eyed and remorseful. He longed to take her in his arms, tell her it was all right, but, somehow, he couldn't make himself move. He might break down if he so much as touched her. And he couldn't—wouldn't—risk doing that in this place, among all these cold-hearted strangers who already thought he was all wet.

"Hey, everybody, it's almost midnight!" someone called out.

Eddie brought the song to a flourishing close. Dot reached up to Charlie's temple and smoothed an unruly lock of his hair back into place.

"Don't be angry," she coaxed. "After all, it was just dinner."

"Here comes the countdown!" came a cry. In unison, the crowd counted down until everyone yelled, "Happy New Year!"

At the stroke of midnight, Charlie pulled himself together, drew Dot into his arms, and kissed her. Even though she returned his kiss, something had shifted between them. Something precious and irretrievable had somehow been lost, and he didn't know how to get it back. He was just a small-town shopkeeper and a half-crippled one at that. She was a butterfly, silky and brilliant, soaring far above him. Who was he to think he could pin her down to the kind of life he could offer?

"'Auld Lang Syne,'" someone called out, and again Dot was propelled back to the piano.

"Sorry," she mouthed to Charlie over her shoulder as Veronica pulled her away. Just one more song, she told herself, and she'd return to his side.

She took a sip from the cup she'd left sitting on the piano lid. Sometime during the evening, her ice water had gotten switched out with champagne. Not that she minded. The sparkling liquid relaxed her tight nerves. She didn't drink much liquor anymore, for Charlie's sake. But he was way over there, sulking. And it was New Year's Eve. One little glass wouldn't hurt. Or maybe it had been two little glasses. She hadn't been paying attention. In any case, the liquid felt bubbly and cool in her throat. She signaled to Eddie. He sounded the opening chords of

"Auld Lang Syne," and she sang the familiar tune about old friends.

Between the effect of the champagne and the sentimental song and Charlie's chilly response to her apology, tears pricked her eyelids. Her voice warbled a little around the lump in her throat. How she loved these people! They may have been kooky lunatics, but they were *her* kooky lunatics. How dare Charlie look down on them? By looking down on them, he was looking down on her.

How had she ever believed she could make their romance work?

As the last note faded, she watched Charlie snake his way through the crowd to her.

"Time to go." His voice was low but firm.

"Now?" She wanted to go on singing … singing so she didn't have to feel anything other than the music. What was the point of leaving now, anyway? They'd blown dinner; they might as well enjoy the rest of the party.

"Now." His voice crackled with exasperation. "We've rung in the New Year. What do you want to do, stay here all night?"

She felt her patience slip a bit. "If you'd relax a little and talk to a few people, maybe you'd start having some fun in spite of yourself."

"Nobody here worth talking to. And what's the deal with that guy?" He cast a sidelong glance toward Eddie.

Her patience slid another few notches. She set her chin. "I told you, he's going to let me audition. Don't be an old stick in the mud."

His voice deepened like distant thunder. "Maybe it's better if I just leave. You can find your own way home."

"Fine," Dot spat the word as her last drop of patience splattered on the floor. "Eddie will see me home. Won't you, Eddie?"

Charlie flinched as though she'd struck him. The room rocked like she was seasick. *What am I saying? No! I don't want to be with Eddie. Don't leave!* But her mouth refused to form the words.

Eddie's face lit up as if he'd just won a longshot bet at the racetrack. "Yeah, sure, baby. I'll make sure you get home safe."

The flush on Charlie's face deepened from pink to red. He started to say something, then turned on his heel and disappeared into the bedroom. A moment later, overcoat slung over his arm, he stormed out of the apartment. Dot watched in disbelief as the door slammed behind him. Every cell in her being wanted to run after him. But something she couldn't name kept her feet frozen to the floor. Fastening on a bright, misery-masking smile, she turned to Eddie, who had begun reeling out some yarn about a close encounter with some famous musician. She only half listened. *Where is Charlie going? Will he come back?* She kept glancing at the door, willing it to crack open, willing everything to be all right.

"Get a load of this," Eddie was saying. "So I says to him, I says, pick up the tempo, see? And he hits the gas and, man, we're gone."

The small cluster gathered around him burst into laughter. Mechanically, Dot joined in, even though the story suddenly seemed pointless, the laughter brittle, the camaraderie as fake as the rhinestones on her headband. Why had she forced Charlie to bring her to this place?

"Oh, Eddie, that's the funniest story I've heard in ages." She choked back a hysterical sob. "Why, look at me. I'm laughing so hard, it's making me cry."

If Charlie really loved her, he wouldn't have left. He would have stayed, would have seen her safely home. He would have understood how important an audition would be to her singing career. And if he truly thought Eddie was flirting with her, he would have fought for her.

If he thought she was worth fighting for.

Her worst fear had come true. A cold realization settled over her.

Everything her father said about her was true. *No decent man.*

A fellow like Charlie would never truly love a girl like her.

Charlie stomped down the stairs as quickly as his pathetic leg would allow and burst out the front door of the apartment building. He slammed it so hard that the glass rattled in the frame. Freezing air slapped him in the face. He paused to catch his breath. A light snow fell. From far down the block, firecrackers sizzled and snapped as revelers continued to welcome 1929.

He was an idiot. What was he doing? He must be loony to leave Dot at the party like this. He couldn't just walk out on her. For a long moment, his stubborn pride kept him rooted in place. He glanced at shabby old Betty, waiting patiently at the curb. He could crank her up and speed away to someplace, anyplace, where he didn't feel like a farm truck among race cars, and never look back.

Then, slowly, he turned and started back up the stairs. They'd have to work this out like adults. If they were going to be married, they'd have to learn how to argue.

Married. Seemed pretty doubtful right now.

He slowed his ascent, giving himself time to collect his thoughts, preparing what he'd say to her, trying to find words that weren't overly conciliatory and yet expressed what he felt for her in his heart. The heart that was now hammering out of fear that he'd already lost her.

At the top of the stairs, he paused for breath, then placed his hand on the doorknob. Dot's lilting laugh carried through the wood.

"Oh, Eddie, that's the funniest story I've heard in ages!"

He could picture her touching Eddie lightly on the arm, the way she had touched Charlie the night they met. In his mind's eye, he saw her brilliant smile, the dimple in her cheek appearing and disappearing as she spoke.

She'd be all right. Eddie would see to that. And if not Eddie, then some other fellow who could dance and drink and keep up with her, who could match her, wit for sparkling wit.

He turned and trudged back down the stairs and out into the frigid black night.

CHAPTER FOUR

Dot had just finished serving a customer when Marjorie walked into the millinery department of Marshall Field and Company.

"Ready to go, Dot?" Marjorie brushed off a bit of sawdust clinging to her dark blue sleeve, a remnant of her work on the display-building team. "I've spent all afternoon constructing characters for the Tall Tales exhibit in the children's section. You have no idea how much trouble Paul Bunyan has been giving me."

"Yes, but he has such nice biceps," Dot said. "Give me half a sec." She jotted a note in her sales book, then opened a drawer and exchanged the sales book for a handbag. "Okay, let's vamoose."

"Shouldn't you let Mrs. Blandings know you're leaving?"

"I already did. She's in a good mood today and didn't hassle me about leaving early." Dot looped her arm through Marjorie's. "Shall we go upstairs and bag ourselves a bridesmaid dress?"

Dot sounded more eager than she felt, half-dreading whatever frothy pastel concoction Marjorie might have dreamed up. But her friend surprised her as they rode the elevator.

"You'll just love the one I've found," Marjorie gushed. "It's gorgeous, a holly berry–red velvet left over from the Christmas season. I've been waiting for it to go on sale forever, and at last it has. Half price!"

"Red is a pretty daring color scheme to choose for a wedding. I approve. But are you sure Kerryville's ready for that?" The prospect of a red dress cheered her up considerably.

Marjorie laughed. "Why not? It will be Valentine's Day, after all."

"Ah, yes. Red's the perfect choice then."

But when, at Marjorie's request, a sales clerk produced the gown with an enthusiastic flourish, Dot realized she had gotten her hopes up a little too soon. The fabric was indeed red velvet, but instead of the bold, sophisticated lines she'd been envisioning, the style was practically Victorian, high-necked and long-sleeved, adorned with an abundant froth of cream-colored lace at both collar and cuffs. Sweet enough to make a person's teeth ache. Melting at Marjorie's eager expression, however, she vowed to say something positive.

"Goodness!" she said. "Won't we feel all warm and toasty on a cold winter's day?"

"Oh, I'm so relieved," Marjorie said, a bit breathless. "I was afraid you might not like it. And, luckily, it's available in both your size and Helen's."

"Lucky." Dot forced a smile.

"Yes, but there's only one left in each size," the sales clerk warned.

"We really should buy it today," Marjorie said, "before somebody else snatches it up."

"Well, then. I'd better go try it on."

The clerk led the way to a dressing room. As Dot wrestled with a long row of fabric-covered buttons, she tried to think optimistic thoughts. The dress fit perfectly, and the cut of it did flatter her slender frame. And in any case, the fact that the gown didn't exactly suit Dot's taste was beside the point. Marjorie loved it, and that's what mattered.

"Come out and let me see," Marjorie pleaded. When Dot pushed aside the curtain and stepped into the waiting area, her friend gasped. "Turn around. Oh, don't you look scrumptious?"

"Scrumptious as a red velvet cupcake." Dot cast a doubt-filled glance at the three-way mirror and touched the lace at the neck. "And it looks like the baker may have gotten a little carried away with the vanilla frosting." But she had to admit, with her dark hair and eyes, she did look sensational in red. Maybe a tailor could lower the neckline a few notches without creating a scandal.

"Silly girl," Marjorie said. "Charlie won't be able to keep his eyes off you."

Dot snorted. "Believe me, Charlie will be putting as much distance between us as possible."

Marjorie crossed her arms. "Oh, for heaven's sake. That silly quarrel was over a week ago. Don't tell me you two haven't kissed and made up yet."

"No, and we're not going to." Noticing the sales clerk's keen interest, she said, "I'll take it. You can start writing up the sales slip. Employee discount." Then she ducked back into the dressing room to change.

"At least tell me you're returning his phone calls," Marjorie called through the curtain.

"What good will that do? Talking isn't going to fix it."

"Dot Rodgers! He's going to think Mrs. Moran and I aren't giving you the messages."

"Applesauce. He'll think nothing of the kind."

"But you two are perfect for each other."

Perfect? Marjorie had a blind spot where Dot was concerned if she thought Dot, the stained and sullied nightclub singer, could ever be good enough for her successful and dashing brother. No, they'd tried that dance. The rhythm had been all wrong. Of course she'd take her brother's side. It was only natural to stick by family. Blood was thicker than … a Bloody Mary, which sounded good to Dot right at that moment. She buttoned her skirt and returned the red dress to its hanger. Then she emerged from the dressing room to face her friend.

"Your brother's sweet to keep calling me, but I'm sure he knows in his heart I'm not the gal for him." Not good enough. Not smart enough. Not clean enough. Not nearly enough for Charlie.

"You're wrong," Marjorie said, blue eyes wide. "Since the day I brought you home to Kerryville and introduced you, my brother's been the happiest I've seen him in years."

"I should have nixed it from the get-go," Dot said. They walked toward the desk where the clerk was writing up the order. "Marjorie, Charlie's a fine man. And we've had some good times. But I'm just being practical, that's all. He's better off without me."

"How can you say that?"

"Because it's true."

"It is not." Marjorie turned to address the clerk. "I'll take the other dress too, please, for my sister." She turned back to Dot. "He's been moping around and miserable ever since New Year's."

Dot pulled some bills from her purse and handed them to the clerk. "He'll get over it."

"I'm not so sure."

"He seems to have gotten over his former girlfriend, eventually. Not that he's told me much about her."

"That was different. He blamed their breakup on the war. He blames your breakup on himself."

As the clerk finished the transaction, Dot imagined she was disappointed to miss out on the rest of the story. Dot hoisted her dress, now encased in a cloth garment bag, and Marjorie took Helen's. They headed for the elevator.

"Main floor, please," Dot said to the operator. Then to Marjorie, "Look, it's not his fault. It's nobody's fault. We're incompatible. Let's face it. I'm not the kind of girl who's meant to be paired with a good Christian man like him, and that's that."

Marjorie shifted the heavy dress from one arm to the other. "Oh, is that it? You don't want to date a Christian man?"

Dot sighed. "That's not what I mean, and you know it. It's just that he's so, well, *nice*."

Marjorie smirked. "Because dating cads has turned out so well for you."

With strained patience, Dot said, "I don't expect you to understand, sweetie. You're about to get married to the original Golden Boy."

Marjorie pinned her with a gaze. "What you do or don't believe is the first thing to get straight. Your faith is more important than any courtship."

They exited the elevator and headed for the employee locker room. "Here we go. How did we go from my love life to my spiritual life?" Dot huffed. "Honestly, Marjorie, don't wrangle with me about religion. I'll think about all you and Charlie have told me." She shuddered slightly. "I'm just fed up with church people. They're such hypocrites."

Marjorie frowned. "Am I a hypocrite? Is Charlie?"

Dot gave an impatient snort. "Of course not. I'm talking about people like my father."

"Not a glowing example of faith as it was meant to be practiced."

In the lounge, they dropped the garment bags onto a bench. Dot opened her locker and pulled out her coat and hat.

"I'll try to keep an open mind. And about my love life ... I will always care for Charlie. But otherwise, things are over between us, and that's that."

"Point taken. I'll keep my nose out of it. Chop suey?"

"Sure."

A blast of cold air buffeted their faces as they exited the store and joined the rush-hour throng on the sidewalk, lugging the garment bags. "Any news yet from the Northside Eskimos?" Marjorie asked. "Has that fellow called you to schedule an audition?"

Dot's shoulders drooped. "Not yet."

Marjorie looped her free arm through her friend's. "It's just a matter of time. Before you know it, you'll be onstage next to Ruth Etting, and I'll have to pay good money to come and hear you sing."

"You're off your nut." Dot laughed. But a glowing sensation warmed her chest anyway because that was exactly the sort of malarkey she needed to hear.

Shivering in his shirt sleeves, Charlie stood on the loading dock behind Corrigan's Dry Goods and Sundries, watching as the last carton was unloaded from a delivery truck and regretting not having grabbed his jacket. Finally, he signed the paperwork with fingers stiff from the cold and thanked the driver, his breath frosty on the wintry air. Then he reached up with his good arm and pulled the rolling dock door downward, sealing out the cold.

From his desk in the tiny, cluttered office, Pop glanced up from a ledger book.

"Need help, son?" He set down his pencil and regarded Charlie over the top of his spectacles.

"I can handle it." Charlie piled the cartons onto a handcart and pushed them toward a wall of shelves. Though tackling a shipment by himself was a challenge, he relished hard work, the harder the better. It helped take his mind off Dot. Even a few minutes of relief from the ache were better than nothing.

Pop picked up the pencil and turned back to his task. After several minutes, he gave a little grunt. Charlie glanced over with concern.

"You doing okay?"

The older man had only recently returned to work after recovering from a heart attack the previous fall, and his family kept a watchful eye.

"Fine," Pop said. "Just surprised, that's all." He tapped his pencil on the ledger. "We'll see what the auditor says, but if my initial calculations are correct, 1928 was Corrigan's best year ever." He stood and made his way over to a water cooler that stood in a corner.

"Don't know why you're so surprised," Charlie said. "We could barely keep pace with the holiday orders." He walked to the office and leaned against the door frame. "Maybe it's time to take another look at expanding."

Pop shook his balding head, just as Charlie knew he would.

"You know how I feel about that. Too risky."

"We need to hustle. The place next door is opening up soon. We could knock down the wall in between and double our retail space.

Now the way I see it—"

Pop held up his hand. "I know the way you see it, son. But the way *I* see it, we've already got about as big a dry-goods store as a town this size is likely to support. We need to sock the extra revenue into savings against a rainy day." He peered at Charlie over his spectacles. "Which is not a bad idea for you, either. Save your money instead of spending it on a fancy set of wheels."

Charlie's face heated, thinking of the brand-new Packard roadster parked in the alley behind the store. He'd bought the car with Dot in mind, to show her he could keep pace with her fancy friends. He dreamed of driving it up to her place, all shiny and gleaming. She'd look out her window and see it, and see him coming up the stairs with flowers and a profuse apology ... if only she'd answer his letters.

"My investments are doing well. I don't see why I shouldn't spend some of it. And I couldn't keep driving old Betty forever. Sooner or later, she was going to start falling apart. A fellow's got to keep up with the times."

"A fellow's got to save for the future, too," Pop said, "especially if he's thinking of settling down." He took a sip of water and walked back to the desk. "How is the lovely Miss Rodgers, anyway? Haven't seen her around since before Christmas."

"We sort of got into an argument on New Year's."

"Sort of?" Pop's brow creased. "Mighty sorry to hear that. I didn't know."

Charlie shrugged. "I thought the whole thing would blow over. But she hasn't answered any of my letters or telephone calls. She must be really steamed at me."

Pop settled back into his swivel chair. "Nonsense. I don't know what your argument was all about, but I've seen how that girl looks at you. She's mighty sweet on you." Charlie's skepticism must've been clear on his face because Pop lifted his eyebrows. "What? I know a thing or two about women. They don't stay angry forever."

"I'm afraid this one will."

"Why don't you drive over and see her in person? Bring her flowers. Tell her you're sorry. It'd probably mean a lot to her that you'd go to the trouble."

Charlie nodded. "I've been tempted, but I don't want to drive several hours only to make matters worse than they are."

Pop's expression grew serious. He took off his spectacles and wiped them on the hem on his vest. "Now, son, you know I like Dot. I like her a lot. She's spirited. Livens things up around here." He replaced his glasses. "But I don't know that you two are on the same page, spiritually, and maybe in some other ways, too. Maybe you're right to give her some breathing room rather than force the issue."

"I think she believes in God deep down. Or she will, eventually. She just has a lot to work through, with that loony father of hers. He put some strange ideas into her head about God and church and all."

"I won't try to tell you what to do. Just thought I should mention the issue." Pop straightened his chair. "I need to finish preparing these books for the accountant." He picked up his pencil. "Is Helen still out front?"

"If she hasn't wandered off somewhere with her friends."

"Better check on her when you're done with those boxes. Make sure she's paying as much attention to the customers as she is to her movie magazines."

Charlie grinned. "Yes, sir."

Since Marjorie had taken a job at Marshall Field's in Chicago the previous summer, their younger sister, Helen, had taken on the task of serving customers after school and on Saturdays. Still in high school, Helen hadn't yet developed Marjorie's heave-ho work ethic. But her naturally bubbly and outgoing personality was proving an asset when it came to serving the clientele.

When Charlie had shoved the last carton into place on the shelf, he went to the sales floor and found Helen folding remnants on the markdown table.

"Hey, kid. What's the buzz?"

She glanced up. "Mrs. Murdoch just bought scads of yardage for curtains for the new Methodist church hall. I talked her into buying up that crazy-daisy printed cotton we've been trying to unload."

Charlie grimaced. "Hope the Methodists like daisies." He ruffled his sister's wavy blond bob. "Keep it up, and there'll be a soda in it for you."

"I do have another reward in mind." She gave him an appealing glance. "The girls and I were hoping you'd drive us over to Harley for Italian food tonight."

"Oh, no. A carload of chattering girls fogging up my windows? No, thanks."

Helen looked sheepish and flashed her dimple. "I sort of already promised them."

"Don't see how that's my problem."

"But they're all just dying to ride in your new roadster. Come on, Charlie, please?" She drew out the word and blinked her big blue eyes.

"Oh, all right," he said. "I guess I could do that."

Helen stood on tiptoe and kissed his cheek. "Thanks! You're the cat's meow."

"That's me, all right."

He sighed. Saturday night, no date, no girl. Specifically, no Dot. No reason in the world not to shepherd a group of giggling schoolgirls over to Harley and drown his sorrows in a plate of spaghetti.

CHAPTER FIVE

With perfect hat-model posture, Dot stood on the red carpet in front of the altar and did her best to look dewy and serene, as suited the occasion of her best friend's wedding. Dewy, not sweaty. Despite the raw February weather outside, heat shimmered off the steam radiators as they hissed and clanked beneath the stained-glass windows. Dot caught the bride glancing her way and lifted her rouged lips in what she hoped was a brilliant smile, all the while striving to rise above the scratchy lace trim torturing her collarbone. *This gown is the absolute limit.* The dainty shoes, too, that had looked so scrumptious in the footwear display at Marshall Field's, proved no match for the length of Pastor Rooney's droning remarks about the blessings of holy matrimony and whatnot.

Across the chancel, she caught Marjorie's eye and gave her a reassuring wink.

Dot's biggest problem, of course—much bigger than scratchy lace and shoes designed by the House of Torquemada—was the gentleman standing across the aisle, the best man, who had some nerve to stand there looking annoyingly devastating in a well-fitted morning coat, his sandy hair parted neatly and slicked back with brilliantine. Noticing these details while refusing to look directly at the man was no mean feat, but Dot managed to pull it off.

Stick-in-the-mud, she told herself. *Wet blanket. Self-righteous squasher of anything the least bit fun.*

But deep inside, her heart died just a little. More than a little, if she were honest. Their breakup had taken place six long weeks ago. Why couldn't she forget about it? Obviously, *he* had. He hadn't looked at her except to offer an awkward greeting when she'd arrived at the Corrigan home the previous evening. In the excited flurry of last-minute tasks and activities, there hadn't been time to worry about it. But now, during the seemingly endless ceremony, she had plenty of time to muse about how their budding romance had gone so wrong.

With a flourish, the organ pealed the opening strains of the recessional, snapping Dot out of her melancholy thoughts. She turned and accepted the arm of somebody's second cousin, a scrawny young man whose Adam's apple worked nervously above his necktie. Together they walked up the aisle behind Helen Corrigan, the young maid of honor, and Charlie Corrigan, Bore-in-Chief. Studiously avoiding the way his broad shoulders filled out his jacket, Dot beamed her smile upon the bride's father, who was dabbing his eyes with a white linen handkerchief. Now there was only the reception to get through, an afternoon tea dance at Kerryville's own hotspot, the Tick-Tock Cafe. Once the cake was cut and Marjorie and Peter climbed into his Buick sedan and drove off in wedded bliss, Dot would be free to change into something less torturous and catch the evening train back to Chicago.

In the vestibule, she hugged and congratulated the bride and groom, then joined in the flurry to form a receiving line. She took a spot at the very end, but the bride's stepmother, Frances, sailed forth in a cloud of Chanel No. 5.

"Oh, dear, this is all wrong." She grasped both Dot and Adam's-apple by the elbows and moved them like chess pieces. "The line-up must be boy-girl-boy-girl. There!" And because nothing could go right on this day, Dot found herself standing shoulder to shoulder with Charlie. Well, shoulder to biceps. He smiled down at her, a familiar dimple appearing on his left cheek.

"Hello, there," he said in a cordial tone.

"Why, hello yourself!" Dot said a little too brightly, eyes wide, as if she'd only just noticed his presence.

After a brief pause, he said, "You look well."

"Thank you." Well? She looked *well*? What kind of a thing was that to say? How had he expected her to look since their breakup—pale and wan and wasting away? Not her. No sirree, not Dot Rodgers.

He started to say something else, but the first guests had started coming through the line, and all they could do for the next half hour was shake hands and mutter predictable responses to predictable remarks.

Wasn't the ceremony lovely? Yes, lovely.

Wasn't the bride lovely? Yes, quite lovely. So lovely.

And Marjorie was. Guided by Dot's fashion advice combined with her own innate sense of style, Marjorie had designed and sewn in record time a drop-waisted satin sheath with a tulle sash and a lace-trimmed bodice. She'd added pale stockings and slippers and a short veil gracing a beaded headband. Only those closest to the bride knew that the white satin had been originally intended for a different gown, for a different wedding, to a different man. Peter Bachmann had stepped onto the stage of Marjorie's life right on cue, around the same time that Dot had.

And then Dot had met Marjorie's brother Charlie, and he'd stolen her heart. For a while, they'd enjoyed a flirtation. Deep down, she'd understood that she could never measure up to his standards. Sure, he thought she was pretty. Men always thought she was pretty. She'd been overwhelmed by his kindness, his tenderness, his patience—so different from the men she was used to dating. Men like Louie Braccio, who liked to show off her looks and her singing voice but cared nothing about the person she was inside.

But Dot was nothing if not practical. She had to face facts. She knew who she was. And no decent, upstanding, serious fellow like Charlie Corrigan could ever truly love a silly, shallow, good-time girl like her.

Charlie leaned against the wall and surveyed the dance floor of the Tick-Tock Cafe, wishing the glass in his hand held something stronger than fruit punch and hating himself for the wish. Fortunately the bar was closed. The entire restaurant had been rented for the reception, and fruit punch and coffee were the only options. There Dot was, all flying limbs and high-wattage smiles as she danced the Charleston to the beat of the Tick-Tock Orchestra. He tried not to stare, but he couldn't help it. She was the most beautiful creature God had ever put on this earth, and he'd let her slip away.

When he'd first met Dot, they'd come to this very restaurant with Marjorie and her date. Charlie had grumbled when Marjorie telephoned to say she was bringing her new roommate home for a visit and would Charlie be her escort? He hated blind dates. Until this one. He and Dot had sat in a booth and talked and talked while the others danced. She hadn't wanted to dance, hadn't been disappointed to stay by Charlie's side. She'd seemed genuinely interested in learning who he was. He could have talked with her forever. But watching her now, he understood. She would never be happy sitting with him on the sidelines. She was the kind of girl who needed to dance.

"Hello, Charlie." A low, feminine voice broke into his thoughts. He turned, and something inside his chest gave a hitch.

"Catherine Bailey. I … I didn't expect to see *you* here." Realizing how that must have sounded, he regrouped. "I mean, how nice that you could make it back for Marjorie's wedding. I thought you'd moved somewhere out of state. Arkansas, is it?" He forced himself to stop rambling.

"Texas. Chet's stationed at the military airfield there."

He gave a nervous chuckle. "I knew it was someplace warm."

"And it's Woodruff now."

"Huh?"

"Catherine Woodruff."

"Oh. Right."

She tilted her head and gazed at him. Same reddish-brown curls and hazel eyes. Those eyes that had stayed in his mind all through the long months of fighting in France. He'd thought he loved her. But he'd been wrong.

She was saying something. "… happened to be in town, visiting my parents, and Frances said it would be all right if they brought me with them today." She paused, frowning a little. "I hope you don't mind."

"No, not at all."

"Good. For a moment there, your face looked … Well, anyway, how have you been? You look good."

"So do you." He took a swig of fruit punch and searched his mind frantically for something to say. "Golly. Air Corps, huh?"

Catherine nodded. "Chet couldn't take any time off, so it's just me. Visiting my parents."

"So you said."

They stood for a moment in silence. Then Catherine said, "Well, I guess I'd better go mingle."

An almost giddy sense of relief rushed through him. "I'm sure lots of people are eager to speak with you. Thanks for saying hello."

He watched as she walked away, then turned his eyes back to the vision in red on the dance floor.

He had to have the worst luck with women of any man alive.

"You've been standing here all afternoon." Peter Bachmann clapped Charlie on the shoulder. "You know, the ceiling won't come crashing down if you stop holding up the wall." He jerked his head toward Catherine, now halfway across the room. "What did Lucrezia Borgia want?"

"Just to say hello."

"Uh huh." Peter took a swallow of punch. "She has some nerve, if you ask me, showing up at your sister's wedding as if nothing happened."

"It's been a long time since she cast me aside like a broken toy. Besides, she's married." Charlie forced a grin. "Speaking of marriage, you're finally hitched, old man. How's it feel?"

"Fantastic," Peter said. "Your sister makes me the happiest man in the world."

Charlie followed Peter's worshipful gaze across the room to where Marjorie stood, radiant, speaking animatedly to a group of well-wishers. She glanced up at her brother and lifted a lace-gloved hand with a smile. He winked back.

"Marriage is the greatest thing, pal," Peter said. "You should try it sometime."

Charlie shook his head. "I don't think so. I'm not much of a hand at this romance business. A guy like me does better striking out on his own."

Peter grimaced. "Sorry, old pal. Sounds rough. But you can't throw in the sponge that easily."

Charlie shrugged. "It's probably for the best. A girl like Dot would be bored stiff living with a quiet fellow like me in a nowhere backwater like Kerryville."

Peter's face brightened. "Hey, listen, she's not the only pebble on the beach." He clapped Charlie on the shoulder. "Have you met my cousin Lola from Detroit? She's single, and she hates to dance. C'mon, I'll introduce you. And I'm told we're going to cut the cake soon. Help yourself to an extra big piece. You could use some sweetening up."

Hoping the girl had more to offer than "single and hates to dance," Charlie followed Peter to a nearby table, where he made polite conversation. But he didn't feel like meeting any cousins from Detroit or eating cake or being cheered up. He didn't want to reminisce with any old flames, either. He only wanted to be left alone, to stand quietly in a corner and watch in helpless wonder as the only woman he'd ever truly love shimmied straight out of his life.

CHAPTER SIX

The Tick-Tock Orchestra sounded the final notes of "You're the Cream in My Coffee." Breathless, Dot thanked her dancing partner and made a beeline for the punch bowl. She took a long, grateful sip of the cool sweet liquid and discreetly pressed a napkin against her brow. She saw a middle-aged man coming her way and turned away, pretended not to see him. He was going to want to dance with her, and she was tired of dancing.

She wished she had someone to talk to, but she didn't know anyone besides the Corrigans, and they were all busy. All day long, she'd felt some of the ladies didn't care for her. It was hard to put her finger on it, but she'd caught them looking her over with hostile eyes, whispering to each other out of the corners of their mouths. She knew it wasn't her clothes and doubted it was her perfume. Perhaps they didn't like the way she danced with their husbands. Whatever the reason, they didn't like her.

Before the eager man could reach her through the crowd, Marjorie swept up beside her, lifted the cup from her hands, and drained the contents.

"Hey! You're allowed to have your very own cup, you know," Dot said, quirking an eyebrow at her friend. "It's one of the privileges of being the bride."

"Sorry." Marjorie gave a sheepish giggle and set the cup on the table. "My mind's all a-muddle. I just wanted to warn you that we're about to cut the cake. Then it'll be time to change into my traveling clothes."

"I'm standing by," Dot assured her. "Gee, I can't believe it's almost over. This whole day passed by in a flash."

Marjorie winked at her. "Could be because you never left the dance floor. Kerryville's never seen the likes of you before." She took Dot's hand. "And neither have I. I'm so glad you came today, even though you and Charlie ... Well, you know."

"Are you kidding? I wouldn't have missed it for the world."

Marjorie's eyes misted. "If it weren't for you, I might be married to Richard by now."

"And you'd have been rock-ribbed enough to make it work. But this"—Dot nodded toward the cake table, where the photographer was setting Peter into position and gesturing wildly for Marjorie to join him—"this is the genuine article. You did it, Marjie. You got the happily ever after." She ignored the lump in her throat and gave her friend a playful push. "Go on now. Your groom's waiting, and we're all dying to dig into that cake."

Dot watched as Marjorie and Peter grasped the beribboned knife, flashed goofy grins when the camera popped, and sliced into the elaborately decorated cake. She was applauding along with the crowd when Helen dashed up and handed her a small red lace bag filled with rice.

"Here, take this," she said excitedly. "We'll all stand around outside, and when they come out the door, we'll let 'em have it." She pantomimed the overhand pitch that had earned her Most Valuable Player on the Kerryville Kittykats girls' baseball team.

"You toss it *gently*," Dot corrected. "Just a few grains at a time. Preferably underhand, so you don't take someone's eye out."

Helen's mouth turned down. "What fun is that?"

"Clearly this is your first wedding."

"Second," Helen said. "Frances and Pop's was my first. But I was just a little kid then."

"You're not a little kid now," Dot said. "You look so sophisticated with your hair like that."

Helen reached up and patted her blond bob. "Thanks. I can't believe Frances finally let me cut it, can you? I guess I wore her down." She held up the basket. "Say. I've got to hand out the rest of this rice before it's time to throw it. Will you come back to the house after the party?"

"I have to get back to the city."

"Too bad. It was fun to be in the wedding party with you." Helen gave Dot a quick hug.

"Same here, kid." Dot's heart squeezed. She missed Helen's puppy-like exuberance, and she didn't suppose she'd be visiting Kerryville again anytime soon.

As Helen twirled away, Marjorie signaled to Dot that she was ready to change clothes. Together they slipped away to a small private dining room, where Marjorie's suitcase waited. Her blue tweed traveling suit hung from a hook on the door. Dot helped her friend remove her beaded headpiece and slide the white satin gown over her head. She slid the gown onto a hanger while Marjorie put on the tweed suit, chattering all the while.

"It was just beautiful, wasn't it?" Marjorie said. "I loved every minute. Did you get some cake?"

"No, but that's all right. I'm trying to slim down."

"You! You're skinny as a spindle already. Be sure to take a piece home with you."

"I will."

"You must have had a great time, too. You barely left the dance floor at all." Marjorie bent down to buckle a shoe.

Dot smiled. "The band is great."

"I know! They sound so professional. You'd never know that the band leader is the high school music teacher." She glanced up. "Did you get a chance to speak to Charlie?"

"No." At Marjorie's concerned expression, Dot quickly added, "I mean, yes. Yes, I spoke to him. But just briefly." She kept her tone casual. "I saw him talking to a woman in an emerald-green dress with curly hair. Is she one of your cousins?"

Marjorie shook her head. "That was Catherine, his former fiancée. She lives out of state now. I never would have put her on the guest list, but our parents are still friends, and when she showed up for a visit, it hardly seemed polite not to invite her." She sighed. "I ought to have warned Charlie that she'd be here. I meant to, but I forgot."

"He didn't look too shaken up when I saw them together." Dot modulated her tone, trying not to sound overly curious. "What happened between them?"

"She called off their engagement when he came home from the war. She didn't want to marry a cripple."

Dot gasped. "She actually said that?"

"Not in so many words, but she made it clear by her actions. He's better off without her." Marjorie grasped her friend's narrow shoulders. "I wish you two would kiss and make up already. He's been absolutely miserable without you."

"I'm not his type," Dot said. "It never would have worked."

Marjorie looked about to say something, then apparently thought the better of it. Instead, she pulled Dot into an embrace. "I love you, and

I'm very glad you agreed to be my bridesmaid. And I won't bring up Charlie again if you don't want me to."

"Thanks." Dot returned Marjorie's embrace. "I do wish you and Peter all the happiness in the world." She bent to pick up the suitcase. "Come on, Cinderella. Your carriage awaits."

They walked back into the reception room. Dot handed the suitcase over to Peter, then stepped aside while he and Marjorie said good-bye to their family. Marjorie whispered something in her brother's ear. He nodded, and she gave him a big hug. Dutifully Dot followed Helen and the rest of the guests out to the main entrance, little bag of rice in hand, and shivered in the winter gloom. She ought to have grabbed her wrap.

Minutes later, the door burst open, and Marjorie and Peter flew down the steps to Peter's decorated roadster, laughing and shielding themselves from the shower of rice. Then it was over. Marjorie was gone. Married.

Dot, feeling like a canceled stamp, trudged back into the reception. The band swung into an upbeat number, but dancing no longer held any appeal. Finally, guests started saying their good-byes. Time to change back into a pumpkin.

Charlie intercepted her. "Let me give you a lift to the station."

She remembered seeing Marjorie whisper to him; she'd bet dollars to doughnuts this was all her idea. She lifted her chin. "Thanks, but I can walk."

"It's too cold and icy out there. You'll ruin your pretty shoes. Besides—" he glanced at the dwindling crowd, "—I need a good excuse to get out of here, or they'll put me to work taking down the decorations or something."

A tingle of excitement coursed up her spine, but outwardly she kept her cool. "All right. I just need to change my clothes and say good-bye to your family."

"Meet you out front in a few minutes."

In the small private room, Dot shed the uncomfortable velvet dress and changed into a dark-green wool frock and matching cloche with a cluster of artificial cherries pinned to one side. Carefully she folded the gown and laid it in her suitcase, vowing to donate it to the rummage bin at the settlement house on her next visit. It would find a second life on some other woman's body—preferably a woman with skin like rhinoceros hide, impervious to scratchy lace. Dot replaced her dainty pumps with sensible snow boots that looked a little schoolmarmish, but who cared? It was time to be comfortable for the long train ride home.

She closed the suitcase, set it in the hallway, and slipped into the ladies' room. As she refreshed her powder and lipstick in front of the mirror, she had second thoughts about accepting a ride to the station with Charlie. What would they say to one another? At least the ride would be brief. They'd chitchat, she'd get out, say thank-you, and wait inside the station with the other lonely, unattached souls heading back to the city.

"Stop it," she muttered sternly to her reflection. "You're not lonely, and you're not one to feel sorry for yourself, so don't start now. All this wedding business has put ideas in your head, that's all. But it's over now."

Head high, she strode out to pick up her life where it had left off.

CHAPTER SEVEN

Dot buttoned up her fur-collared coat, said good-bye to the Corrigans, and headed out the front door of the cafe, where Charlie's new roadster, a sleek cream-and-chrome touring car with leather upholstery, idled at the curb. In his black wool Chesterfield and driving gloves, he looked like a Field's ad for the Man About Town. He opened the passenger door for her, and she slid onto the seat. She ran her hand over the smooth leather while he climbed in beside her.

"Nice ride."

He beamed. "You like it? Picked it up a couple weeks ago." His tone was casual as if it were a new scooter. "She never stalls on me, never backfires. She could not be more different from Betty, the old hay-burner."

"I know, but I kind of liked old Betty. What'd you do with her?"

"Sold her to an old buddy of mine, Riley O'Rourke."

"Have you named this one yet?"

"Haven't come up with just the right moniker."

"Well, for now you can just call her Better-than-Betty. No lap blanket?"

"This model came with its own heater." Charlie pointed to a box near the floor.

"A heater! How luxurious." Despite her skittishness about being alone with Charlie, Dot wished the station were a little farther away just so she could enjoy the ride.

"Yeah, they figured out how to draw hot air off the engine and use it to warm the interior."

"Genius," she marveled. "What will they think of next?"

"You probably won't need the blanket," he continued, "but it's on the back seat if you do. And let me know if you get too hot. The heater is either on or off—I can't really adjust it."

"I'm very comfortable." *At least physically.* "Thanks."

Catching a whiff of his Burma-Shave, she felt warmth that had nothing to do with the heater.

Charlie shifted gears and steered the car onto Main Street.

"Lovely wedding, wasn't it?" Dot said.

He laughed. "If I hear that phrase one more time, I'm going to pull a Daniel Boone."

"A what?"

"Shoot my supper."

"Me, too." She grinned. "I'll bet it was nice for you to catch up with your relatives and friends." *Like a certain auburn-curled lady*, she thought.

"It was," Charlie said. "The folks would have liked you to stay an extra day."

They? Not you?

"I wish I could, but we're launching a special sale in Millinery this weekend. It's been advertised all over the place, and it's important I be there first thing in the morning to help corral the herd."

His eyes crinkled as he smiled. She'd always loved that about his eyes.

"I hope they realize what a dedicated employee they have in you."

"It's completely self-serving," she said. "Whoever has the highest sales by the end of next week wins an extra day off."

"I see." Too soon, Charlie pulled the car to the curb in front of the station. He set it in park, then turned to face her. "I've been wanting to talk to you about what happened on New Year's Eve. I feel awful that I didn't see you home. That things between us ended that way."

Unexpected tears pricked her eyelids. "I'm sorry too," she said, looking at her gloves. "I do wish you all the best. Truly."

His touch on her shoulder sent a surge through her, even through her thick wool coat. "I've been thinking. Can't we get together sometime? Maybe have lunch in the city?"

Her voice sounded unnaturally bright to her own ears. "Sure. Give a call to Mrs. Moran's next time you're in town, and we'll schedule something."

He leaned closer. She felt his breath on her cheek. "Dot, listen …"

If she looked at him, she'd be a goner. "I really must be going. Thanks so much for the lift." Panic swelled as her tears threatened to spill for real.

He sat back. "It's awfully cold out there. Maybe you should wait here until your train comes."

Dot forced a smile. "I need to buy my ticket. And you need to get back to your family. They'll be needing someone tall to help pull down the streamers." She winked. He reached for his door handle, but she said, "No, no, you stay put. I'll just hop out. No need to fuss about opening my door for me." She looked at him and swallowed hard. Who knew when they'd see each other again? "Good-bye, Charlie. Thanks for the lift."

"Good-bye, and good luck on the sale this weekend. Hope you don't get stampeded. The next time I'm in Chicago, I'll call you."

"Do that." She forced her gaze away from his mesmerizing blue eyes and stepped out of the car.

The bracing air slapped her face, waking her back to reality. She entered the station and purchased her ticket at the window. Then she headed for a long row of slatted wooden benches that took up the center of the passenger waiting room. She nodded to a few fellow wedding guests, whose names she did not know, and smiled hello. She sat, set her traveling bag on the empty seat next to her, slumped against the scrolled iron armrest, and pondered whether she had the energy to dig her latest detective novel out of her bag. She perked up when she overheard a familiar name.

"I was surprised to see Catherine Woodruff there. Looked quite fetching, I might add. Wonder if he has any regrets about how their engagement ended."

Dot sat stock-still. The speaker was a woman whom Dot didn't recognize. She spoke quietly to her companion, but since they were sitting directly behind Dot, she could hear every word and couldn't help but listen in.

"Regrets?" the woman's companion replied. "Well, I don't know about *him*, but I'm pretty sure *she* has some." She lowered her voice. "They say her marriage is on the rocks."

"I'm not surprised," the first woman said. "I knew that flyboy was trouble from the start. But surely she wouldn't expect to pick up with Charlie again. Not after the way she treated him. And now they say she's practically a divorced woman."

Divorced? Dot turned her head slightly to hear better. *Divorced*, as in *no longer married*, as in *free to flirt with Charlie*? Not that she cared, of course.

"She's not divorced yet," the second woman said. "At least, if she is, the news hasn't been made public."

"Oh, I know. She's just home 'visiting her parents,'" the first woman said in a tone that implied she didn't believe it for a second. "But I tell you, even a divorced woman's a better choice for Charlie than that little number he was dating. You know, that friend of Marjorie's? That bridesmaid with the bangs."

Dot's hand flew to her forehead and fingered the silky hair peeking out from under the brim of her cloche. Her face burned.

"She and Charlie were an item? Do tell!"

"Only briefly. He must have come to his senses. I heard she …" The woman lowered her voice further, and Dot couldn't make out the words, although she strained to hear. But the other woman's sharp intake of breath let her know that it was something delicious and, most likely, highly uncomplimentary.

"No!" breathed the second woman.

"Yes! And I also heard that her most recent boyfriend was a gangster, and now he's doing time."

"Those Corrigans. You never know what they'll be up to next. First, Marjorie throws over that good-looking doctor for that policeman—"

"Prohibition agent," her friend corrected.

"Whatever. And then Charlie has a dalliance with that speakeasy floozy. Who do you suppose young Helen will take up with? Pretty Boy Floyd?"

The women laughed.

Where is that stupid train? It should be here by now. Shielding her face in the thick rabbit-fur collar of her coat, Dot walked to the ticket window. On another day, she might have delighted in confronting the women, of revealing her presence and watching the horror cross their doughy faces as they realized she'd heard every word. Not today. Somehow the emotional marathon of Marjorie's wedding day had taken all the starch out of Dot.

Especially since every word they'd spoken was the truth.

"Excuse me," she said to the clerk. "Will the train be here soon?"

"I was just about to make an announcement." The clerk lifted a device, and the intercom crackled to life. "Ladies and gentlemen, I regret to say that the Number 34 train to Chicago has been canceled due to a derailment near Rochelle. I repeat, the Number 34 train to Chicago has been canceled due to a derailment. The railroad apologizes for the inconvenience. All fares will be refunded." He set down the microphone and looked at Dot, a weary expression on his bewhiskered face.

"Oh, dear," she said. "What time is the next train to Chicago?"

"Tomorrow morning if the tracks are cleared by then. Got your ticket?"

She handed him her ticket, and he counted out the refund. "I need to get back to the city tonight. Is there another way to get there? A bus, perhaps?"

"No bus." The clerk leaned over and peered at the line forming behind her. "Next!"

Dot stepped aside and considered her options. *What a bother.* She supposed she'd have to trudge over to the Corrigans' house and ask to spend the night. Or find a hotel if one existed in this tiny town. Her first priority was to get away from those awful gossips.

She exited the station, got her bearings, and had started to walk toward Main Street when she heard a honk. There was Charlie's car, still idling next to the curb. She walked over as he rolled down the window.

"What are you still doing here?" she asked.

"Waiting to make sure you made the train all right. Where are you going?"

Dot explained the delay.

"Hop in," Charlie said. "I'll drive you to Chicago."

"Oh, Charlie. All that way tonight? You don't have to do that. I'll get a room at the hotel."

He laughed. "What hotel? Besides, I thought you had to be at work in the morning. The big hat sale, remember?"

She pulled her fur collar more tightly around her throat. "They'll have to start without me. It's not my fault the train is canceled."

"Just get in the car," Charlie said. "If we leave now, you'll be home at a decent hour."

"But what about you? You'll be staying in a hotel, or driving half the night to get back."

He shrugged. "Not like I haven't done it before."

"If you're sure." Dot acquiesced, tossed her bag in the backseat, and got in.

She sank into the leather seat. The car felt cozy and warm, like a cocoon.

"I really appreciate this," she said. "I'd be in big trouble if I didn't make it into work tomorrow. Plus, this fancy new car of yours is oodles more comfortable than the train." *Especially a train carrying people who think I'm a speakeasy floozy.*

They drove in silence. A few big, fat snowflakes fell, illuminated by the headlamps against the darkening sky. Charlie kept his eyes firmly fixed on the road. Finally, he spoke.

"Dot, I've been asking the Lord to give me a chance to speak to you alone. I guess this is as good a chance as any."

Oh, boy. "It looks that way," she said lightly, even though she dreaded what he had to say. "I'm a captive audience from here to Chicago."

He glanced at her, his expression grim. "You haven't answered any of my letters, nor returned my telephone calls. I know I shouldn't have left you that night. I wanted to … I went back, but you seemed to be having the time of your life."

She lifted one penciled eyebrow. "You came back? I didn't see you."

"I heard you laughing with that piano player. So … Anyway, I've been trying to apologize. Which you'd know if you'd returned my calls."

She looked down at her gloves. "That was rude of me. I'm sorry."

"I don't care about your manners," he said, less gently. "I care that you think so little of me that you won't even take five minutes out of your life to speak to me."

So little of him? Jeepers, had he read her wrong. "I think a lot of you, Charlie." She looked out her window at the passing fields, their frost tinged purple in the twilight, as she grappled for the right words. "I didn't return your calls because I didn't know what to say. I didn't see any point in continuing as we had been. We were so ill-suited as a couple. Can't you see that?"

A frown creased his handsome profile as he glared out the windshield. "I thought we were great together."

"We were, when we were by ourselves, or with Marjorie and Peter. But anywhere else …" She released a harsh chuckle. "Well, you didn't exactly fit into my world. You can't stand my friends." She paused to give him a chance to deny it. He didn't. "And I don't exactly fit into yours." *Speakeasy floozy.*

"How do you know? We only dated a few months, and most of that was long distance, with me in Kerryville and you in Chicago. Seems to me you didn't give us much of a chance."

"Your life in Kerryville seems a galaxy away from mine in the city. I didn't want to give you any false hope that things would work out between us."

A muscle worked in his jaw. "I understand that we don't run in the same circles, Dot. Clearly, I'm not in your league. You're very sociable, and I spend most of my time working. And when I'm not working, my idea of a good time is a quiet evening in front of the radio. But, gee whiz, you have to know I'm crazy about you. I'd do anything for you."

"Except make an effort with my friends."

He said nothing. Her indignation dissolved. She laid a hand on his arm. "You're a nice guy. You really are. But we're from two different worlds. I didn't see any point in prolonging things. But you deserve an explanation. And I'm sorry, too, that I was so stubborn about the party and caused us to miss our dinner reservations. I was having fun singing with Eddie, even though the band audition hasn't panned out, and I didn't want to leave. I guess deep down I was angry with you, but I didn't know how to say so."

His eyebrows rose. "You were angry with me? About what?"

She hesitated, considered her options. She didn't want to have this conversation, but she couldn't see a way out of it now. Her own fault for bringing it up. "About making me go to Indiana."

He sat forward in his seat. "I didn't *make* you go anywhere."

"You encouraged me."

"I merely suggested that Christmas might be a good opportunity to make peace with your family."

"The Barkers are not like the Corrigans. We aren't some little-birds-in-their-nests-agree household."

"Neither are the Corrigans. Don't know where you got that idea." He passed a hand over his eyes. "But you're right, I shouldn't have interfered. Truce?"

"Truce."

They drove in silence for a while. The snow started to build up on the roads, but Charlie seemed unconcerned.

"But speaking of your family … have you read *Elmer Gantry*? It's a novel that came out last year," he said.

"I've heard of it. Hard not to. It's made lots of waves and ruffled plenty of feathers. Banned in Boston and whatnot. Why do you ask?"

"I read it over Christmas."

"What did you think of it?"

"For the most part, it's garbage. The author has some gripe in his kidney regarding Christianity, especially evangelicals. Every Christian in the book is portrayed either as a faker, a hypocrite, or a naïve idiot." He shrugged. "As I said, garbage. Clearly, the fellow has no idea what the heck he's talking about."

"Why'd you read it, then?"

"I wanted to know what all the fuss was about. Figured I should read the thing before parroting others who were saying how bad it was."

Dot smirked. "Well, that's pretty much what I thought about Christians, too. That is until I met you and Marjorie and your family and other believers who aren't like that at all."

Charlie leaned forward, energized. "I know. And why did you think that?"

"Because that describes my father exactly. A faker. A hypocrite. Not easily duped, though. He's the one who does the duping."

"That's the reason I'm bringing it up. The main character, Elmer Gantry, is exactly like your father."

"How so?"

"He's a faker through and through. But he's awfully good at fleecing people and putting on a front, and so people keep flocking after him."

"Why does he bother? Why doesn't he go into some other line of work?"

"Because he loves the sense of power it gives him, and the fame, and of course, the money." Charlie had an excited gleam in his eyes. "See, that's why I think your father does what he does—for the power, and the money. It has nothing to do with genuine faith."

Dot snorted. "Who cares why he does it? Deceiving people is criminal. That's all there is to it."

"But if you understand why he does it, maybe you'll be able to separate yourself from him and his type. Maybe then, you'll be able to get to know true faith."

"As I've told you, *many* times, I do believe in God." She gave him a sidelong glance. "The world had to come from someplace. It didn't just pop into existence. But I don't believe He's all that involved in our daily lives, healing people and such. He's just sort of … out there." She gestured to the night sky.

"At least pray about it. Read your Bible. Open up a line of communication with the Almighty. Maybe then, you'll be able to get to know true faith."

"Because mine's not true."

"No. Frankly, it's not."

"I see." She smiled. "You never give up, do you?"

Charlie glanced at her and grinned. "No. I'll never give up."

The tension between them eased, and they drove along the country roads, exchanging stories and laughing.

With no warning on the silent snowy night, the car lurched and spun on a patch of ice. Dot let out a scream, and Charlie clutched at the wheel. Despite his strenuous effort, the car veered, bumped over the edge of the pavement, and came to an abrupt halt in a snow-filled ditch.

CHAPTER EIGHT

"Holy cats!" Dot gripped the dashboard until she was sure the car had stopped moving. Her pulse pounded.

Charlie muttered an expletive, followed by, "Are you all right?" He touched Dot's arm and looked at her with concern.

She placed a gloved hand on her chest to quell the hammering. "I'm fine. What happened?"

"Black ice," he said grimly. "You don't see it until you hit it." He shifted into reverse and tried to back the car out of the ditch, but the wheels spun in the snow. He got out of the car, slammed the door, and tried pushing it out of the snowbank. No luck.

Dot rolled down her window and leaned out. Soft snowflakes landed on her cheeks and eyelashes.

"Want me to help?"

"Won't do any good. She's stuck fast."

No amount of pushing, cajoling, or strong language would move the car out of the ditch.

Charlie walked to the driver's side door, reached in, and switched off the engine. An eerie silence settled around them. Somewhere in the distance, a dog howled.

Dot got out of the car and stood shivering with her arms wrapped around herself. "What do you think we should do?"

He squinted up and down the highway. "No traffic coming in either direction," he said. "That's what I get for taking a shortcut. We should have stayed on the main road."

"Well, you couldn't have known she'd land in the ditch," Dot said.

Charlie looked around, and she followed his gaze. They were surrounded by acres of snow-covered fields. In the distance, she could make out a large barn and a few scattered outbuildings. The only visible light shone from the windows of a farmhouse.

"I guess our only option is to walk to that farmhouse and ask to use their telephone," Charlie said.

"Let's hope they have one."

"You want to come with me or stay here with the car?" Charlie asked. "Maybe you should wait here. It looks like quite a hike. You could bundle up in the lap robe, and I could leave the car running."

"I've got my walking boots on," Dot said. "I'd rather go with you than stay here alone in the dark."

"All right, then. Let's go."

They trudged down the road toward the farmhouse.

"Let's look for a driveway," he said, "so we don't have to tramp across the field."

Dot tightened her coat. "I just hope they're nice people and don't come after us with a shotgun for trespassing."

"Farmers are generally nice people. Hey, you're shivering." He put an arm around her shoulders and drew her close.

She leaned into his embrace. For warmth, of course. And, well, just because. They continued arm in arm.

She ought to have been frightened or at least annoyed, having to trudge down an icy road in the dark for help. But the snowfall had subsided, the moon shone clear and white between scattered clouds, and Charlie's arm was a comfortable weight around her shoulders. His very nearness made her feel in high spirits. Even the cold seemed chased away by his presence. They walked along together, teasing and laughing until the rumble of a motor came up behind them, and a pair of headlamp beams fell across their path. A worn blue pickup truck slowed down and stopped a few feet in front of them. A man with white hair leaned out the window, his ruddy face clear in the moonlight. "That your car in the ditch back there? You kids need some help?"

"We sure do," Charlie called back. "Think you could help pull us out of the snowbank?"

"I'll give it a try. Got some chains in the back."

"Oh, thank you," Dot breathed. "I was afraid we'd be stuck here all night."

The man stepped out of the truck and extended a work-worn hand to Charlie.

"Name's Cal Bains. That's my place over there." He gestured toward the lighted farmhouse where Dot and Charlie had been headed.

Charlie shook the man's hand. "I'm Charlie Corrigan, and this is Miss Rodgers. We sure do appreciate your help, Mr. Bains."

"Call me Cal. You want I should drop the lady at the house first to warm up? I'm sure my wife would be happy to put the kettle on."

"No, thank you," Dot said, not wanting to leave Charlie's side.

Cal got back behind the wheel. "You kids hop in."

Charlie opened the passenger door and helped Dot climb into the cab, then he followed. Cal steered the truck to where the Packard sat cockeyed at the side of the road. He backed up his truck until it was positioned near the roadster. They all got out, and Cal surveyed the situation for a moment, then reached into the bed of the pickup, pulled out a couple of pieces of wood, and handed them to Charlie. "Stick these in front of the wheels." Then he reached back in the truck and pulled out a thick length of heavy chain. He attached one end to the rear of the truck and the other to the Packard. "You get behind her and push if she needs it," he instructed Charlie. "Make sure she's in neutral."

"What should I do?" Dot asked, stamping her freezing feet.

"Just stay out of the way," Charlie said, his breath frosty, "in case she slides." He climbed behind the wheel of the roadster, then signaled to Cal that he was ready.

Dot stepped to the side and shivered as Cal revved the engine, then started to pull the truck forward. The chain tightened with a rattle, then slowly dragged the roadster out of the ditch and back onto the road. Dot breathed a sigh of relief.

The farmer hopped out of the truck and retrieved his chain. "There you go. Good as gold."

"Don't see any damage," Charlie said, looking over the car. "I can't thank you enough." In the beam of the truck's headlamps, he reached into his wallet and pulled out a few bills. "Here's something for your trouble."

Cal held up his work-worn hand. "Keep it. Maybe someday you can help out some other poor soul stuck in a ditch. Better keep those boards with you. They might come in handy in the snow or mud."

"Thanks. You're very kind." Charlie helped Dot into the roadster, then climbed in himself. He pressed the starter and turned the key in the ignition.

Nothing happened.

He tried again.

Still no response from the roadster's engine, just a dull click.

Standing nearby, Cal removed his seed cap and scratched his head.

Charlie swore under his breath. He rolled down the window.

"Sounds like you've got some trouble there," Cal said.

"She's on the fritz. Can't seem to get her started."

To Dot's mind, old Betty's hand-cranked starter suddenly wasn't looking so bad.

"Maybe she just needs a jump. I've got some cables back at the farm. Let's hitch her up again, and I'll tow her over."

"Looks like we don't have a choice." Charlie threw Dot an apologetic glance. "Sorry about all this."

"It's all right." She got out of the roadster.

"Have a seat in the truck, missy. We'll be done in no time," Cal said.

Dot climbed back into the dusty, unheated cab of the battered old truck and pulled her fur collar around her face while Cal and Charlie hitched up the vehicles again. Her breath fogged the windows. Then Cal climbed into the driver's seat while Charlie got behind the wheel of the Packard. Dot twisted in her seat to keep an eye on him out the truck's rear window.

With a lurch, the chain pulled taut, and the truck towed the car a short distance down the highway, then down a long dirt drive toward the farm. They stopped between the barn and the farmhouse.

"We'll get you inside where it's warm, missy," Cal said to Dot, "and then Charlie and I will figure out what's wrong with this flivver."

They entered the farmhouse through a side door into a bright, cheerful kitchen, where a plump woman in a gingham dress and flowered apron stood washing dishes at the sink. She turned, and a smile creased her broad face.

"Well, hello there," she said cordially. "Who have we here?"

"Ellie, these folks are having a bit of car trouble. Maybe you can rustle the lady up a cup of tea while Charlie here and I see if we can get the engine running."

"Why, sure. Come on in, dear, and have a seat by the stove. You must be frozen stiff. My, is that a real fur collar?" The woman kept up a steady patter as she took Dot's coat and hung it on a peg near the door. Then she motioned for her to sit at the table next to a glowing iron stove while she pulled two cups and saucers out of a cupboard and set them on the counter.

"We're so sorry to interrupt your evening," Dot said. "My name's Dot Rodgers, by the way."

"Ellie Bains. It's no bother at all." The woman poured water from a steaming kettle into the cups and added tea bags. "I'm happy for the company. Although I must say, you've picked a cold night to have car trouble. You poor thing. Where are you folks headed to?"

"Chicago," Dot said. "We've just been to a wedding in Kerryville."

"Oh, a wedding! I love weddings." Ellie set the steaming cups on the clean blue-and-white checked oilcloth. She reached into a ceramic jar, pulled out a few cookies, and put them on a plate. Then she joined Dot at the table. "Here's the cream and sugar," she said, setting them on the table with the cookies. "I'm afraid I have no lemons."

"That's all right. Those cookies look good." Dot picked up a heart-shaped cookie sprinkled with red sugar. "So pretty."

Ellie beamed. "I made them for Valentine's Day. I'm a sentimental old fool, but it's just Cal and me here, and I like to spoil him."

Dot took a bite. "*Mmm.* He's a lucky man."

"Will you and your fella do something special for Valentine's Day?"

"Oh, we're not … He's not my fella. We're just friends. The train was canceled, so he offered to give me a ride home."

"Oh, I see."

The two women sat in the cozy kitchen. Dot talked mainly about the wedding they'd just been to, and Ellie pitched in with some wedding stories of her own, mostly involving her three grown daughters. After a while, the two men came through the door, stamping their snowy boots on the doormat. Dot glanced up. "Success?"

"After all that tinkering, we still haven't been able to get the blasted thing started," Charlie said with a grimace.

"I think I know what's wrong with it," Cal said, "but I'll have to get a part. It can't be fixed until morning."

"Oh, dear," Dot said.

Charlie held his cap in his hands and said, "We'd be awfully grateful if you could give us a lift to the nearest town that has a hotel."

"Nonsense," Ellie said. "You two will stay right here. We have plenty of room."

"Oh, that would suit us first rate. If you're sure we'll be no trouble …" Charlie looked doubtful.

"Absolutely no trouble at all." Ellie smiled as she stood and went to the cupboard for two more teacups. "Charlie, go and get your things out of the car. I'm afraid we have only one guest room."

"Dot can have that room," Charlie said. "If it's all right with you, I'll bunk on the sofa."

"It's nice and warm in the parlor," Cal said. "I've slept in there a time or two myself." He winked at Ellie.

"Oh, you." She set the cups on the table and flicked her apron as if shooing him away.

Charlie left and, a moment later, came back carrying Dot's bag. He set it on the linoleum floor and took off his coat and gloves.

Ellie said, "Now sit down and have some tea. You look half frozen." She carried the cookie plate over to the jar and refilled it.

Dot lifted the pot and filled the cups. "How early in the morning do you think you can get the part, Mr. Bains?" she asked, her stomach tight with anxiety. "We still have over an hour's drive."

"Don't you worry. The hardware store opens early here in farm country. Once I have the part, the repair should be pretty simple. You'll be on your way in no time."

"That's good. I'll need to get to work as soon as possible."

"Where do you work?" Ellie asked.

When Dot told her, Ellie's face lit up.

"Goodness, how interesting." She slid into a chair and picked up her teacup.

Charlie grinned, his blue eyes sparkling. "That's how we met, you know. She sold my sister a hat."

"Well, now, that's a story we need to hear." Cal slapped his knee.

Dot kept them all laughing with a lively account of selling shy-violet Marjorie a bold yellow cloche, which eventually led to a whole new look for the girl, as well as a close friendship.

"And was her stepmother ever scandalized when Marjie brought me home to Kerryville for a visit," she said, laughing. "I thought she was going to hit the roof when she saw us with our bobbed hair, short skirts, and lip rouge."

"Frances might have hit the roof, but my jaw hit the floor," Charlie said. "She was the prettiest thing to hit Kerryville since … well, since forever."

Dot caught his gaze and felt herself blush—and she wasn't the blushing type. Ever since childhood, she'd heard people say she was pretty, and it had always made her uncomfortable. Her self-righteous father had acted as if her good looks were some kind of curse, a key poised to unlock a Pandora's box filled with all sorts of evil temptations. When she'd dated Louie Braccio, he'd been proud of her appearance in the same way he might have been proud of a diamond stickpin or a sable coat—something to be admired and envied by other men. But when

Charlie said it, it really meant something. He made her feel appreciated and cherished all the way to her toes.

Why couldn't she let go of her fears and fall in love with him?

Because she didn't deserve him. That's why.

She fixed her gaze on her teacup.

Ellie spoke up. "How about you, Charlie? What do you do?"

Charlie filled them in on Corrigan's Dry Goods and his family in Kerryville and his plans for the business.

"I think we should open a second store," he said, "maybe in Dubuque or Galena. Business is good, and they say the chain store is the wave of the future."

The two couples talked and laughed well into the evening as if they were longtime friends instead of strangers. A warm tingle spread through Dot's chest. She felt welcome and included, the way she felt around the Corrigans—with the exception of Frances. Her own family had not joked and told stories. As for her friends from the Villa Italiana, their humor was often mean-spirited, their laughter snide and cynical. Whatever attraction they'd held for Dot softened in the warmth of a glowing farmhouse stove and an older couple who clearly loved and respected each other. She remembered what Charlie'd said about enjoying quiet evenings around the radio. Here in the Bains' kitchen, that sort of life seemed more appealing than the most glittering nightspot.

She didn't notice the time passing until a cuckoo clock on the kitchen wall struck nine. Cal stood and stretched.

"Morning comes early for a farmer," he said. "Time to call it a night. What do you say, Mother?" He smiled at Ellie.

"We should get some sleep, too," Charlie said. "We'll want to hit the road as early as possible."

Ellie stood and carried cups to the sink. "Come on, Dot, I'll give you the grand tour."

While Cal helped Charlie get settled in the parlor, Ellie led the way upstairs and down a hallway. "Here we are," she chirped, opening the door to a darling little room directly over the kitchen. Calico curtains graced the windows, and a rag rug warmed the wooden floor. A Blue Willow china washbowl and pitcher sat on an oak dresser. An iron bed covered with a patchwork quilt cozied up to a stovepipe that ran from the floor to the ceiling. For a moment, the image of waking up in this room next to Charlie flashed through Dot's mind. She closed her eyes, refusing to complete the thought, ashamed of even having it. No use pining for what she wouldn't allow herself to have.

"It's perfect. So cozy," she said.

"This was Cal's and my room when the girls lived at home," Ellie said. "They all shared the bigger room down the hall. But after they moved out, I insisted we switch rooms. With that big old stovepipe running through, this room got a little *too* cozy for me if you know what I mean." She made a fanning motion and stage-whispered, "Change of life."

Dot grinned. "I'm sure I'll be very comfortable here."

Ellie showed her the rest of the upstairs, then the women returned to the kitchen, where Charlie was holding her overnight bag. He'd removed his suit jacket and loosened his tie.

"I'll carry it upstairs for you," he said.

"That's all right. It's not heavy." As she took the bag from him, her hand touched his, and a pleasant jolt shimmied up her arm.

"Good night, you two. See you in the morning," Cal said with a yawn. He and Ellie climbed the stairs. Dot turned to follow them when Charlie touched her shoulder.

"Stay a while. You're not tired, are you?"

Although it had been a long day, she was used to staying up well past nine o'clock and wasn't the least bit sleepy.

"All right." She set her overnight bag at the bottom of the stairs and joined Charlie in the cozy parlor. They sat together on a sofa near the woodstove, to which Cal had added a fresh log to warm the room for Charlie's comfort. Dot pictured Cal sitting in the wing chair flanked by a table holding a pipe, a book, and reading glasses. The floral-cushioned rocker was apparently Ellie's, for beside it rested a basket holding bright blue yarn and a pair of knitting needles. A cat purred on the hearth in front of the stove. As she settled next to Charlie, Dot felt as if she'd entered a sentimental old painting, so very different from her modern life in Chicago.

"Cold?" Charlie asked as he slid his arm around her shoulders.

"Not at all." Nestled in the circle of Charlie's arm, Dot was peaceful and happy. It had been a crazy day—first a wedding, then a canceled train, then a car accident, and now a night spent in a strange farmhouse. But oddly, Dot felt as comfortable as if she'd lived here all her life.

"I like the Bainses," she said to Charlie. "It must be wonderful to grow old with somebody like that. To still be in love after all those years."

"This is the kind of future I think about having with you." Charlie turned slightly to face her. His voice was low and husky. "Dot, we could be so happy together. I know we come from different backgrounds, and I know you're used to a much more exciting life than I'm used to, but if you only knew how much I—"

She put her finger against his lips. "Charlie, hush," she said. Her chest burned. "It's such a beautiful evening. Let's not spoil it with that kind of talk."

But the warmth of the fire and the sweetness of the cookies must have gone to her head. Because when he leaned closer, she made no objection. He brushed his lips against hers, gently, tentatively at first, then firmly. His kiss tasted of tea and sugar cookies, of missing her, of making up for lost time. She froze for a moment, her breath caught in her throat. A note of caution bubbled to her mind, then burst. She curved her hand around the back of his neck and pulled him closer.

The hour was very late when Dot finally climbed the stairs to the guest bedroom carrying her bag, her heart wrapped in the warmth of Charlie. But soon, the chill of clear-headed thinking took over. *What are you doing?* she scolded herself. *You told him you could only be his friend, not his sweetheart. You told him you were not the right woman for him. But once again, you let your heart take over. Now he has the wrong idea. He'll think you have a future together. But one day, when he realizes how poorly you fit into his world, he'll be sorry. He needs a nice, wholesome woman to be his wife and the mother of his children, not a torch singer with a complicated past.*

You silly, selfish girl.

Wearily she pulled on her nightgown and crawled between the immaculate sheets under the patchwork quilt. She needed to get back to her life in the city and forget all about Charlie. No matter what, she mustn't slip up again. It wasn't fair to him to keep his hopes on a string like a yo-yo. He wasn't strong enough to break it off for good. That was up to her.

Before dawn, she woke from a fitful sleep in the strange bed and wondered where she was. Then, as her situation seeped back into her brain, the chug of a freight train puffed across the dark winter fields. Her ears perked up. That meant the train tracks must have been cleared since last night's accident.

She pushed back the warm quilt and swung herself out of bed. She tiptoed across the cold wooden floor to the window. Peering out into the darkness, in the dim light of a waning moon, she saw a lantern swinging from the hand of a lone figure heading toward the barn. *It must be Cal,* she thought, *off to do the morning's milking.* Quickly, she wrestled out of her nightgown and back into the previous day's green wool dress. When she was dressed, she grabbed her overnight case and tiptoed down the stairs in stocking feet. As she passed the door to the parlor, she peeked in to see Charlie's shape huddled under a quilt, fast asleep on the sofa in front of the embers of a dying fire. He looked so sweet, lying there. Her heart lurched. She touched her lips where he'd kissed her only hours before. Then she tiptoed to the kitchen door, put on her boots, and quietly unlatched the door. Leaving her bag on the step, she crossed the yard, her footsteps crunching on the snow, to the barn where Cal sat on a stool, milking a cow.

"Excuse me," she said.

He turned. "You're up mighty early, missy. Sleep well?"

"Yes," she lied. "Listen, it's really important that I get back to the city as soon as possible. It sounds like the trains are running again. Do you think you could possibly give me a lift to the nearest train station?"

"Sure thing. That'd be Aurora, just about a fifteen-minute drive. I'll go warm up the truck while you tell Charlie you're leaving."

"I'll let him sleep. He was just doing me a favor, driving me to Chicago. He lives in the opposite direction. So if I can take the train instead of making him drive the rest of the way, I'm sure he'll be very grateful."

The farmer nodded. "All right. You go fetch your bag, and I'll meet you out here."

A few minutes later, Cal and Dot climbed into his pickup truck and drove the few minutes into town. He let her off at a small brick train station. It was nearly empty at that hour, but a few early-morning passengers were starting to congregate. Dot thanked him profusely, then waited for her train in the warmth of the depot, watching through the thick window glass as the horizon grew more pale.

The sooner she could get back to Chicago and forget all about Charlie Corrigan—and make him forget all about her—the better.

CHAPTER NINE

In direct contrast to Charlie's mood, the midday sun shone brightly, pouring in through the windshield of the Packard as he pulled into his usual parking spot in the alley behind Corrigan's Dry Goods. The car's engine purred, good as new after he and Cal had tinkered with it at the farm earlier that morning. The good man hadn't even accepted Charlie's offer of payment, had only let him pay for the new part. And Ellie had refused to send him off without a good hearty breakfast of bacon and eggs. Charlie was grateful there were still good people in the world. They helped to balance out the other kind—the kind of people who ran off before it was even light out and left a fellow sleeping like a stone.

And just when he'd thought things were going well between them. The memory of Dot's kiss made him ache with loss. What had he done wrong that she left him like that?

He shut off the engine and slid out of the car. Snow crunched beneath his boots. He glanced at the car's normally gleaming cream-colored exterior. She was going to need a wash and wax later. Not that she deserved it.

Troublemaker.

"Not your finest moment, sweetheart," he muttered at the headlamps. "Maybe it wasn't your fault we skidded off the road, but the fact that you refused to even *start*—well, that's all on you. You're brand new. You don't need to get all temperamental and start having things go wrong."

Thinking the car looked remarkably unrepentant for her deeds, Charlie left her in the alley. Old Betty would never have let him down like that.

He pulled a set of keys out of his coat pocket and let himself in the back door.

He paused at the door of the office. "Hi, Pop."

"Well, the hapless traveler has returned. Glad to see you made it back safely, son. Thanks for telephoning the house. We'd have been worried. What was the problem?"

"Something faulty in the ignition. A part must have gotten jarred loose when we hit the ditch."

"Can't trust some of these new automobiles. They don't make 'em like they used to. Hope you didn't get stuck with a lemon."

"I wouldn't go so far as to call her a lemon," Charlie said defensively. "She's a smooth ride—just needs some careful handling."

"Well, the important thing is that neither you nor Dot got hurt."

"Yeah. I tried to get back sooner. I really made tracks, once we got her going, but when I got back to town, I had to stop home to wash up and change my clothes. I was still in my wedding duds."

"No matter. Things haven't been too busy this morning, and Helen will be here after school."

"I thought you might keep the store closed an extra day, to recover from the wedding."

"No can do. Being closed one day was enough. Besides, Frances needs the rest, and I wanted to stay out of her hair. Did Dot get home all right?"

Charlie shrugged. "I suppose so. She took off very early. Caught the train. She didn't even wake me up to say good-bye. Just took off without a word."

Pop stood and put a hand on Charlie's shoulder. "Maybe it's for the best, son. She's got her own life to live. And so do you."

Charlie nodded. He was just about done with feeling miserable over that girl.

Now, all he had to do was get his heart to agree.

It was still relatively early morning when the train chugged into Union Station. Dot stopped at her apartment only long enough to drop her suitcase, wash up, redo her makeup, and change into a black dress suitable for work. *Oh, crumbs.* One of her favorite gold drop earrings was missing. It could have fallen off anywhere between Kerryville and Chicago: the train, the station, the Bains' bathroom .... With a sigh, she debated whether it was worth even trying to track it down. But the earrings were genuine gold and worth a lot of money. Not that she'd paid for them herself, of course. They'd been a gift from Louie. He'd given her lots of jewelry while they were dating, saying he wanted his singer to look good on stage. The earrings held no sentimental meaning for her. She supposed that if she were a more principled woman, she'd welcome the loss, considering who gave them to her. But the plain truth was, she didn't care who they came from. They were her favorites, and she wanted the missing one back.

After she cast a longing glance at her comfortable bed, she left to use the public telephone at the bakery on the corner to call her supervisor and explain she'd be late. She was tempted to call in sick altogether and take another day off. Nonetheless, she steeled her resolve and headed straight for the streetcar after purchasing a coconut-sprinkled doughnut to tide her over until lunch. Professionals didn't call in sick on the first day of a big hat sale, and Dot Rodgers was nothing if not a pro.

Yawning broadly, she approached the employee entrance at Marshall Field & Co. feeling as if it took her very last ounce of strength just to push open the heavy revolving door. She clocked in and arrived at the millinery section, which was already bustling with customers. She got right to work helping ladies choose hats and answering customers' questions about the winter-season headwear on sale and the new styles coming in for spring. Being the best sales clerk in Millinery meant more than winning an extra day off; it was a point of pride. To make up time for arriving late, she skipped her morning break and didn't stop moving for a moment until lunch.

In the cafeteria, her friends peppered her with questions as she sipped a third cup of coffee.

"What was the wedding like? Was it beautiful?" Agnes-in-Books gushed. "Gosh, I wish I could have been there."

Betty-in-Hosiery nodded. "Yeah, I wish she hadn't held it in the middle of the week like that."

"She had her heart set on a Valentine's Day wedding," Dot reminded them, "and I think they wanted to keep it small, although I know she would have loved to have all of you there."

Dot filled them in on as many details as she could remember, ending with "I'm sure Marjorie will bring in her photograph album and answer all your questions when she returns."

"When will that be?" Ruthie-in-Stationery asked.

"In a couple of weeks, when they get back from their automobile trip to Florida."

"I'd love to go to Florida in the middle of winter." Agnes sighed.

"I can't believe she's coming back to work," Betty said. "If I ever get married, I'll stay home and become a lady of leisure."

"Better pick somebody richer than Stanley Novak, then," Ruthie said, citing Betty's boyfriend-of-the-month.

Betty shrugged. "He's got prospects."

"Well, you ladies know Marjorie," Dot said. "She absolutely adores her job, especially since Mr. Fraser made her a window trimmer. She'll be eager to come back."

"Yeah, and she'll probably get a zillion big ideas while she's down there," Ruthie said. "And the next thing you know, we'll be looking at some wild window display with surf and sand and palm trees, and a scale replica of Mar-a-Lago or something."

"It's easy for her." Betty sniffed. "Her honey works at Marshall Field's, too. She gets to see him whenever she wants."

"Isn't it wonderful that Peter was named head of security after that big bootlegging fiasco last year?" cried Agnes, who, as a bookseller, had a strong sense of the dramatic. "I still can't believe we all trusted the likes of Kurt Steuben and Stella Davenport. Imagine, criminals in our very midst!"

"I don't know," Betty said. "I think it would be boring for him to work in store security after being a Prohibition agent for so long. Less chance of catching any really big criminals."

"Less chance of getting tossed in the river wearing cement shoes, too," Agnes said.

"Speaking of criminals, have you girls seen today's headline?" Ruthie reached into her handbag and pulled out a copy of the *Chicago Tribune*. "There was some big shootout yesterday over on the North Side. Seven men got killed. They say George Moran's men were gunned down by, they think, Al Capone's gang. Luckily none of the names were familiar to me." Ruthie volunteered at a settlement house in a neighborhood infested with gangsters, and she was on a first-name basis with some of the worst of them.

"Even if the Capone gang did it," Agnes said, "it says Al Capone himself is down in Florida, hundreds of miles away from the scene of the crime."

"Maybe Marjorie and Peter should drop in and say hello while they're there," Betty drawled.

"Careful, or next thing you know, it will be all over the moccasin trail that they're in on it, too," Agnes said, citing Field's version of a rumor mill.

"Capone still could have ordered it done," Ruthie said. "The blood would still be on his hands."

"Let me see," Dot said. Ruthie handed her the newspaper, which gave front-page coverage to the incident. Her gaze slid down the victims' names. None of them were Louie's friends, she noted with relief, although one or two had been customers of the Villa Italiana. At least one of them had been at the New Year's Eve party at Veronica's. She shuddered as she handed the newspaper back to Ruthie. It was one thing to act a little sketchy, to skirt the law. But out-and-out gang warfare and murder? Too close for comfort. She really needed to cut all ties with these kinds of people.

Why was saying good-bye to them so hard?

With a shiver, she suddenly realized that the gossipers at the Kerryville train station had been right.

Dot Rodgers was just a speakeasy floozy with gangster connections.

The following Monday, the shop was busy with customers, which suited Charlie fine because it helped keep his mind off Dot. Around three thirty, he took advantage of a lull in the action to sweep the shop floor. The bell over the front door tinkled merrily as Helen burst in. She dumped her schoolbooks on the counter and reached for her work apron, talking a mile a minute all the while.

"Hi, Charlie. Say, wasn't Marjie's wedding the cat's whiskers? The girls and I couldn't stop talking about it all day. Mrs. Larson had to reprimand us for talking during chemistry lab."

She'd been going on about the wedding all week. "That's nothing new, I'm sure."

Helen continued chattering as if he'd not spoken. "Everyone said that having a wedding on Valentine's Day was absolutely brilliant. So romantic, all those hearts and cupids strung up over the dance floor. Say, wasn't the band great? I never thought Frances would go for jazz, thought she'd insist on having some musty old string quartet or something. Wasn't that clever to have a heart-shaped wedding cake? I'd love to get married on Valentine's Day, except I don't want to share an anniversary date with Marjie, plus, I don't want to get married in the middle of winter. I want a summer wedding, with rose petals down the aisle and a white wedding cake three feet high, maybe four. Natalie

Brinker says she wants a fall wedding, but I wouldn't want to be married in fall. I hate chrysanthemums. They make me sneeze."

"I don't think you need to worry about planning your wedding for a while yet," Charlie teased when his sister paused to take a breath, "seeing as how you're still 'sweet sixteen and never been kissed.'"

She lifted her chin. "How do you know I've never been kissed?" she teased back.

"Well, I hope you haven't," he said in sudden alarm. "*You* might be ready for that, but I'm not."

"Oh, don't worry. I'm not going to kiss anyone until somebody comes to town worth kissing. Anyway, everyone said they've never been to such a fun wedding …"

His mind drifted as she prattled on about cakes and photographs and dresses. How could he convince Pop to at least consider opening a second store? The time was ripe, and so were the finances. It wouldn't have to be in Chicago, necessarily. Dubuque might be just as—"

"—and didn't Dot look sensational?"

"Huh?" The mention of Dot's name snapped him back to the present.

"Dot. Didn't she look pretty in that red dress? It was a better color on her than on me."

"Oh, I don't know … if you say so." He cast about for words.

Helen gave him an incredulous look, then rolled her eyes. "You men are blind as beetles when it comes to fashion." The bell over the door gave a tinkle. "May I help you?" While Helen stopped talking about weddings long enough to wait on a customer, Charlie collected his thoughts. Dot had looked sensational, no matter what she was wearing. But that wasn't the point. He was almost thirty years old. Most of his friends had married and settled down. But a fellow couldn't build a marriage on good looks and fancy dance steps. He needed to forget all about Dot Rodgers and find himself a girl who was serious, who would love being married to him and would stick by him, no matter what. If such a girl existed.

Helen finished with the customer and held the front door open for her as she exited. "Thank you! Come again."

He was crouched down, rummaging under the counter for some display materials, when the bell jangled as a customer walked in the door. Above his head, he heard Helen offer a routine, "Welcome to Corrigan's. May I help you?" Then, "Oh, hello. I remember seeing you at Marjorie's wedding. I'm her sister, Helen."

"Yes, I know who you are," said a smooth female voice.

Charlie stood. The auburn-haired woman smiled at him. "And I know your brother, too. Hello, Charlie."

"Catherine." He ran a hand through his hair. "Nice to see you again. Um, what can we help you with?"

"I was just walking by and wondered if you might like to take a break and join me for a cup of coffee at the cafe. We hardly got to talk to each other at the wedding. It would be nice to catch up, don't you think?"

"Oh. Um … Gee, that would be swell, but I'm afraid we're too busy." There wasn't a topic in the world he was eager to discuss with his old flame.

He glanced at Helen, who quirked an eyebrow.

"I can cover the store for a while." His sister's voice was laced with curiosity.

Charlie wracked his brain but couldn't conjure up another excuse. "Okay. Just let me grab my coat." He took his time going back to the stockroom.

"I'm going out for a while, Pop," he called as he lifted his jacket from the wall peg. "Not for long." He paused, then walked over to Pop's office and leaned against the doorframe as he pulled on his gloves. "It's the darnedest thing, Pop. Catherine's here. Wants to have coffee with me."

"Catherine's here?" Pop raised an eyebrow. "I saw her at the wedding. Heard she's in town visiting her folks." He smiled at Charlie. "Well, that's nice. It's been a long time since you two split up, and you've never been one to hold a grudge. Give her my regards."

As they headed down the snowy sidewalk, Catherine remarked, "Oh, it's slippery," and took his arm. "Nice to see the sunshine, though."

They exchanged comments about the weather and other topics of no consequence during the short walk to the cafe. Charlie pushed open the door, and a warm burst of cinnamon-scented air greeted them.

"Let's grab a table near the window," she urged.

"Two coffees," Charlie said to the waitress, and then to Catherine, "Would you like anything else? A cinnamon roll?"

"No, thank you." When the waitress placed their steaming coffee cups on the table, Catherine immediately reached for Charlie's and stirred in some sugar. "Two cubes, no cream. Right?"

"Good memory." The hot liquid felt comforting as he swallowed.

"Some things I never forget," she said with a coy smile.

He cleared his throat. "I'm surprised you're still in town. Figured you'd have headed back to Arkansas."

"Texas." Her smile faded, and she stared down into her cup. "Near San Antonio." She glanced up and said brightly, "Well, of course, now that I'm in Kerryville, it seems silly not to stick around a while and …" Her voice wobbled, and she looked as if she might cry. Then, "Who am I kidding?" Her tone turned scornful. "I'm not home for a visit. I'm getting a divorce."

His thoughts scrambled. "You're … what?"

She arched an eyebrow. "You needn't look so shocked. This is 1929, after all."

"No. I mean, that's not what I … golly, I'm sorry."

As she launched into a story about a husband and his temper and her deep unhappiness, a knot of confused emotions tumbled through him. Almost a decade earlier, when he'd come home from the war with permanent injuries and recurring nightmares, she'd broken off their courtship without a backward glance. Not long after that—at least it hadn't seemed very long—he'd heard she'd gotten married to someone from out of town, an airman who'd managed to come back from Europe unbroken. For years, Charlie had sworn off women. He hadn't dated anyone until Dot had given him fresh hope, only to dash it again. And now here was Catherine, telling him her happily-ever-after had crashed and burned.

He swallowed. "I'm sorry to hear that. Truly, I am. But why are you telling me all this?"

All at once, her tone softened, and he swore he saw a tear glisten at the corner of her eye. He'd forgotten how mercurial her moods could be. She reached across the table and laid her hand on his. "Because I knew you'd understand. We were close once."

As gracefully as he could, he withdrew his hand and used it to grasp his coffee cup.

"I'd forgotten what a backward place Kerryville is," she continued. "Everyone in town is treating me like some sort of pariah."

"Oh, that can't be true."

Her eyes bore beseechingly into his. "I knew I could count on you to still be my friend."

Friend? He wasn't her friend, and she wasn't his.

"Friends don't kick a man when he's down," he said quietly.

She was silent, biting her lower lip. "You can't still be angry with me that I broke off our engagement. Surely not, after all these years."

He didn't respond.

"I was just a girl," she continued. "A silly girl who didn't know what she wanted. But she knows now."

His throat threatened to close. "Look, Catherine," he said, as gently as he could. "I'm sorry you're having such a rough time of it. But I don't know what you want from me."

"What I want," she said, her hazel eyes hopeful, "is another chance."

After telephoning everyone from the Union Station lost-and-found to Ellie Bains on her farm near Aurora, Dot faced the fact that she'd have to call Charlie if she had any hope of recovering her lost earring. At her break, she used the pay phone in the employee lounge.

"Kerryville, please. Corrigan's Dry Goods," she told the operator, then dropped in the requested number of coins.

"Corrigan's," a young voice chirped on the line.

"Hi, Helen. It's Dot."

Helen's words came in a rush. "Dot! I got a part in the school play. I'm to be Helen of Troy. Isn't that the craziest thing, Helen playing Helen?"

"That's wonderful, sweetie. I'm afraid I'm at work, so I have to rush. May I speak to your brother?"

"I'm sorry. He's gone off with Catherine Woodruff. Can I give him a message?"

Catherine. Dot tried to ignore the cold burning sensation in the pit of her stomach. She didn't care. She couldn't care. He was free to do as he pleased. As was she.

"Just tell him that I've lost an earring and am wondering if it might be in his car. Thanks."

She rang off and headed back to Millinery, blaming her sudden tummy ache on the cafeteria coffee but knowing, deep down, it was something else entirely.

CHAPTER TEN

The next day, on her final coffee break of the day, Dot rode the elevator to the book department to buy the novel Charlie had been talking about.

"Have you read it?" Dot asked Agnes as she wrapped up the purchase.

"No, but everybody's been talking about it," Agnes replied. "Mrs. Hahner wants to get Sinclair Lewis back in to sign copies." Marcella Hahner, the manager of the book section, was something of an industry pioneer in the matter of author book signings, which had proved to be among Field's most profitable and well-attended events.

"Also, do you have any good mysteries?" Dot asked. "I've finished the most recent Lord Peter Wimsey."

"I believe we have a new Dorothy Sayers, something different. Yes, here it is."

Agnes wrapped up the books, and Dot paid for them. Then she headed to her locker, where she tucked the books into her handbag. It had been a crazy couple of days with little sleep. She hoped a new book would hold her interest so she wouldn't fall asleep on the streetcar home and miss her stop. Besides, she was curious about this character Charlie said reminded him of her father.

When she got back to Millinery, she was surprised to see two uniformed police officers standing in the department, talking to her coworker, Isabel Nafwitz. As she approached, Isabel lifted her hand and pointed at Dot, who quickened her step. No doubt one of the officers needed a hat for a wife or sweetheart or something, and Dot was just the one to sell it to them.

"Good afternoon, officers," she said brightly. "How can I help you today?"

Neither of the men smiled back. Out of the corner of her eye, Dot saw Isabel slither away toward the stockroom.

"Are you Miss Dorothy Rodgers?" the taller of the two said.

"Yes." Dot's throat constricted. Had something happened to someone she cared about? Her mother? One of her sisters? Charlie? She raised her hand to her chest. "What's the matter? Has something happened?"

Another voice responded. "Yes, what's this all about?" Her supervisor, Mrs. Blandings, appeared at her side.

The tall man continued to address Dot. "I'm Officer Marino, and this is Officer O'Rourke. We'd like you to come with us down to the station for questioning."

Questioning? Her?

Mrs. Blandings frowned. "Why?"

The shorter officer spoke to Dot. "Please, just come with us, Miss Rodgers."

Dot put her hands on her hips. "Am I under arrest?"

"No, ma'am. But it's in your best interest to come down to the station."

Everyone was staring at her, store employees and customers alike.

"Go with them, Miss Rodgers," the supervisor said. "We don't want to make a scene."

"I'll have to get my coat and purse."

The officers accompanied her down the elevator to the employee locker room. Dot tried to look nonchalant for the sake of the curious elevator operator, but her mind was whirling. What could be the matter? Had she done something wrong? Forgotten to pay a bill? Been observed jaywalking across State Street? She honestly could not think of a thing worth getting pinched for. After she retrieved her things, she buttoned up her coat and grabbed her handbag.

"Our patrol car is parked this way," one of them said, steering her toward the Madison Street exit.

Icy rain poured down in sheets. As they stepped onto the sidewalk, Dot was vaguely aware of someone snapping her photograph. Umbrellas lifted as bystanders turned their heads her way in mild curiosity. Instinctively, she turned up the rabbit-fur collar of her coat, concealing her face. Soon she was bundled into the back of the patrol car traveling up the street. At least they didn't turn the lights and the siren on.

"What's going on? Please tell me."

Officer O'Rourke shrugged. "We don't know ourselves. Guess we'll find out when we get there."

Dot wasn't so sure about that. But they gave no further information, and she asked no more questions.

The remainder of the ride to the grim building at the intersection of

Hudson and Blackhawk was accomplished in silence. Once there, Dot was hustled to a messy little office. The man seated at the desk, who rose briefly at her appearance, was introduced to her as the district attorney. Another man sat silently off to the side, examining his cuticles.

"That will be all, gentlemen," the DA said to the officers. They backed out, closing the door behind them.

Dot stood in the middle of the room, waiting, watching. The DA motioned toward a hard wooden chair, but she didn't feel like sitting.

He peered at her out of eyes ringed with dark circles. His lined, ashen face looked as gray as his hair, as if he were sorely in need of sleep.

"Miss Rodgers, I'm Sam Bradshaw, district attorney. And this is the assistant district attorney, Clyde Greeley. We understand you're a close acquaintance of one Mr. Louis Braccio."

"I know him. I wouldn't say that we're close, but—"

"But you and he are friends."

Dot swallowed hard. "He was my boss. What's this about?"

"It appears Mr. Braccio may have some connection to the shootings last Thursday at the SMC Cartage Company. We're trying to find out what that connection is."

She sank into the wooden chair after all, her knees suddenly threatening to give way.

"He can't have been involved in that," she warbled. "He's in jail." Her voice grew small. "Isn't he?"

"That he is." Bradshaw tapped a pencil on the scarred surface of his desk. "We're trying to make all the pieces fit. We just want to know what you know."

"Me?" Dot's voice trembled. "I don't know anything."

"We have reason to believe members of Mr. Braccio's gang might have been involved. He hasn't talked with you? You haven't discussed anything pertinent to the case, perhaps while visiting him in jail?"

She gripped the arms of the chair. "I haven't visited the jail. Surely you can simply look at the visitor's log to verify that fact."

The DA eyed her for a long moment. "You could have written in a false name on the log. Happens all the time. Lots of dames fitting your description visit the jail."

Dot lifted her chin. "Well, I didn't."

"Letters? Telephone calls?"

"No."

"You've had no communication with Mr. Braccio since his

incarceration."

"That's correct."

Bradshaw consulted his notes. "You were lately seen fraternizing with one Eduardo Valencio. At a New Year's Eve party, I believe."

"Who? Eduardo Valen—oh, you mean Eddie? The piano player?" A nervous hyena-type sound escaped her throat, although nothing was the least bit funny. "I met him that night. He's a Northside Eskimo."

In the corner, Greeley looked up sharply from his cuticles. "Northside Eskimos … that some new street gang?"

"It's not a gang." Dot's head pounded. "It's a dance band. And I'm a singer, and Eddie—Mr. Valencio—told me he'd set up an audition for me."

"'Audition,' eh? Is that what he called it?" Greeley settled back in his chair with a smirk.

Anger at his insinuating tone seized her throat, but she forced herself to speak calmly. "Yes, that's right."

Bradshaw leaned forward. "Miss Rodgers, we have reason to believe Eduardo Valencio is connected to the Braccio gang. And we further suspect the Braccio gang's involved somehow in the shooting on Valentine's Day. No one is accusing you of anything, but as you appear to have connections to both men, you might have some information that will help us. That's why you're here. The sooner you answer our questions, the sooner you can leave."

"I see." Reassured that she wasn't in trouble, Dot sat up straighter. "Well, I'm not connected to anyone. I used to sing at Mr. Braccio's restaurant—"

"Restaurant." Greeley snorted.

She ignored him. "And I met Mr. Valencio one time at a party. That's all."

Bradshaw flipped through his notepad. "This audition you speak of. When and where did it take place?"

Dot shrank back in her seat. "It hasn't. He hasn't telephoned me. Yet."

"I see."

"But I'm certain he will."

Bradshaw tapped his pencil on the pad. "And the night of the party, he didn't give any indication of knowing Mr. Braccio?"

"He asked me if I was Louie's girlfriend."

Bradshaw's eyebrows raised. "Are you?"

"No. I mean—not anymore." This was not going well.

Bradshaw sighed. "Miss Rodgers." He pounded his fist on the desk, and she jerked like she'd been shot. "Listen, Miss Rodgers. Although I believe your name is actually *Barker*, isn't it?" He held her gaze as he paced around the desk then returned to his seat.

How did he know that? "Barker is my father's name," Dot explained. "I use Rodgers now. My mother's maiden name." Because the further she distanced herself from Oliver Barker, the better. But Bradshaw didn't need to know that. It unnerved her that he'd been checking up on her.

"Okay, Miss Barker"—emphasis on the name—"I'm thinking you know plenty, and you're going to spill it. Now, are you ready to talk nice?"

Clearly, the man's nerves were shot. Dot realized he must have been working on this case day and night. But that was no excuse for his behavior. She drew herself up.

"Look, I'd like to help you. But I don't know anything. Honest." She spoke firmly, even though her palms sweated. "I haven't seen Louie Braccio since a few days before his arrest. I used to sing in a speak ... in a restaurant he owned, the Villa Italiana. And we may have dated each other a few times. But that was it, and it was over months ago. And I only met Eddie Valencio at the party on New Year's Eve. I didn't know him at all before then."

"Aw, chief. Can't you see she's had enough?" Greeley's bored voice broke in. "Lay off her. She don't know nothing."

Bradshaw heaved a weary sigh.

"All right. Lock her up for safekeeping, then. She might be dangerous."

Dot's mouth gaped. Lock her up? And what was that last part? "Dangerous? Are you"—she was about to say *insane*, then thought the better of it—"sure you have the right Louie?"

"Go easy, chief," Greeley said. "I don't think she's in the know."

Dot looked gratefully at the man who moments before she'd wanted to throttle. Hysteria threatened to bubble up through her chest, but she bit her lip to keep it back.

"Don't leave town, Miss Barker ... Rodgers," Bradshaw said gruffly. "We may want to speak with you again." He turned abruptly on his heel and left the room.

Greeley crossed to where Dot was sitting and leaned against the desk so they faced each other.

"I'm sorry, kid. You all right? The guy's been working on this case for days. His nerves are shot."

Dot tried to smile.

"Now promise that you won't take it on the lam, and I'll spot you carfare."

Dot promised.

That evening she took a bath the minute she got home and went to bed with no thought of supper. Hoping for a light read to soothe her mind, she picked up *Elmer Gantry*, then set it down again. The last thing she needed before bed was to have images of her father floating through her mind. She picked up the other book she'd recently purchased, the one by Dorothy Sayers. A good mystery would be just the ticket.

Contrary to her expectations, this Sayers book turned out to be not a mystery at all but some kind of religious book. With a rush of disdain, she set it aside. Good grief, were even her favorite authors going to start prodding and poking at her about her lack of faith?

At last she fell into a fitful sleep. Sometime around midnight, however, she jerked awake from an exhausted, dreamless sleep to the insistent shrill of the door buzzer.

"Holy cats," she muttered as she slid a robe over her shoulders and shoved her feet into house slippers. Who on earth could be here at this hour?

"It's me. Veronica," came the response to her sleepy inquiry over the speaking tube. She pressed the button to unlock the outer door downstairs, then opened the apartment door to admit her friend.

When Veronica reached the top of the stairs, Dot said, "Is everything all right?"

Veronica muttered an expletive. "Ever thought of getting a telephone installed?" she wheezed, cranky from the climb. Chain-smoking wasn't doing her lungs any favors.

"Here, let me take your coat." Dot reached for her friend's snow-dampened fur. Veronica shrugged her away.

"I can't stay."

"What are you doing here, then?" Dot was wide awake now.

Veronica's dark eyes glittered beneath the low brim of her cloche. "I've come to give you a message."

"From whom?"

"Doesn't matter." She pulled a cigarette out of her handbag. "You got a light?"

Dot folded her arms and waited.

Veronica dug in her own bag for a lighter, then flicked it against the tip of the cigarette, took a drag, and puffed out a cloud. She closed her eyes for a moment, then returned her gaze to Dot.

"Look, kid. You and I are friends, right?"

"I suppose so."

"Then, as your friend, I've come to do you a favor." She took another slow drag on the cigarette. "Rumor has it you've been talking to the police."

Dot's grip on her arms tightened. Talking to the police? How had that gotten out, and what were these rumors saying? More importantly, who cared? Dot didn't know anything to tell them. "What if I have?"

Veronica's dark gaze flicked over Dot's face. "You know the kinds of work our men do. Carlo and Louie, and the others."

"Louie's not my man."

A plume of smoke rose lazily from one corner of Veronica's mouth.

"Whatever. Just be careful what you say when you're talking to the cops."

"What do you mean, what I *say*? I haven't said anything. I don't *know* anything."

"That's what I told them." She spoke around the cigarette perched jauntily between her lips.

"Told who?"

Veronica's gaze slid to the side. "I'm just warning you. You wouldn't want to accidentally say the wrong thing at the wrong time like your friend Marjorie did." She turned. "I gotta go. I shouldn't even be here."

"But what ... who ...?" Dot called ineffectually as Veronica hurried down the stairs and out the front door, letting in a blast of cold air.

Shivering, Dot closed the door to the hallway, locked it, and slumped against it. Then she hurried over to the front window and peered out, but the dark street was empty and silent, snow swirling crazily under the street lamps. It was true that Marjorie had made an innocent observation that set off a chain of events that had ended with Louie behind bars. But that was old news. And Louie deserved to serve time; he'd broken the law by running a liquor-smuggling ring. Think what she may about Prohibition—and she didn't care for it at all—there was no denying that Louie had violated it. What did any of that have to do with her visit to the police station?

Slowly she turned and collapsed onto the sofa, all thoughts of sleep abandoned.

What had *that* been all about?

CHAPTER ELEVEN

It was nearly closing time at Corrigan's Dry Goods when the telephone rang. Charlie looked up to see Helen lean over the counter and scoop the receiver to her ear with one hand, grabbing the base with the other.

"If it's Catherine, say I'm not available," he stage-whispered.

"Oh, brother." She glanced upward, then chirped into the mouthpiece, "Good evening, Corrigan's Dry Goods and Sundries. Oh, hi, Frances."

Relieved, he returned to his task at the register, where he was tallying the day's receipts. He tried to drown out his sister's voice.

A moment later, Helen said, "What? All right, we'll pick one up at the drugstore on the way home. What's for dinner?" Another pause, and then, "*Mmm*, sounds good. All right, see you soon." She replaced the receiver on the hook.

"What'd she say?" Charlie asked.

"Beef stew and biscuits."

"No, silly, I mean what are we supposed to pick up on the way home?"

"Oh, a newspaper. Specifically, one of the Chicago papers." She pulled the shade down over the front door, turned the key in the lock, and flipped the sign from Open to Closed.

"What for?"

"She didn't say. Probably wants a recipe or something." Clearly Helen's mind was on food.

"I'm just about done here," Charlie said. "Go ask Pop if he's ready to go."

"He went home a little while ago. Said he felt tired."

"Oh." Charlie enclosed the cash in a leather pouch. "All right, let's go."

They bundled themselves into jackets and scarves in the stockroom, then went out the back exit into the alley. Charlie locked the door behind them, and they climbed into the roadster. He stepped on the starter, and the engine purred to life.

"It sure is nice you don't have to crank it," Helen said. "Remember huffing and puffing to get Betty started up in winter?"

"Sure do." He had a fleeting moment of nostalgia for his old car. He bit back a comment about the new car's fickle engine and tendency to stall in cold weather. No need to have Helen join Pop in thinking he'd made a less-than-wise purchase.

They stopped first at the bank, where Charlie made the day's deposit. Then they stopped at the drugstore, where Helen bought the Chicago paper, among other things. "Took you long enough," Charlie grumbled when she returned to the car.

"Shut up or I won't share." She tore open a Baby Ruth bar and handed him a piece.

When they got home, they didn't even have time to take off their coats and boots before Frances came flying in from the kitchen wearing a flour-covered apron and a look of utter panic.

"Did you bring the paper?"

Helen handed her the folded newspaper.

Frances flipped it open and gasped. "She was right! Oh, dear, oh, dear."

"Who was right?"

Frances heaved a sigh. "Sadie Miller. She telephoned this afternoon and asked if I'd seen the Chicago paper. Said Marjorie's friend Dot Rodgers made the front page."

Charlie's stomach filled with acid.

"Dot did?" Helen cried. "Let me see."

"What are you talking about?" Charlie jerked the paper out of his stepmother's hands. He stared at the photograph of Dot being escorted by two policemen. There was no doubt it was her. He swatted Helen's hand away as she tried to grab the paper and read the headline aloud.

"Showgirl taken in for questioning."

"Showgirl! Our Dot?" Helen exclaimed.

"My land." Frances looked as if she might swoon.

"Shh. Listen," Charlie said. "'Miss Dorothy Rodgers, former showgirl at the Villa Italiana and alleged associate of gangster Louie Braccio, was taken in for questioning at the 36th police district yesterday and released. Braccio is currently serving six months in the Cook County Jail for his role in a bootlegging ring. Nonetheless, he is under suspicion, along with several of his associates, of having some knowledge of information connected to last week's shooting at the SMC Cartage Company, in which seven men died. The victims, all members or known associates of George Moran's gang, are alleged to have been killed at the hands of a rival gang led by notorious gangster Alphonse Capone.'"

"I heard about that shooting at school," Helen said. "They're calling it the St. Valentine's Day Massacre."

"How dreadful," Frances said, fanning her face with her fluttering hands.

"But I heard some cops did it," Helen continued, a look of confusion on her face.

"They say it wasn't real cops, just some guys disguised as cops," Charlie said. "Listen, there's more. 'Capone, reached at his Florida residence, denied any involvement in the crime. However, authorities think he may have given the order for the mass execution, which was then carried out by his henchmen.'"

"Does it say anything more about Dot?" Helen asked.

Charlie scanned the article. "Just that she hasn't been arrested or charged with any crime."

"A gangster's moll! And to think she's been in our home," Frances wailed, throwing her arms around Helen as if to protect her from evil influences. "She's eaten dinner at our table. Why, she was here in this very house just last week! She might have robbed us blind while we slept in our beds."

Anger heated Charlie's chest. "Come off it, Frances. Dot's anything but a gangster's moll. She may have made some poor choices of companions in the past, but that's all. You don't have to scorn her for it."

"But I love Dot!" Tears poured down Helen's cheeks. "Frances, how can you say such terrible things about her?"

"What's going on out here?" Pop shuffled into the foyer in his house slippers, blinking as if freshly woken from a snooze in his easy chair.

"Dot's been arrested!" Helen wailed.

"Not *arrested*, you ninny," Charlie said. "*Questioned*. And released."

Pop's eyes widened in surprise. "*Our* Dot?"

"Oh, for heaven's sake. Will everyone stop saying *our* Dot?" Frances interjected. "Clearly she has connections to the underworld we've known nothing about. I never did trust that girl. All that lip rouge and eye liner."

Charlie handed Pop the newspaper and pointed to the article. "See for yourself."

"Charlie," Frances said, "you must break off your relationship with her at once. I insist."

"Now, Frances, calm yourself," Pop said. "Let's not jump to any conclusions. I'm sure there's a good explanation behind all this."

"As a matter of fact, Frances, I'm not seeing her anymore," Charlie said, his voice rising. "But she was the one who broke it off, not me. And I certainly wouldn't have done so just to suit you and your so-called sense of—"

"Will everybody please calm down?" Pop said firmly. "Frances, dear, why don't you go into the kitchen and start putting dinner on the table? Helen, go and wash your face. And then we'll all discuss this over dinner like reasonable people."

Charlie didn't feel reasonable at all. He felt like punching the wall. Pop placed a comforting hand on his shoulder.

"Son, I know this news is a shock for you. It is for me too. But we don't have all the facts yet, and I for one think Dot deserves the benefit of the doubt. Don't you?"

"Sure I do. But gosh, the things Frances was saying—"

"You let me take care of Frances. Don't worry about that. Do you think maybe you should drive to the city and see Dot?"

"She doesn't want to see me. It'll probably make matters even worse for her if I show up out of the blue."

"Well, let's go and have ourselves a good dinner. After that we can think about what to do next."

Charlie relaxed a little under the weight of Pop's hand on his shoulder. What would he ever do without Pop's clear-headed guidance?

That evening, Charlie sat at the desk in his room and tried to write a letter to Dot. When he'd found her lost earring on the floor of the Packard, he'd attempted telephoning her via Mrs. Moran but had gotten no answer. Which was probably just as well since he'd get tongue-tied on the telephone, anyway, and he wasn't in the mood to listen to the landlady's friendly banter. He didn't think Dot would appreciate his showing up at her place unannounced, not considering the way she'd left him at the Bains's place. She hadn't been too keen on answering the letters he'd sent her in the weeks following their New Year's Eve fiasco. But maybe she'd be willing to do so now after their fleeting reconciliation at the farmhouse. In any case, he figured a letter might be the best way to reach her. He had to let her know he was thinking about her and was on her side. If only he could think of the right words to say.

As for the earring, the golden object lay on his desk and glinted in the lamplight. He picked it up and turned it over in his hand, wondering if she'd received it from Louie. In any case, it looked too valuable to risk sending it through the mail. To get it back, she would have to see him in person, a thought that gladdened his heart. He'd use any excuse to see her.

He turned back to his letter. He'd gotten as far as "Dear Dot." Outside his dormer window, a winter storm was kicking up. The eaves creaked in the wind, and the glass rattled in the window frame. At his desk, warm and well fed on beef stew and biscuits, he was comfortable. Maybe *too* comfortable. He thought of Dot, living all on her own now that Marjorie had gotten married and moved out of their shared apartment in the big city. How was she feeling? Nervous after being hauled down to the police station? Maybe more than nervous. Maybe scared out of her wits. Of what, though? The police? The people she'd run around with? If only Charlie could help her.

Here he was, as safe and snug as a turtle under his parents' roof. It didn't seem right.

Dot was no shrinking violet. He knew that as well as anyone. She could take care of herself. But maybe if he'd been there, maybe if they'd still been together, she wouldn't be in trouble now. Not that she was in trouble, necessarily. She'd only been questioned, after all, and let go, probably when the police understood she no longer had any connection to Louie Braccio and his shady underworld friends. Still, he couldn't shake the feeling that something was wrong. He should be with her now. If she'd given him the slightest hope she cared for him, he'd jump in the car and go.

Chewing absentmindedly on the cap of his fountain pen, he looked around his bedroom as if seeing it for the first time. It still looked exactly as it had most of his life. A red plaid bedspread, a bookcase housing trophies from his prewar days as a high school athlete, several books by the likes of Mark Twain and Horatio Alger, and colorful Chicago Cubs pennants lining the walls. It was a boy's room, not a man's room. He shifted on his chair. What kind of way was this for a man approaching thirty to live?

He should be out of the house by now, out on his own, making his way in the world. Not working for his father and living comfortably in his parents' house. Not that he didn't help out with household chores and bills—he did, at least as much as Pop would allow.

Pop. He was the key. If Charlie could get Pop to agree to open a second store, Charlie could run it. He'd finally have something he could call his own. And regardless of whether or not he and Dot ever got back together, he'd never again feel as stuck and useless as he did tonight.

And forget Dubuque or Galena. The new store should be located in or near Chicago. If Dot loved the city that much, he would never make her leave it. Not even if they ended up getting back together. *Especially* if they got back together. He'd be the one to adjust to city life, not force her to adjust to life in the country.

He turned back to the blank sheet of paper, and the words started to flow. He wrote to her about the article in the paper, about how brave she was, and about how he would stand by her no matter what. He wrote about his ideas for the second store and where it should be located and how he would broach the subject with Pop. He wrote about his plans for the future and how he hoped they'd include her. If not, he wrote about how he hoped they'd always be friends. He reassured her about the earring, said he'd like to return it in person if she'd consent to see him. He wrote and wrote and wrote, not stopping until it was time to sign it.

He dickered on the closing. Should he write *Sincerely* or *Yours truly* or *Truly yours* or *Very truly yours?*

At last he shook his pen to freshen the ink and scrawled out his heart onto the page in big, bold strokes.

Love, Charlie.

CHAPTER TWELVE

Only ten days had passed since Marjorie's wedding, but to Dot, it felt like ten weeks.

"This brimmed style is very becoming to your profile and will remain stylish for several seasons to come," she promised the silver-haired customer seated before the mirror. In spite of the drama swirling in her personal life, her professional demeanor never wavered. She had a job to do, and she did it well.

"I'll take it," said the well-dressed matron, turning her head to admire the hat from various angles. "It might even work with my Easter outfit. Do you think so?"

"It will do nicely for church, Mrs. Dunsworthy. Hard to believe that Easter's only a few weeks away." The thought cheered Dot, even as the February snows swirled up and down State Street. In the five days since she'd been taken in for questioning, it seemed the sun hadn't come out once, but the spring sunshine would eventually arrive. It always did.

The customer turned and gave Dot a warm smile. "Thank you for your help today, Miss Rodgers. You're a gem."

To her own surprise, a lump formed in her throat. She clung to the warmth of that smile as if to a life raft.

The snow-blanketed city wasn't the only atmosphere that was chilly. Since the news broke of her past involvement with Louie Braccio and the fact of Louie being investigated in connection with the St. Valentine's Day massacre, the other clerks avoided her as if she had a contagious disease. It didn't matter that, though the crime remained unsolved, Louie had been cleared of any suspicion, as had Eddie Valencio, and the police had not questioned Dot further about either one of them. The stain on her reputation was permanent, as far as the moccasin trail was concerned.

No decent man will ever want you.

At lunch, instead of putting on a false face of gaiety in the cafeteria, she found a quiet corner and pulled out the Sayers book she'd been reading. In spite of her initial distaste for spiritual topics, her fondness for Sayers' writing and incisive mind won out. It was a short, thought-provoking book about a man: Jesus Bar-Joseph, the carpenter of Nazareth. It showed Jesus in a way she hadn't considered before. Not the way her father misrepresented him. And to her surprise, she found she could scarcely put it down.

After work, the snowstorm slowed the streetcar's progress, and she arrived home tired, wet, and bedraggled. She unlocked the front door, onto which Mrs. Moran had tacked a small decorative bouquet of silk hyacinths in cheerful defiance of the miserable winter weather. God bless Mrs. Moran. At least she hadn't turned Dot out into the snow on account of that dreadful newspaper article. She'd given no speech about needing to maintain the reputation of her building. She hadn't even clucked her tongue or given Dot the side-eye, as so many others had done. Maybe she didn't read the papers.

As Dot collected her mail from the small metal box in the vestibule, Mrs. Moran's door swung open. "There you are," the landlady said cheerfully. "This letter got mixed in with my mail by mistake."

"Thank you." Dot accepted the white envelope.

"It's postmarked Kerryville," Mrs. Moran continued.

Dot looked at the return address, and her heart gave a lurch. "So it is." The envelope bore Charlie's handwriting. With a pang of guilt, she thought of how she'd run out on him at the Bains farm. No doubt his letter would be filled with scoldings and recriminations. Or worse … news of his reconciliation with the auburn-curled wonder. She couldn't blame him. The woman was an attractive Kerryville girl who would fit smoothly into his life, whose parents were friends with his. Frances would not feel the need to give Catherine the evil eye over the length of her skirts or the strength of her perfume.

With a weary sigh, Dot slid the envelope to the bottom of the stack and started up the stairs. "Well, good night."

"Isn't Kerryville where that nice young man comes from?" Mrs. Moran called after her. "I believe I once heard you mention that he …"

"Good night, Mrs. Moran," Dot called again. She gently closed the door to her apartment and slumped against it. Coming home to an empty flat felt lonely and cold in a way it hadn't before Marjorie'd moved in the previous summer. But Dot hadn't spent much time in the apartment before Marjorie. She'd spent most evenings either singing at the Villa Italiana, modeling for life-drawing classes at the Art Institute, or going out with Louie and friends like Veronica. Now she did none of those things.

She thought of Veronica's strange late-night visit and veiled threat and shuddered. Some friends. Sure, Veronica had given her a place to sleep, helped her get the job at Field's. But at what price? Louie had let her sing three nights a week in exchange for a good meal and tips. She'd been grateful. But when the place had been raided by the feds, she'd narrowly escaped arrest. And now she was being questioned by the police because of her ties to him. Charlie was right. Her friends were bad news.

She dropped the mail on an end table, shrugged off her coat and hung it on a peg near the door, and turned on a lamp to dispel the twilight gloom. In the kitchen, she lit the burner under the tea kettle and poured a can of tomato soup into a saucepan. While waiting for her dinner to heat, she sat on the sofa and riffled through the mail. Bills, bills, and more bills. Not only did she miss Marjorie's company, she'd soon miss her help with the rent. She'd need to find another roommate, and soon. She'd hoped to get hired as a legitimate singer with a legitimate band like the Northside Eskimos, but not only had Eddie not called her, according to the DA, he, too, was a shady character. She seemed to attract them like metal shavings to a magnet. Finding another singing job at a speakeasy was a possibility, but not one that Dot found attractive. Not with the quality of the clientele.

She resolved to contact the Art Institute about getting back on the roster as a model, if not for the spring semester, then for summer school. The idea didn't hold much appeal, but she didn't have many options for evening work on top of her day job at Field's.

At last she turned to the letter she'd been avoiding. She picked it up, then set it on top of the pile. Surely nothing good would come of reading it.

She returned to the kitchen and poured boiling water into a teacup, along with a tea bag and a spoonful of honey. She was tempted to add a shot of whiskey—it was a cold night, after all—but decided against it. Ever since she'd started seeing Charlie, she'd avoided alcohol. The one night she'd slipped off the wagon, they'd broken up. It seemed no surprise that the taste of alcohol no longer appealed as it once had. She poured the tomato soup into a bowl and buttered a piece of bread. Then she sat down at the kitchen table to eat her simple meal.

"And how was your day, Dot?" she spoke brightly into the silence. "Oh, lovely, thank you. Mrs. Deane bought two sun hats to wear on her cruise to Havana, and more than one customer had Easter bonnets on the brain. My sales book looked pretty good by the end of the day, I'll tell you that. And was my supervisor pleased? She most certainly was not. In fact, her attitude was downright frosty. And Miss Jantzen snubbed me at coffee break, and Miss Nafwitz ignored me at lunch, so among them, they had the whole day covered. Can't wait to do it all again tomorrow!"

She sighed and toyed with the tea bag. Deciding that Elmer Gantry would make a better dinner companion than her own pathetic self, she pushed back from the table and went to the bookcase to grab the novel. Charlie was right; the story of the false-hearted evangelist seemed to shed new light on the character of her father. As she passed the end table, Charlie's letter glowed up at her from the stack of letters.

Read me, it seemed to say.

"No," she said out loud. "Go back where you came from."

C'mon. Just slit me open. You know you're curious.

Even the darn envelope sounded like Charlie.

She snatched up the letter, grabbed two corners to tear it in half, then stopped. Stupid to open it. It would only make this harder. But she slid her finger under the flap. Might as well take it like a woman and get it over with. He had every right to be angry. She couldn't blame him for taking up with Catherine again if that was the news contained on the ink-covered pages. Dot had made her intentions clear. She always knew he'd find someone more suitable. She had no right to complain now that he had, even if the thought made her insides shrivel.

She sat back down at the kitchen table and began to read.

Several minutes later, she set the letter beside her bowl and stared at it, mystified.

He'd said such kind things. He would always be her friend. He knew the kind of person she was, and he'd stand by her, always.

Where was the anger? Where was the recrimination? The name Catherine hadn't appeared once.

Her finger traced his closing word: *Love.*

She picked up her spoon and stirred the now-cold soup.

He was on her side. And what had she done to deserve it?

She stood and carried her dish to the sink. She turned on the tap and let the water flow, and with it, the tears.

Charlie couldn't believe it. He sat on a stool in the stockroom and read her letter through two, three, a dozen times. It had taken a couple weeks, but she'd actually written back! She'd thanked him for his letter and said she looked forward to his returning the earring in person. She said they could remain friends, that she appreciated his support and was happy to have him in her life. Not in the way he'd hoped, perhaps, but it was a start. At least she wasn't shutting him out completely.

He folded the letter and slid it into his breast pocket, next to his heart. He felt as if he could do anything, including selling his father on the idea of opening a second store. A second store that would be closer to Chicago. Closer to Dot.

"See here, Pop," he said later that day. He and his father were leaning over either side of Pop's desk, looking at financial reports. Charlie pointed to the glowing assessment provided by the accountant. "Now is the time to jump on expansion. You're correct that Kerryville can't support another dry-goods store. But a bigger metropolitan area can."

Pop sat up, removed his spectacles, polished them with a cloth, and shook his head. "I don't think Chicago is desperate for another dry-goods store either, son."

"I'm not talking about Chicago, necessarily. Look." Charlie pushed aside the financial reports and spread out a map on Pop's desk. "This is the greater Chicago area. 'Chicagoland,' the developers are calling it. Now see"—he outlined an area of the map with a pencil—"here you have the Chicago city limits. On the east side, obviously, you have the lake. And all this"—he drew a long, curving C-shape from north to south—"is the suburbs. These suburbs are booming, Pop, all along the train lines. See?" He indicated the rail lines that spoked out from the city in all directions. "New houses are going up like crazy, and people are snapping them up. People no longer want to travel all the way downtown to do their shopping. Look, Marshall Field's recently opened a branch store in Lake Forest." He tapped the north end of the map. "And out here, this is Oak Park, where they're building another branch." He pointed to an area west of the city.

Pop replaced his spectacles and fastened his gaze on the map.

"So you're thinking we should open a second store in one of these new suburbs?"

"That's what I'm thinking."

"I don't know. Seems like a pretty big risk to me."

Changing the display in the front window seems like a pretty big risk to you. "I know. But businesses don't move ahead without some risk. You took a mighty big risk when you opened up this place."

Pop nodded slowly. "That I did, son. You and Marjorie were just little tykes then, and Helen wasn't even born yet. Your great-aunt Betsy helped behind the counter, and sometimes your mother helped, too, when we were especially busy. You used to play under the counter while she waited on customers." His eyes took on a faraway look.

"I remember," Charlie said quietly. "And, see, it turned out all right. Corrigan's Dry Goods has kept a roof over our family's heads and food on our table for all this time."

"Yes, it has. But not without sacrifice. There have been some lean years, too."

Charlie's exasperation level spiked. He fought to keep his tone respectful. "Of course. But 1929 isn't one of them. That's why I think we should jump on this opportunity. You've seen the report I drew up about the kind of revenue I think we could get, the going rates for rents and such. Don't you see, Pop?" He looked his father straight in the eye and spoke with as much earnestness as he could muster, just a few hairs short of begging. "This is the opportunity of a lifetime. I think we need to seize the brass ring while it's within reach."

Pop regarded his son for several minutes as if sizing him up. Charlie waited, holding his breath. Finally Pop spoke.

"I remember how it was, wanting my own business. Nothing unusual about a grown man wanting to strike out on his own."

"I wouldn't be completely on my own. It will be our business, a new opportunity for *us*. For the whole family. The new store would still be Corrigan's—just a branch store." He blinked in rising excitement. "Maybe the start of a whole chain of stores."

Pop raised a hand. "Whoa. Let's not get ahead of ourselves."

Charlie backed down. "The point is, we'd still be working together, you and I. Just at different locations. You'd be here, running the flagship store, and I'd manage the branch, closer to Chicago." He liked the word "flagship." It sounded powerful and reassuring.

"You've worked alongside me since you were a boy." Pop's tone was thoughtful. Charlie knew he was weighing the prospect and hope surged. "You know the business inside and out. Which makes you a valuable asset. It'd be tough trying to get along without you. Helen can't do everything you do. Not yet, anyway."

"There are plenty of young fellows around town who'd love to hire on here. Heck, they'd do a lot better with physical work, the lifting and carrying, than I do, with my ... limitations."

"You do fine, son. No job you can't tackle if you set your mind to it." Pop hesitated another minute, then looked at Charlie and sighed. "I suppose we can give it a go with one store. *One*, mind you."

Charlie's breath whooshed out in relief, and he slapped his hand on the desk. He could hardly contain his excitement. He grabbed his father's hand and pumped it up and down. "That's great, Pop. That's just great. You're the tops, you know that? You won't be sorry."

Pop adjusted his glasses. "I hope not."

At last, Charlie was getting his chance to shine. Best of all, he'd be moving closer to Dot, could see her more often—a prospect she seemed open to, according to her letter, even if merely "as friends." He felt sure that, with a prosperous store and a brilliant future, with money to spend and the proximity to woo her, he'd be able to win her back in time. And they'd *have* time when he lived closer to her.

"Best get started right away." Charlie dragged a stool over to the desk. "What do you say we go over those numbers one more time, and I'll tell you all about what I'm thinking?"

CHAPTER THIRTEEN

Wearing a rooster-printed cotton apron that Marjorie had received as a wedding-shower gift, Dot stood at the white porcelain sink in the Bachmann kitchen, rinsing green beans in a colander under the tap. The sight of a robin fluttering on the budding branches outside the second-story apartment window made her smile. Spring at last!

Beside her, Marjorie reached into a cabinet and pulled out a stack of plates.

"I hope it's not awkward for you that Charlie will be joining us for dinner tonight."

Dot kept her voice light. "Awkward? Not awkward at all. We're on friendly terms, after all."

Marjorie looked relieved. "Well, that's good to hear."

Dot set a plate on the drain board. "We've decided the best thing to do is simply move on. Go forward as friends."

Marjorie quirked an eyebrow. "Does Charlie know that? You've talked about it?"

"Of course. Why?"

Marjorie shrugged but didn't say anything else. Instead, she turned her concentration to pulling a hot pan of rolls out of the compact apartment-sized oven.

"Anyway," Dot continued, "it'll be good to see him. We've exchanged a few letters, but I haven't seen him since your wedding." *Or shortly thereafter*, she thought, but she hadn't filled Marjorie in on the whole Bains-farmhouse incident, and what her friend didn't know wouldn't hurt her. "I'm eager to hear about the new store and everything. Have you seen it?"

"Not yet," Marjorie said, "but Peter has. He says it needs some fixing up, but it sounds like only surface work—painting and such. The building seems sound, and it's in a great location."

"I understand he's hoping to open on May first."

"Sounds like he'll make it. You'll come, won't you? To the opening?"

"I wouldn't miss it."

Marjorie used a spatula to transfer the rolls from the pan to a platter, then covered them with a clean dishtowel to keep warm.

"Frankly," she said, "I'm relieved he's finally moving out of Pop's house and out of Kerryville altogether."

"Why?"

Marjorie glanced around as if making sure Peter was out of earshot. "The word around town is that Catherine Bailey—I mean, Woodruff—has her hooks out for him."

"His old girlfriend?" A familiar burning sensation settled in Dot's stomach. So it wasn't just a fluke, that time she'd called the store and learned Charlie'd gone out with Catherine. Maybe she was wooing him back. When he'd written Dot that beautiful letter, friendship, and friendship only, had been his intention. She swallowed around her disappointment, even though friendship was what she'd thought she wanted, too. "I thought you said she lived out of state."

"Not anymore. She left her husband and moved back to Kerryville to live with her parents."

"Oh, my." So the gossiping biddies at the Kerryville train station had been right. Dot slid the green beans into a pot of boiling water on the stove and added a pinch of salt. "I remember you said she broke up with Charlie after the war. He never told me much about her."

Marjorie sighed. "She's not a bad person, really. We all liked her. The problem was, she dumped Charlie like a hot potato when he came back from the war not quite … himself. She gave some other reason, of course, like they'd 'grown apart' and developed 'separate interests,' but we all knew it was because he was no longer the prime specimen of masculinity she'd agreed to marry." She shrugged. "It's been hard to feel kindly toward her after she broke my brother's heart."

"Poor Charlie." The scorn in Marjorie's tone matched Dot's indignation on Charlie's behalf.

"Anyway," Marjorie continued, "not long after that, she up and married a fellow who was in the Army Air Corps, and she moved away. Charlie went into sort of a tailspin. He took to drinking, as you know, and it was a long time before he risked approaching a woman romantically. Then you came along and …" She shrugged again. "We'd all hoped you two would work out as a couple, of course. But at least you're on friendly terms, and neither of you seems traumatized by the breakup."

Dot did, in fact, feel traumatized, even though the breakup had been her idea. But she didn't want to let on, not even to her best friend. The thought of Charlie finding someone else made her lose her appetite, but she put on a brave face.

"I suppose he'll be dating someone else soon enough."

"I suppose so," Marjorie agreed. "I just hope to high heaven he chooses someone—anyone—other than Catherine."

***

Charlie recruited Helen to help him transform an empty storefront into the Corrigan's Dry Goods and Sundries branch store. The burgeoning suburb of Oak Park had been selected as the site. A mere eight miles to the west of Chicago and easily reached by streetcars, elevated trains, and the Chicago Burlington & Quincy commuter line, Oak Park was perfectly situated to serve exactly the sort of prosperous high-hat clientele Charlie had in mind. With the help of a rental agent, he'd found and signed the lease on a storefront property just a few doors down Lake Street from the new branch of Marshall Field & Company. He'd secured a bank loan for fixtures and inventory, which he'd be ordering in the next few weeks. Then all that was needed was a little feminine assistance to transform it from a former tobacco shop into a fabrics emporium.

Now, as he stood in the middle of the empty store and watched his kid sister apply a coat of fresh white paint to a wall, deep satisfaction welled up in his chest. In his fondest daydreams, the store would be a great success. Dot would transfer to the Oak Park branch of Field's, and then she and Charlie would work just a few doors away from each other and would meet up nearly every day for companionable lunches and dinners, just friends at first, and then eventually ... But it was too soon to think about all that. There was a great deal of work to be done if the store was going to be ready to open in early May.

"You could help, you know, instead of standing there daydreaming," Helen chided from her perch atop a ladder. "I didn't give up my spring break to help you fix up the store so you could leave me to do it all by myself."

Charlie snorted. "Give up your spring break? Hey, I don't think you've had it so bad. You've only worked here two days out of the whole week. The rest of the time you've been living high on the hog—shopping with Marjorie and Dot, going to the theater, dining in restaurants, sleeping at Marjorie and Peter's place …"

"Their sofa is lumpy," she said, turning back to the wall and lifting her paintbrush. "But I guess you're right. It hasn't all been child labor."

"We have to knock off now, anyway. We've been invited to Marjorie and Peter's for dinner."

Helen glanced at him with a grin. "Dot, too?"

"I don't know. I suppose so." He tried to sound nonchalant.

"That's good. She's the bee's knees."

Yes, she is, kid. Yes, she is.

"Be sure to rinse the brush out really well," he gruffed. "I don't want to find it all stuck with paint in the morning."

Together they washed up using the sink in the tiny stockroom at the back of the store. Charlie finished putting away their tools while Helen changed from paint-stained overalls back into a skirt and sweater. Then they headed outside to wait for the streetcar that would carry them to Marjorie and Peter's West Side apartment.

The breeze blew warmth around them, redolent with the springtime scents of rain and earth. Tulips bloomed in concrete planters lining the curbs. Shoppers and office workers strolled up and down the sidewalks at a more leisurely pace than the unending frantic rush of the Loop. Charlie fervently prayed some of them would become customers.

They soon arrived at the apartment, a two-flat like Dot's, except that the Bachmanns occupied the ground floor instead of the upper floor. Charlie pressed the buzzer marked "Bachmann." He still hadn't gotten used to the fact that Marjorie's last name was Bachmann now. Peter and Marjorie, still sporting traces of their honeymoon suntans, welcomed Charlie and Helen with warm hugs and handshakes. Pop was there, too. He'd be driving Helen home to Kerryville after dinner.

"Didn't Frances come with you?" Helen asked after she kissed her father.

"No, she didn't, kiddo. She sends her regrets, but she had an important club meeting tonight that she didn't feel she could skip out on."

Charlie worried at first when he didn't see Dot, but disappointment turned to relief when she appeared in the kitchen doorway, wiping her hands on a dish towel. As Marjorie's dear friend, she was still practically part of the family, even though she and Charlie were no longer an item.

"We're so excited you could join us," Marjorie said to him. "You're our first official dinner guests since we've been married." She smiled at Peter, who winked back. Charlie's chest tightened, hoping that one day he'd find a wife who'd look at him that way.

He walked over to Dot. "Here, I brought you this." He produced the gold earring from his trouser pocket. "I found it on the floor under the passenger seat."

"Thanks so much for remembering to bring it," she said. "I hated to think I'd lost it forever."

"It's awful to lose something you love," he agreed. He waited for her to say something more about it, like where it came from or why it meant so much to her, but she merely smiled, carried it to the coat rack, and slid it into a purse hanging there.

The family gathered around the table in the small dining alcove that opened off the front room. It was a tight squeeze, but Charlie didn't mind. He spent the entire meal within inches of Dot, which suited him fine.

Over fried pork chops and green beans, Marjorie and Peter took turns telling stories of their honeymoon trip to Florida. Then the conversation turned to books.

"I read a book Charlie recommended," Dot said. "*Elmer Gantry*."

Charlie's eyebrows lifted. "I didn't exactly recommend it. I said the main character reminded me of your father."

"You were right," she said. "I didn't like it very much, but it did make me think. I also picked up another book called *The Greatest Drama Ever Staged* by Dorothy Sayers."

"What did you think of that one?" Marjorie asked.

"I think Sinclair Lewis and Dorothy Sayers do not run in the same circles." She laughed, then said, "It's clearing some things up for me. About faith and church and ... things like that."

"Sounds interesting," Charlie said. "We should talk about it sometime."

"I'd like that." She gave him a smile that warmed him to his toes.

"Maybe you should be opening a bookshop instead of a dry goods store," Helen said.

With that, the conversation turned to the new Marshall Field's branch in Oak Park and plans for the new Corrigan's store.

"You're smart to choose Oak Park," Dot said. "It's a very up-and-coming suburb."

"I've heard that several employees have asked to be transferred out there from the main store," Marjorie remarked. "There are lots of opportunities opening up."

"Yes, I've heard that, too," Dot said.

"How about you?" Charlie said eagerly. "Why don't you put in for a transfer?"

"I don't know," she said in a noncommittal tone. "I have it pretty good where I'm at."

"But think of it. A brand-new store." *Right down the street from me*, he added silently.

"How long are you planning to live above the store?" Helen asked Charlie. "You should see it," she announced to the rest of the table. "He's got a cot, a table, a lamp—and that's just about it."

"Sounds luxurious," Peter murmured.

Helen turned back to Charlie. "You should look for a nice apartment like this one."

Charlie laughed. "All in good time, kid. All in good time." Unknown to his family, he had toured a stately new apartment building called the Oak Park Arms. The high rent would have made Pop's remaining hair curl, but Charlie's soaring stock market investments brought it within reach, provided the new store flourished as he intended. However, the large apartments seemed better suited to married couples or families. With God's help, he'd reach that state eventually, with a certain dark-haired lady at his side. For the time being, a flat above the store would suit him just fine.

After a delicious dessert of apple pie and vanilla ice cream, Pop leaned back in his chair and patted his stomach. "Helen and I had better hit the road. We have a long drive."

Good-byes and promises to visit again soon were shared all around.

After they'd gone, Charlie eased himself onto a sofa and groaned with satisfaction.

"That was a great dinner, Marjie."

"Thanks," Marjorie said. "Let's all sit in the living room where it's more comfortable. More coffee, anyone?"

"Yes, please," Charlie said.

"I'd like some, too. I'll help." Dot started to go with Marjorie to the kitchen.

"Everyone sit down," Peter ordered. "You too, Marjorie. You served up that great dinner. The least I can do is get the coffee."

He went to the kitchen and returned with a tray bearing the shiny new percolator and four wedding-china cups and saucers.

"So how are the renovations coming on the store?" he asked Charlie as he poured hot coffee into the cups.

"Helen's been a big help, but there's still a lot to do." Charlie sipped his coffee. "I can finish up the painting. That's no problem. I may have only one good arm, but that one arm is pretty darn efficient with a paintbrush."

"I can come by and help you out after work," Peter offered.

"I'll take all the help I can get." Charlie shifted on the sofa. "What I'm especially hoping, though, is that you girls might help me out, too." He looked at Marjorie and Dot in turn. "I could sure use a feminine touch when it comes to choosing inventory and creating displays. I've never been too talented with that froufrou stuff."

Marjorie lit up. "Sure, I can help. I can practice some of the decorating techniques Mr. Fraser's been teaching me. We might even have some supplies at Field's that we're not going to use. You could probably snap them up on the cheap. I'll check."

"That would be fine." Charlie's gaze shifted to Dot. "What about you? Do you think you could give us a hand?"

Dot's dark eyes flicked from Marjorie to Charlie and back again. "I suppose I could help, too, a couple of evenings a week. As long as Marjorie's going to be there."

Charlie sensed her unspoken wish not to spend long stretches of time alone with him. The thought squelched his growing hope that she might one day return his affection.

Dot stirred her coffee. "I suppose it would be a lot more convenient to come over and help you if I were already working in Oak Park. Maybe I should put in for that transfer."

Charlie grinned. "Maybe you should."

"But I won't give up my job at Field's," she added firmly.

"I would never ask you to."

Charlie didn't miss the undercurrent of reluctance in her tone. He couldn't blame her for not wanting to work two jobs, and Field's offered a lot more security than a small shop that hadn't even opened its doors yet.

"It'll just be temporary, until the store's ready to open," Charlie said. "Any time you can spare would be more than appreciated."

And if working together helped her warm up to him, well, that would be the frosting on the cupcake.

※

Working at Field's all day and then at Corrigan's most evenings, helping to bring in new inventory and set up the displays, proved to be a challenge, but it was a challenge Dot relished. It was the kind of work she loved to do, and it filled her evenings. She'd lost her appetite for going out to the speakeasies. Her old friends, who once seemed so glamorous and sophisticated, now seemed shallow and vapid. Further, she hadn't appreciated the threatening tone of Veronica's late-night visit. While she owed Veronica a debt of gratitude for past kindnesses, it no longer felt fun or daring or clever to be part of a circle that scoffed at the law. It felt stupid, even dangerous. Her priorities had shifted. If she thought about it at all, she blamed it on Dorothy Sayers, who had enticed her to pick up a few other books about faith, even a small copy of the New Testament. It was hard to read familiar verses without hearing her father's booming voice misquoting them or applying them out of context for his own shady purposes, but she persevered to read with fresh eyes and an open heart.

At Corrigan's, as she unpacked crates and arranged goods on the shelves, she mused about how someday, the possibility of owning a little shop of her own didn't seem all that far-fetched. Shopkeeping would probably be more secure than singing in restaurants. The fact that Eddie Valencio hadn't called about an audition still stung, though she tried to shrug it off. Good riddance if he was an associate of Louie's.

Right now, this extra job allowed her to work alongside Charlie and Marjorie, two people she admired more than almost anyone in the world. What could be better?

She knew what could be better. Being Charlie's sweetheart again would be better. But that was out of the question. The cloud of scandal still hadn't lifted, and she couldn't stand to harm his reputation by association. Though she'd done nothing wrong but choose the wrong friends, people had long memories. She felt distant from almost everybody except Marjorie, Peter, and Charlie. But they were friends, and that's all they ever could be. Someday he'd marry a nice Kerryville girl with no past and no whiff of scandal following her around. Dot would throw rice at their wedding, then go home to her little flat, where she would have only a cat for company. She'd had her mind set on getting a cat ever since the sweet one at the Bains' farmhouse had helped set such a cozy scene. She'd grow old with a cat, a radio, and an African violet.

In the middle of a particularly hectic day, Dot stopped by the candy counter at Marshall Field's to treat herself to a bag of chocolate-covered almonds. She didn't make a habit of stopping at the candy counter, unwilling to risk her fashionably flat figure. But a crazy day like this one simply cried out for chocolate.

"Where ya been, Dottie?" Veronica said as she scooped the candy into a small paper bag and weighed it on a scale. "We've missed you." She looked completely different on the job—scrubbed clean of makeup and wearing a uniform and hairnet—than she did in her going-out attire.

"You haven't been to any of the nightclubs in weeks and weeks," she continued.

"I've been working two jobs, sort of," Dot said. "Just temporarily. But it fills up my evenings." She told Veronica all about the Oak Park store and her role in helping to set it up. "Besides," she added, "I don't spend as much time at parties and such as I used to. Those places kind of lost their appeal for me since the Villa Italiana closed."

"You're not planning to leave Field's, are you?" Veronica quirked an eyebrow.

"Oh, heavens, no. As I said, this second job is just temporary, to help out a friend."

"Not Charlie Corrigan, is it?"

Dot nodded.

Veronica sighed. "Honestly, Dottie, I don't know what you see in him. I mean, sure, he's good-looking and all, but could there be a wetter blanket in all of Chicago?"

"I'm not dating him," Dot insisted. "We're just friends."

Veronica rolled her eyes. "Sure, doll. Whatever you say. But what about your singing? If you don't hang around the speaks, where are you going to get a chance to sing?"

"Church, maybe." She realized as she said the words, she was serious. Why not? She'd judged all Christians by her father. But Charlie and Marjorie were Christians. Peter, too. And they were nothing like her dad. They were kind and sincere and forgiving. Maybe Dot could sing in church. Maybe she could be happy in church like she'd never been when her father was at the pulpit.

"Church? You?" Veronica sputtered. "You're so funny." She leaned on the counter—a definite Field's no-no. "So what kind of store is it?"

"Dry goods."

"Sounds boring."

Boring? Dot thought of Charlie, and a glow spread over her chest. "Maybe boring is exactly what I need."

CHAPTER FOURTEEN

One evening in late April, Dot and Marjorie caught the streetcar outside of Marshall Field's and rode to Oak Park after work, as they'd been doing for weeks. Dot felt flat-out exhausted after a long day of helping ladies choose their summer hats. Nonetheless, her energy picked up as the streetcar neared the leafy suburb. Maybe the smartest thing, after all, would be to ask for a transfer to the suburban store. Maybe Charlie was right—more opportunities would open up out here. And she could continue to help him in the evenings. If that's what he wanted.

Helping to build the new store from the ground up was exciting, and they were making great progress. Along with Charlie, they worked hard getting the new store painted, plastered, preened, and polished to perfection in preparation for the fast-approaching grand opening. Often Peter helped out, too, when he was off-duty as Marshall Field's head of security. He contributed many good ideas to the layout of the store and the flow of customer traffic. The idea of having enough customers to call them "traffic" brought grins to all their faces.

Dot chose many of the fabrics and notions that made up the inventory. Marjorie helped, too, by suggesting staple fabrics and supplies that sold well in the Kerryville store, and she was having a grand time planning what to put in the oversize display windows, which let in plenty of natural light.

"You know, I love working at Field's with Mr. Fraser," Marjorie told Dot. "I mean, the fellow's an absolute genius when it comes to designing merchandise displays. But I must admit, it's kind of nice to do a project out from under his shadow, too."

Together the women decided on a garden theme to welcome May and had a lot of fun choosing floral fabrics and coordinating ribbons to put on display.

"Maybe you could teach sewing," Dot suggested to Marjorie as she carefully stepped over a drop cloth. "You know, hold classes in the store two or three evenings a week, and students would naturally buy all their supplies here."

Marjorie laughed. "I think the fresh paint fumes might be going to your head. I've got a full-time job on my hands as it is. Besides, I'm not sure Peter would appreciate my being away from home so many evenings."

Dot, for whom working two or three jobs at a time to make ends meet seemed completely normal, realized she didn't know the first thing about being someone's wife. Charlie might not have known it, but he'd be much happier in the long run that they'd put the brakes on any romantic notions.

The following afternoon, business was slow in Field's millinery section. Dot yawned broadly and waited until her supervisor's back was turned before looking at the clock. Two more hours to quitting time. She tried to focus her bleary eyes on arranging some feathers on a hat. Her supervisor, Mrs. Blandings, walked over.

"Posture, please, Miss Rodgers," she said in a warning tone.

Dot straightened her spine and gave a feeble smile. "Sorry. Late night."

"It appears you've had a great many late nights recently. I've observed much yawning and slouching," the supervisor said. "Need I remind you we expect our employees to get their rest and be at their brightest and most cheerful on the job."

"Yes, ma'am."

"We don't want to burden our customers with our haphazard personal habits."

Dot felt a jolt. "Have there been complaints about my work?" Other than a minor kerfuffle with Isabel Nafwitz over where to display the veil-trimmed derbies, she couldn't think of a reason for dissatisfaction.

"Not yet. But there will be if you continue to slouch about in this manner."

"Yes, ma'am," Dot repeated. Maybe it was time to put in for that transfer, after all. With less riding back and forth to Oak Park, it would be easier to get her rest.

On her break, Dot smoothed her hair and her navy-blue skirt and took the elevator up to the eighth floor. As she entered the frosted glass office marked "Personnel," she remembered her earliest days at Marshall Field's and how happy she'd been to land a job so soon after leaving Indiana. Louie helped by introducing her to Veronica, who in turn introduced her to Mrs. Carlson. But her subsequent success on the job was all her own. She had a knack for hats. She didn't want to leave Field's, but something had to give.

Mrs. Carlson, a fortyish woman dressed in tweed, greeted her and motioned for her to sit down.

"What can I do for you, Miss Rodgers?"

Dot cleared her throat. "I'm wondering how hard it might be to put in for a transfer to the Oak Park branch."

Mrs. Carlson's eyebrows shot up. "The Oak Park store?" An incredulous smile crossed her face. "You, in the suburbs? I picture you as more of the sophisticated city type."

"So do I," Dot admitted. "But I've been thinking that such a move might be good for me. For my career, I mean."

"I see." She looked at Dot over the top of her spectacles. "Mrs. Blandings would find it difficult to run the department without you."

Dot doubted that very much.

"Much as you would be missed here," Mrs. Carlson continued, "I think you might be right. There are opportunities in the new suburban stores that would be harder to achieve here in the flagship store." She stood up, signaling Dot that their chat was over. "Well, I can't make any promises," she said cordially, "but if you're serious, I'll suggest it to the branch manager on your behalf."

"Thank you." Dot sprang to her feet and hurried back to her hats. Now that a transfer seemed within reach, she suddenly wanted it more than anything. A new store, a fresh start, far away from the judgmental eyes of Isabel and Mrs. Blandings. Being stationed in Oak Park would make helping at Corrigan's so much easier.

CHAPTER FIFTEEN

The evening before the grand opening, the Oak Park branch of Corrigan's Dry Goods and Sundries looked perfect down to the last detail. Charlie, Dot, Marjorie, and Peter had stayed late to put the finishing touches in place.

"What do you say we all go to the Orange Garden to celebrate?" Charlie suggested, naming a favorite Chinese restaurant near Dot's apartment. He drove the four of them in the Packard, which for once behaved itself and didn't stall out or backfire or get a flat tire. Contrary to everything he'd believed about new automobiles, the roadster was twice as temperamental as good old Betty. As Peter and Charlie discussed the details of the car, Dot and Marjorie went over the details of the following day's event.

"Mr. Fraser was a dear about letting me off for the day," Marjorie said. "He understands how important this new store is to me and my family."

"Wish I could say the same about my new supervisor," Dot said ruefully. "My word, you'd think Field's isn't able to sell a single hat if I'm not there to personally oversee each transaction."

"You might not be too far off there," Marjorie said. "You're the best sales clerk they've got."

"That may have been true in Chicago, but now that I'm in Oak Park, I'll have to prove myself all over again. Still, I was able to talk her into giving me the day off."

She looked out the car window at the shimmer of the street lamps in the rain. "You know, helping set up the store has given me some ideas. Maybe I don't want to stay at Field's forever. Maybe I'd like to open up a little store of my own somewhere. A store where I'd choose the merchandise and hire the staff, where I could be the boss." She glanced at Marjorie and gave a snort. "You must think those paint fumes are still affecting my brain."

"On the contrary," Marjorie said. "I think you'd be great at it."

"Really? Trust you to see my brilliance," Dot said with a toss of her head.

A few minutes later, they were seated at a square table under a glowing scarlet paper lantern, where they laughed and joked over large platters of chicken chop suey mounded over rice and steaming bowls of wonton soup. Dot settled back against the leather banquette, warm and comfortable, and wished it could always be like this, two couples together, enjoying each other's company. *But we're not two couples*, she reminded herself. *We're one couple and one pair of good friends who would eventually make each other miserable if they tried to be anything else.*

At the end of the meal, the four sipped tea from small china cups and discussed plans for the new store.

"I hope I did the right thing by hiring Bianca Montalto as a clerk," Charlie said. "I know you think highly of her, Marjorie, but she seems awfully young."

"She may be young," Dot said, "but she's smart as a whip and good with figures."

"You absolutely did the right thing, Charlie," Marjorie said. "Yes, she's young, and she's terribly sad about having to quit high school in order to help support her family. But I've volunteered with her at the settlement house, and she's extremely honest and trustworthy. As Dot said, she's good at math, and she's familiar with sewing, too. She helped me with all those costumes for the children's choir concerts."

"Customers will appreciate a sales clerk who knows her way around a sewing machine," Dot added, stirring her tea. "I'm hopeless at it."

Charlie held up his hand. "You two can stop selling me on her skills. She's already hired." He removed his napkin from his lap and set it on the table. "I just said she's awfully young, that's all. Not much experience in the work world. I wish it were one of you two who was staying on permanently." He looked meaningfully at Dot.

"Charlie, you know I can't give up my job at Field's," Dot said firmly. "It's secure, and I've finally got some seniority."

"I know," he said quietly.

"But I can continue to help out after hours. If you still want me."

"I still want you." His words hung in the air.

Peter cleared his throat. "From what I've observed, this Bianca is very conscientious and a hard worker. A harder worker even than

Helen."

"*Anybody's* a harder worker than Helen," Charlie quipped, "unless she's practicing for a play."

"Well, I think you're a dear for giving Bianca a chance," Marjorie said with a grateful glance at her brother. "As she works alongside you, she'll pick up the procedures quickly and be able to fill in for you in no time."

"I hope so," Charlie said.

Along with the bill, the white-aproned waiter brought each of them a fortune cookie. Charlie took a bite of his, pulled out a little slip of paper, and read aloud, "Success is on the horizon."

"Hear, hear." Peter lifted his teacup. In response, the other three raised their teacups and clinked a toast across the table.

"You next, Marjie," Dot urged. "What does yours say?"

Marjorie cracked open the small brown cookie. "Hard work and perseverance are your best course of action." She sighed and tossed the slip of paper onto the table. "Tell me something I don't already know."

"Well, I'm relieved to know you'll be holding down the fort," Peter teased, "because mine says, 'An exotic journey awaits.'"

"Florida was exotic enough," Marjorie replied with a mock shudder. "All those alligators."

Dot broke open her cookie and read, "True love is right in front of you." Heat rose to her face as Marjorie let out a little giggle.

"Is it?" Charlie said, grinning from across the table.

She looked back down at the paper. "Why, it's absolutely true. There's nothing I love more than a good plate of chop suey."

After a split-second of awkwardness, everyone laughed, including Charlie. But when Dot dared to glance back up at him, his expression was closed. She looked away and bit into the cookie with a decisive crunch, inexplicably sad.

They left the restaurant amid promises to be at the store extra-early the next morning. Since Dot lived the closest, Charlie dropped her off first. As he opened her door, she longed to reach out and kiss his cheek. She suspected that her stupid, flippant joke at the restaurant had hurt his feelings. But with Peter and Marjorie present, she said only, "Thanks for the yummy supper, Charlie. See you tomorrow."

"Yep."

He kept the roadster idling at the curb until she'd safely entered the vestibule. She waved to let him know she'd made it inside, then watched through the glass door until she saw the taillights turn the corner at the end of her block. She determined to be particularly sweet to Charlie the next day to make up for her comment. Turning to the row of brass mailboxes, she used her tiny key to open hers and idly flipped through the small handful of envelopes. *Bills, bills, and more bills.*

Though she'd followed this same routine every night, tonight, something was different. Creepy, even. The tiny hairs on the back of her neck stood at attention. Slowly, almost afraid to look, she turned. The vestibule was empty. She tried to peer out through the glass of the front door, but she could only see her own face reflected back. She shivered and hurried up the stairs and into the sanctuary of her apartment. Without turning on a lamp, she made her way through the darkened room to the front window and looked down at the dim front yard, which was illuminated only by a street lamp. No one was there, and the sidewalks in either direction looked empty as well.

"Scaredy cat," she chided herself. She flipped on a lamp and walked to the bedroom, momentarily wishing she still had a roommate. Still, she'd lived alone, off and on, many times over the past several years. It wasn't like her to be all high-strung and jumping at shadows. She just needed to get a good night's rest before the excitement of the next day's grand opening.

She drew the bedroom curtains, switched on the bedside lamp, and got ready for bed.

A few minutes later, she switched off the lamp and took another quick peek out the window. Her breath caught when she thought she detected a slight movement near the lilac bush, but it was only a branch swaying in the wind. Only later, moments before sleep, did she jerk awake. A sense of dread crept up the back of her neck. There was no wind that night. In fact, all evening, the air had been deathly still.

CHAPTER SIXTEEN

By two o'clock on the afternoon of May first, just hours after flashbulbs had popped at the ribbon-cutting ceremony marking the opening of the new Oak Park branch of Corrigan's Dry Goods and Sundries, the store teemed with customers. Even though it wasn't her store, Dot swelled with pride.

"You look like a million bucks," Charlie murmured to her. He slipped past on his way to greet a new group of well-wishers who'd entered by the front door.

Dot smiled and squeezed his arm, feeling particularly pleased with her choice of outfit for the grand opening: a low-waisted lemon-colored georgette crepe and a small brimmed yellow hat that set off her dark hair to perfection.

"How's everything going, Miss Montalto?" Dot said to Bianca, who was stationed at the cash register. The girl smiled broadly, but her large brown eyes carried the slightest hint of apprehension.

"Just fine, I think," she said bravely. Dot patted her arm, then walked over to the large cutting table at the back of the room.

"Jeepers. Can you believe this turnout?" she murmured to Marjorie as she refilled a plate from a large white cardboard box of fancy cookies Frances had provided. Sunshine poured through the plate-glass windows at the front of the store. The sweet-starchy smell of factory-new fabrics wafted off bright bolts of cotton, silk, and wool, mingling with the scents of fresh paint, furniture polish, and floor wax, and the various perfumes of the ladies who wandered through the store.

Marjorie, who, along with Helen, was serving customers at a long cutting table, beamed. "It's wonderful," she agreed, "but would you mind carrying those cookies someplace far away from the merchandise? The thought of powdered sugar on this navy cotton is giving me palpitations." She turned her attention to a customer and smiled brightly. "Here you go. What else can we help you with today?"

"Three and a quarter yards of this ribbon, please. I'm so glad you've opened up your shop right here on Lake Street," the customer commented as she surrendered a spool of pastel-striped grosgrain ribbon. "So many stores carry only ready-to-wear nowadays, but I still prefer to make my own clothes."

"Such stunning upholstery fabrics, too," said another woman, admiring a display of brocades. "I'll simply have to have my decorator come take a look."

Dot smiled at the remarks as she carefully carried the plate of cookies across the store to where Frances and Pop were seated in a couple of folding chairs.

"Thank you, my dear," Pop said, helping himself to a butter cookie.

"These are delicious, Mrs. Corrigan," Dot said politely. "You were so kind to bring them. Won't you try one?"

Frances offered a tight, polite smile and shook her head. She still had not warmed to Dot after the gangster's-moll newspaper incident, even though Dot had been spending hours and hours helping Charlie and Marjorie get the store ready. Dot decided to shrug it off and concentrate her attention on dear Pop.

"I'm so glad you could make it all the way from Kerryville." Dot gave his arm a squeeze. "I know it means a lot to Charlie to have you here."

"Well, it's my store, too," Pop said, his pride evident. "It's in my best interest to give the lad my full support."

"Did you have to close the Kerryville store for the day in order to be here?"

"No. Since Charlie's been in Chicago, I've taken on a part-time worker to help serve customers during the day while Helen's in school."

"You have? Who is it?"

"She's a cousin of mine. Second or third cousin, something like that. Her name's Elvira Meeks. She's a widow lady who had some time on her hands and seems happy to help us out. I was able to leave the store in her capable hands today."

"That's great news. With the addition of Mrs. Meeks and our Bianca, Corrigan's is expanding beyond just the family."

"That's progress, so my son tells me."

Dot smiled. "Well, I'd better see if Charlie needs anything. Good to see you ... both." In an awkward moment, she realized that during the time she'd lived with Marjorie and dated Charlie, she'd fallen into the habit of calling their father Pop, as his children did. She'd felt almost like one of the family. But now "Pop" felt inappropriately familiar, given the circumstances. To call him "Melvin" seemed odd, but "Mr. Corrigan" seemed too stiff and formal. So she ended up not calling him anything at all.

Nodding to the older couple, she turned away and set the plate of cookies on an empty shelf, well away from the merchandise, then wove through the crowd to find Charlie and help wait on customers.

By a quarter to six, the crowd had dwindled. Exhausted but happy, Dot helped Marjorie finish the task of putting away bolts of fabric and restoring the merchandise displays to order. Peter swept the wooden floor with a brand-new broom, and Charlie counted up the day's receipts with a big grin on his face. It had been a profitable day. With Bianca's help, Frances washed up the plates and cups in the sink, then Helen placed them in a crate to go back to Kerryville. Pop brought the car around to the front of the building and parked it at the curb, then came inside. The bell over the door gave a merry tinkle, just like its Kerryville counterpart.

"I think today calls for a celebration," Pop called. "What do you say we all enjoy a nice celebration dinner at the Georgian Room?"

"Followed by ice cream at Petersen's," Helen said.

"We'll see. In any case, my treat."

"No, Pop, *my* treat," Charlie protested. "I'm the one who put us all to work today."

"*Our* treat, then." Pop grinned. "Dinner is on Corrigan's Dry Goods Empire." He clapped Charlie on the back. "Well done. I'm proud of you." To the rest of the family, he said, "Shall we go? You too, Miss Montalto. You were a big help today."

"You all go on ahead and get a table," Dot said impulsively. "I'll help Charlie finish up, and then we'll be right along as soon as we make the bank deposit."

The Corrigan clan and Bianca trooped out to the car, leaving Dot alone with Charlie in the empty store.

"Sticking around to keep me honest?" he teased as he sealed the deposit in its leather pouch.

"It was such a crazy day. I just need a moment of quiet to catch my breath."

Suddenly he grabbed her around the waist, pulled her to him, and gave her a hard, fast kiss on the mouth. Then, just as quickly, he released her.

So much for catching her breath.

"Wh-what was that for?"

"For being so great today," he said with a smile. "For giving me so much of your time these last few weeks, getting the store set up. For ... for being you."

She felt a glow warm her face.

"I was happy to do it."

Together they walked toward the back of the store. "No, really," he said. "You and Marjorie worked like Trojans to fix this place up, and on top of your regular jobs, too. I can never thank you enough." He tugged on the back door to make sure it was locked.

A wave of disappointment that his impulsive kiss had been spurred more by hard work on her part than romantic passion on his rolled over her. *That's what you wanted,* her inner voice nagged. *You just wanted his friendship, nothing more.*

Beware of what you ask for, she thought gloomily. *You just might get it.*

He moved to a panel on the wall and switched off all the lights except for those in the front display window. The setting sun bathed the store in an amber glow.

Whether it was the success of the day, the aching beauty of twilight, or just the insistence of her heart, love surged for this kind, gentle, hard-working man. Not friendship. Love. Impulsively, she moved closer to him, placed her hands on his shoulders, and tried to consider her next words over the rushing in her ears.

"Charlie, I—"

The bell over the door jangled, signaling someone's arrival. Over Dot's shoulder, Charlie said, "I'm sorry, sir. The store is closing."

"Is it?" a man said in a deep baritone voice. "What a pity. It appears I'm too late."

At the sound of the voice, Dot gasped. Immediately, she let her hands fall from Charlie's shoulders and spun. She stiffened as if jolted by an electric shock.

"Hello there, Dottie." A tall, well-dressed man with crisp dark hair, aquiline features, and burning black eyes gave a lazy grin, his teeth gleaming white in the dusk.

"Dot, who is this?" Charlie said behind her. His voice barely masked his concern.

She and the man stared at each other for a long moment. Then she swallowed hard.

"Ch-Charlie Corrigan, may I introduce Mr. Louie Braccio."

CHAPTER SEVENTEEN

"How do you do, Mr. Braccio." Charlie stood tall and fought to keep his expression calm, though his voice had come out in an uncharacteristically high-pitched squawk, like a choirboy on the cusp of puberty. He'd survived bloody combat, but he'd never been face to face with a convicted criminal before, much less one walking through his store and eying his girl. Quietly he slipped the bank deposit into a drawer and turned the key.

"So pleased to meet you … Corrigan, is it?" The dark-haired stranger moved easily into the room. "You're the owner of this—*establishment*—I take it?" It wasn't really a question. Some mixture of contempt and amusement glittered in his black eyes as he took in the bolts of fabric and spools of ribbon. "How nice. You seem to have everything the ladies could want." He turned and faced Charlie directly. "Am I right?" He turned to Dot, his expression unchanged. "Is he giving the lady everything she wants?"

"Shut up, Louie," Dot said. She tried to sound brave, but a quiver slipped into her voice.

"Now, Dottie, is that any way to talk to a friend?"

"You're not my friend."

All of Charlie's nerves stood on end. Wasn't this man supposed to be in jail? He was a notorious gangster and bootlegger. He used to run a speakeasy, where he coaxed Dot to sing. And who knows what else.

He stepped between the stranger and Dot, who stood frozen.

"I'm afraid we're closed," Charlie said with more bravado than he felt.

"No matter." Louie fingered a fragment of silk that hung from a bolt. "I'm not looking to buy anything. I just came by to see how my Dottie is doing. It's been such a long time. What, six months?"

Dot didn't reply.

"And all that time, you didn't even come to see me. Your attention must have been drawn elsewhere." A shadow passed over the sharp planes of Louie's face—whether from the darkening sky outside or a darkening mood within, Charlie wasn't sure.

"Six months," the man repeated slowly. "Six months in the slammer, thanks to your little chickadee friend tweeting about what she thought she saw at Field's."

"You leave Marjorie out of this," Dot said fiercely.

Electricity surged through Charlie's nerves. The story he'd tried to forget rushed back to his mind. The liquor-smuggling ring that had stolen Marshall Field's delivery trucks to shepherd illegal booze around the city. People were so used to the familiar sight of Field's trucks, the criminals had been able to drive openly through every neighborhood in the city and suburbs without arousing suspicion. It had been a cool set-up. Then Marjorie, working late one night, had seen some trucks being loaded. She'd gotten suspicious and told Peter what she'd seen. Thanks to that tip, the ringleaders had landed in jail, including Louie Braccio, who stood before them now, mad as a hornet at Charlie's sister and Dot's best friend. Possibly even seeking revenge.

Charlie clenched his fists. A few minutes earlier and Braccio would have encountered Marjorie in this very store!

How did Louie know about the store, anyway? How did he know Dot would be here?

But Louie was smiling now. He no longer looked angry, but amused, which somehow felt even more unnerving than his scowl.

"Oak Park's a nice town," he said. "Clean and wholesome-like. I wouldn't mind setting up a little business here myself." His bejeweled fingers touched another bolt of silk. "Would be a shame if anything went wrong here. A robbery, a fire, and *poof*. Gone." He spread his hands. "I would be willing to offer you protection, for a small monthly fee. So you and Dottie wouldn't have to worry about such ... unpleasantries."

Heat flushed through Charlie's body. "I'm not paying you or anyone else for protection. Get out."

Louie's dark gaze shifted to Dot. "Can't you talk some sense into this fellow?"

She stood taller as if steeling her spine. "Please leave us alone."

Louie stared at her for a moment. Then his mouth broke into a smile that didn't quite reach his eyes.

"Suit yourselves. I'll leave you two to your little tête-à-tête," he said.

"After all, you're closed." He turned and flicked the store sign from *Open* to *Closed*. "But I look forward to seeing you later, Dottie. We have a lot to catch up on. And I'm glad to hear you're still living in the same place, so I know where to find you."

He walked out, closing the door behind him. The happy jingle of the bell terribly out of place in the suddenly sinister atmosphere.

Charlie went to the door and locked it, then turned to Dot and took her in his arms.

"Are you all right?"

"I'm all right. He doesn't scare me." But he could feel her shaking. He tightened his hold. "It must have been him, lurking outside my building last night."

"What?" Charlie held her at arms' length so he could look in her eyes. "You didn't tell me?"

"I wasn't sure. I mean, it was dark out. I didn't see anyone. Just sort of felt it. Besides, we were so busy, I didn't give it another thought."

"Well, you're certainly not staying there alone tonight. Is there someone you can stay with?"

"Don't be silly. He won't do anything to hurt me."

But the tremor in her voice gave her true feelings away.

CHAPTER EIGHTEEN

Dot tried to enjoy the celebration with the boisterous Corrigans, but it was hard to keep her mind off of Louie and what sounded like his veiled threats. After dinner, Pop, Frances, and Helen set off for Kerryville, with a detour to drop Bianca off at her family's apartment in Little Italy. Still seated at the table in the Georgian Room, Charlie explained to Marjorie and Peter what had happened at the store with Louie.

"Shouldn't we tell the police?" Marjorie asked.

"I don't know what we'd tell them," Dot said. "Besides, he probably has them in his back pocket. Remember how they let him off with a warning about running the speakeasy."

"But he did time for smuggling," Marjorie said.

"That was different," Peter said. "That time he couldn't shake it off."

"You could report that he's threatened you," Marjorie persisted.

"He didn't exactly threaten, just implied. And he hasn't actually done anything," Dot said. "And I don't think he will. I think Charlie is being overly cautious."

"Sure you'll be all right on your own?" Charlie said when he dropped her off. "I don't like it. I wish you'd stayed with the Bachmanns."

"I'll be fine," Dot said. "That apartment is way too small for three people. And even if I stayed one night … what about the next? And the next? Besides, Mrs. Moran is right downstairs. If anyone tries anything, she'll clobber him with her broom handle."

"I'm sure she will." Charlie walked her to her door and gave her a brotherly hug. From the safety of the vestibule, Dot watched him drive off, then dragged herself upstairs, exhausted after a long, busy day.

No sooner had she put the kettle on to heat for her bedtime tea than the buzzer rang. No doubt it was Charlie again with some last-minute words of advice to double-check the door to the fire escape or latch the bathroom window.

But it was Veronica's voice that floated up the speaking tube.

"This is getting to be a habit," Dot muttered to herself as she pressed the buzzer.

But when Veronica appeared in the doorway, Dot gasped. Her friend's left eye was swollen, bruised, and purple.

"What happened to you?" she sputtered.

Veronica stalked past her, appearing more angry than upset. "Carlo lost his temper."

"Not again." Dot moved her friend closer to the window to examine her face. "Why do you stay with that brute?"

Veronica looked at Dot, and her voice softened, although it still carried a sneer. "Don't worry, doll. I gave as much as I took."

"The monster. Well, take off your coat and sit down. I'll get some ice." Dot hurried into the kitchen and emerged with a dish towel knotted into a bag shape and filled with ice chips. "Here. Hold this against your eye. Gee, that looks painful."

"Not as much pain as he's in, I'll wager." Veronica winced as she touched the ice bag to her swollen eye. Dot believed her. An angry Veronica was not one to hold back. But now she spoke softly. "I hate to ask this, doll, but can I stay here at your place tonight? Just one night, maybe two, until he cools off."

"Of course," Dot said. "But what happened? What did you fight about?"

Veronica gazed at her with her one good eye. "He found out I've been seeing someone else."

"You have?"

"Yeah."

"Anybody I know?"

Veronica shifted on the sofa. "Nobody worth talking about. It was just, you know, one of those things." Holding the ice bag to her eye with one hand, she fumbled through her bag with the other and pulled out her cigarette case.

The kettle shrieked. Dot went to the kitchen and switched off the stove, then returned with a couple of steaming cups.

Veronica produced a flask from her purse and poured a shot of brandy into her tea. "Want some?" She held out the flask, her wide kimono sleeve brushing against the arm of the sofa.

"No, thanks." Dot held up her hand. "Just honey for me."

Veronica grimaced. "Don't tell me you're becoming a teetotaler like your dull little friend Marjorie."

Dot's blood pressure rose. "I just don't want any brandy right now, that's all. And believe me, Marjorie's anything but dull. Why, she's one of the most creative people I know."

"Creative, maybe, but all those Corrigans seem like wet blankets. If you want my opinion, I think you should give Louie another chance. He's changed. Besides, you don't really want to be tied to a dry-goods peddler your whole life, do you?"

"I don't want to be tied to anyone, thank you very much. And he's hardly a peddler. He wants to expand his family's store into a whole chain."

"Ah, yes. Starting with the fancy new store in Oak Park."

"Have you been out to see it?"

Veronica sipped her tea. "No, but Louie was telling me it's quite swanky."

"Louie." Dot shook her head. "I'm still trying to figure out how he knew I'd be at the opening. He was in jail the whole time we were setting it up. You didn't tell him, did you?"

"I might have. It's not exactly a secret, is it?"

"No, but he showed up there out of the blue on opening day and scared me half to death. He tried to get Charlie to give him protection money. The nerve."

"Well, I'm not sure why you're surprised he's taking an interest." Veronica shrugged. "After all, Charlie did hire his cousin to work there."

"Whose cousin?" A crease formed between Dot's eyebrows. "What are you talking about?"

"Bianca Montalto. The girl Charlie hired as a clerk. She's Louie's cousin." A look of incredulity crossed the half of Veronica's face not covered by the ice bag. "Don't tell me you didn't know."

"How would I know that? I don't know any of Louie's cousins."

"Well, you were dating him."

"Not to the point where we met each other's families. I've never met his parents or brothers and sisters, much less his cousins. Are you sure?"

"Sure, I'm sure. Anyway, maybe she told Louie about the grand opening, or her mother told Louie's mother or something. You know how it goes in these big, close-knit Italian families. Impossible to keep a secret for very long."

Dot didn't know since her own family was neither big nor close. But all she could think of now was how angry Charlie would be when he found out that Bianca was Louie's cousin. He might even fire her, which would be grossly unfair to the girl.

"Marjorie and I both recommended Bianca to Charlie," Dot said. "We know her from the settlement house. Marjorie knows her better than I do, but I met her, and she seemed perfectly sweet and lovely."

"She is sweet and lovely," Veronica confirmed. "A little naive, maybe, but of course, she's still practically a child. Fifteen, I believe."

"She just turned sixteen. And she's a relative of Louie's ..." A headache started coming on. "Charlie will have an absolute fit."

"Why do you have to tell him? What difference does it make?" Veronica set down the ice pack long enough to light a cigarette. "You know, you really ought to be more loyal to your old friends. Louie gave you a chance, remember? When you first came to Chicago, looking for all the world like something washed up with the tide."

Dot nodded. "I know. He took this country bumpkin and gave her a taste of the kind of life she'd only seen at the movie theater. But the taste turned out to be bitter."

"What are you talking about? He made you a star. He gave you your first singing job at his nightclub."

"Speakeasy."

"Whatever. In any case, you got your start, right?"

Dot threw her hands up. "All right, it's true. Louie was exciting. Charismatic. Charming, even, when he had a mind to be. Wealthy, which was great if you didn't think too hard about how he made his money. But he never treated me as if I were someone special. His attitude toward me ran hot and cold. So, if I'm not thrilled to renew our acquaintance now, I should think you'd understand why."

Reclining on the sofa cushions and still holding the ice bag to one eye, Veronica stared at the ceiling with the other as if she weren't even listening. She drew on the cigarette and puffed out the smoke in neat rings. "He helped you, and now Charlie is giving a hand up to his cousin. Seems like a prime example of what goes around, comes around, wouldn't you say?"

"Except Charlie doesn't have the faintest clue that he's giving a hand up to Louie's cousin."

Veronica sat up with a catlike stretch. "Come on, doll, you're making this into a bigger deal than it is. You owe it to Louie to be friendly, at least. Nobody's saying you have to start dating him again."

Dot stirred her tea and frowned. "I suppose not."

"Although I don't see why you wouldn't." Veronica leaned forward and tapped her cigarette into an ashtray. "You could do far worse than Louie, you know. He's rich, he's powerful, he's handsome in that steamy Latin way."

Dot crossed her arms. "Then why don't you go after him yourself?"

"Oh, you know, I'm totally devoted to Carlo." She shrugged. "Most of the time, anyway."

"Which earned you a black eye. May I remind you that Louie's also a convicted criminal? There's no telling what he's capable of."

"Seems to me the real crime is making liquor illegal."

"That doesn't change the fact that he was a lousy boyfriend. He was never faithful to me when we were supposedly an item. He always had his eye on every skirt that sashayed past."

"Oh, you know how men are." Veronica's lip curled. "Besides, when I talked to him, he swore to me that he's going legit. Going to open a nice restaurant that families could bring their kids to."

"Why would he do that?"

"How should I know? Look, doll, this could be a fresh start for both of you. Life with Louie would be a whole lot more fun and interesting than a future with those dreary Corrigans. Why, from what I've seen, they're about as much fun as a lemon-sucking contest. You don't fit in with them and you know it. You're one of us."

Dot held her peace, but she didn't feel peaceful. Just sad. She didn't want to be one of the old crowd. That sort of life no longer suited her. She wished she could belong to the Corrigan clan. Some of the best times she'd ever had were spent laughing and joking with the lot of them around their dining room table. For the first time, she'd felt included in something greater than herself. But now, with Marjorie married, with her relationship with Charlie forever changed, and with Frances treating her as if she had beriberi, she felt more like the hungry child in a Christmas tale, shivering outside in the cold, peering into the happy family's warm hearth through the frosted windowpane.

Her last chance at happiness was slipping through her fingers. And it was going to slip even faster the longer she waited to tell Charlie the uncomfortable truth that he'd inadvertently hired Louie Braccio's cousin to work in his store.

The following day was Sunday. Dot thought about getting dressed and going to church as she'd been doing lately, but she allowed her houseguest to talk her out of it. Veronica's eye looked less swollen but was still shaded an ugly purple. Instead of going out, they stayed home and made pancakes for breakfast, then spent a lazy morning lying in the apartment, reading the newspaper. They were still lounging in bathrobes and slippers when the door buzzer sounded.

"Who could that be at this hour?" Dot muttered, even though it was close to noon and hardly too early for visitors. She leaned toward the speaking tube. "Yes?"

"Dottie, it's me," Louie's smooth voice floated up. "May I come in?"

"Louie? What are you doing here?" She turned to Veronica, who avoided her gaze and toyed with the handle of her coffee cup.

"I saw him last night before all that business with Carlo happened. I may have encouraged him to stop by," she mumbled.

"You what?"

Veronica shrugged. "Don't flip your wig. He just wants to talk to you."

Turning back to the speaking tube, Dot said, "You can come on up. But just for a minute. And take your time. We need to get dressed."

She unlatched the door, then she and Veronica hurried to their rooms. Dot dressed hastily in a shabby dress she normally reserved for weekend chores. She just wanted to be decently clad, not give Louie the idea she was concerned with getting dolled up for him. Those days were over.

When she emerged, Louie was sitting quietly on her sofa, a bouquet of roses in hand. He stood as she entered the room.

"Hiya, Dottie."

He handed her the flowers. She dropped them on an end table.

"What are you doing here?" she said briskly.

His large brown eyes looked contrite. "Sorry to bother you, baby."

"What do you want, Louie?"

He spread his hands in a pleading gesture. "I just want to talk to you. Is that so bad?"

She glanced at the ceiling and folded her arms. "Well, then, talk, and make it snappy."

He took a step closer. "I feel I may owe you an apology for my behavior at your friend's store. I've been thinking about it and worry that I may have come across a little, er, strong."

Dot couldn't believe her ears. Her voice rose. "Strong? You think so?"

He stepped back. "I know, I know. It just made me crazy, baby, seeing you with that fellow. Before I, er, went away last fall, I thought you were *my* girl." His eyes held a beseeching expression.

"Really? Because I recall that the whole time you were supposedly seeing me, you were spending an awful lot of time with other women. Whenever I showed up at the Villa Italiana, I never knew which Louie I was going to get: nice Louie or cold-shoulder Louie."

As if she hadn't spoken, he continued. "Haven't I always taken care of you? What about all those gifts I gave you? All that jewelry? And you never even visited me. Aw, baby, didn't we have something special going?"

"You were my boss, and I was infatuated with you. As I recall, you spent more time looking at other women than spending time with me. Even before you went to jail, you were stringing me along like a toy. I got vertigo just trying to get your attention. And now you're a convicted criminal." She couldn't believe she was talking to him this way, but she had to admit, it felt good.

"I've done my time. I'm going straight. You'll see."

"So I've heard," she said flatly.

"I swear to you, hand on heart, that stint in the slammer has made me a new man. One night I hit bottom, and I said to myself, Louie, what kind of life are you leading? I vowed to change my ways." He placed his hand over his heart as though reciting the Pledge of Allegiance. "I'm going to open a legitimate restaurant. A nice, homey place. Someplace you could bring your grandmother. And I'd like to hire you to sing again, Dottie. The customers always liked it when you sang. I want you to forget that Corrigan loser and come work for me." He stepped toward her again. "You can trust me."

"I'll never trust you again, Louie," Dot said. "I don't want that kind of life." She gave the words a moment to sink in, waited until his look of hope faded. Then she tried a kind smile. "But I suppose we'll still run into each other now and then. I understand we hired your cousin to work for Corrigan's."

"Yeah. That was real nice of you."

"Well, we didn't do it on purpose. I met Bianca when I was helping out at the settlement house."

"Which is a very good thing of you to do," he said. "And Bianca's a good girl, too. You'll like her."

"I already like her. She's nothing like you."

He smiled his slow, lazy grin. "I'll win you back, baby. You know I will. I'll change your mind about me if it's the last thing I do."

And then, he was gone.

Veronica emerged from the bedroom. "Is the coast clear?"

"Yes. You could have come out, you know. I would have appreciated not having to talk to him alone."

Veronica touched her face and winced. "I didn't want him to see my black eye. He might have gotten mad at Carlo."

"He *should* be mad at Carlo. What Carlo did to you was heinous."

"Aw, he just got jealous. It's his way of showing he cares."

Dot shook her head. "That's not caring, Vee. It's control. Don't go back to him. Please."

But in her heart, she knew that Veronica would reunite with Carlo before the week was out. She always did.

No wonder Charlie thought her friends caused trouble. Because, come to think of it, they often did. And Dot was getting darn tired of the drama. She remembered a time when she'd counted herself lucky that, no matter how badly Louie treated her, he never hit her. Now, thanks to Charlie, she knew what it meant to be treated well. Even if she and Charlie were not meant to be together, she would never go back to Louie. She would never stoop so low again.

CHAPTER NINETEEN

As spring melted into summer, Dot had multiple opportunities to tell Charlie that Bianca Montalto was Louie's cousin. But somehow, she never got around to it. She didn't think he'd fire the girl just for being Louie's cousin, but she couldn't be sure. After all, his feelings against Louie ran pretty strong.

After a couple of nights spent at Dot's apartment, Veronica moved back home. She swore she was through with Carlo. Dot could only hope that she'd stick to her resolve. But it seemed unlikely that her friend was ready to change her ways for the better.

One beautiful June night, Dot walked down Lake Street from Marshall Field's to Corrigan's to meet Charlie and continue on to dinner. Her transfer to Oak Park had turned out well. The commute on the streetcar wasn't bad, heading out to the suburbs instead of to the Loop. Certainly there was a lot less traffic going in that direction. And to her amazement, the rumors about her connection to Louie Braccio and hoodlums hadn't followed her to her new job. Her new supervisor and coworkers treated her as if she were just another clerk—a clerk who'd gained a lot of experience at the flagship store and thus earned their respect.

Best of all, the fact that she now worked a mere block away from Corrigan's made it easier to help Charlie at his store in the evenings. She loved spending time with him, letting their friendship bloom without pressure. And although now he'd hired Bianca Montalto and could technically get along without Dot's help, he hadn't asked her to stop coming, and she enjoyed keeping her hand in.

In recent weeks, they'd fallen into something of a routine. After finishing her shift at Field's, Dot would come over to Corrigans and work on the physical appearance of the store while Charlie took care of the end-of-day bookkeeping. Then he'd walk her to the streetcar and wait with her until she boarded. Sometimes he even drove her all the way home. And sometimes, such as this typical Thursday, they grabbed a bite to eat. The weather was so warm that they opted for ice cream at Petersen's.

Over ice cream sundaes in petite silver dishes frosted with condensation, they chit-chatted about the business, which was going even better than expected.

"It's still early days, but Pop's been busting his buttons over the latest sales reports," Charlie said.

Dot smiled. "You are one smart businessman, Charlie Corrigan."

He flushed but looked pleased. "I'm relieved to say Louie Braccio hasn't turned out to be the threat I thought he'd be. I haven't seen him since opening day."

To Dot, this seemed a good a time as any to mention Louie's visit. Keeping her voice casual, she said, "He came over one Sunday, several weeks ago."

Charlie set down his spoon. "He came to your apartment?"

Dot nodded, training her gaze on the sprinkles atop her sundae. "It was one of those days that Veronica was staying with me. She invited him."

"And you didn't kick him to the curb?"

"He just wanted to talk." She toyed with her spoon, making swirls in the ice cream. "He felt bad about the way he spoke to you at the store. He told me he's changed."

Charlie straightened in his chair. "Of course he says he's changed. He'd like nothing better than to get back together with you."

"Now you're being silly." She tried to laugh, but it came out as a hacking sound. She took a sip of water.

Now it was Charlie's turn to act casual. "Do you still like him?"

"If you mean romantically, then no. Of course not. But he did give me my first singing gig here in the city. Even if my illustrious musical career has gone nowhere since then." She lifted her gaze to meet Charlie's. "Honestly, if it weren't for Louie's help, I'd probably be back in Indiana now, chafing under my father's rule and trying to figure out a way to get out."

"Have you seen Louie since that day?"

"No." He'd sent her roses twice, but she didn't mention that.

"Well, I don't like it," Charlie said. "I don't like it one bit. But if you're sure he won't cause any harm …"

"I'm sure. And after all, doesn't everybody deserve a second chance?"

Charlie shook his head and laughed. "Now you're starting to sound like Marjorie."

Dot grinned and took a bite of her mint chocolate chip. Now that Charlie was acting less skittish about Louie being around, she'd soon feel confident enough to reveal the Louie-Bianca connection without fearing he'd fire the girl. One step at a time.

Plus, if what he said was true and she was starting to sound like Marjorie, then maybe there was a little streak of goodness inside her after all.

A few days later, Charlie telephoned Mrs. Moran early and asked to speak to Dot. He heard two thumps as the landlady banged on the ceiling with a broom handle—her signal that Dot was wanted on the telephone. After a few minutes, Dot's voice came over the line.

"Hello?"

"Want to take a ride with me out to Kerryville today? Pop wants to give me some inventory that's not selling too well out there, to see if it will do better in Oak Park."

"Oh, Charlie, I'd love to. I'll call up Field's to arrange a day off. If they let me have it, I'll call you back."

He shot up a quick prayer, and when at last the telephone jangled, the news was good.

"Turns out I still haven't used my extra day off from the last sales contest," she said. "For once, procrastination has worked in my favor. I'll be ready."

But when Charlie rang the buzzer and she flew down the stairs, she saw he held a large carton in his arms.

"What's that?"

Charlie's blue eyes held a twinkle. "Something I've been wanting to give you for a while. Let's go back upstairs for a minute."

Curious, Dot led the way back to the apartment. Charlie set the carton down on the coffee table, opened it, and lifted out an impressive-looking square mahogany box with shiny brass fittings and a leather handle.

"What is it?" Dot ran her fingers over the satiny finish.

Charlie clicked open the fasteners and lifted the lid.

"It's a portable Victrola."

"A Victrola!" Dot gasped in delight when she saw the turntable and tone arm.

He stood tall and puffed out his chest a little. "It's called a Victor Reliance Portable Phonograph."

"But it's so small. And where's the horn?"

"No horn. The sound comes out of the speakers here." He pointed to a grille next to the turntable.

"Well, I'll be," Dot breathed. "Show me how it works."

He produced a metal crank from inside the lid. "You attach the crank to the side like this." He slid the end of the crank into a hole. "Like on a regular Victrola, only the salesman said it will play two and a half records with just one winding."

"How marvelous!" She tapped the tone arm. "Too bad I don't have any records, or we could test it out."

"I've thought of that, too." He reached into the carton and pulled out a wax disk in a paper sleeve. He slid the disk from the sleeve and placed it on the turntable. Then he gave the machine a few good cranks. The turntable spun. He lifted the tone arm and set the needle in the groove. After a few crackles and pops, the opening strains of Fats Waller's "Ain't Misbehavin'" poured out.

Dot stared at the machine and shook her head. "It's a marvel."

"Look, I've brought more." He reached into the carton, pulled out a small stack of records, and handed them to Dot. Her heart fluttered as she read the labels.

"Sophie Tucker … Al Jolson … Ruth Etting. Oh, my." She hugged the stack of records to her chest. "I adore Ruth Etting."

"I know you do." His voice was gentle.

She gazed up at him. "But you don't. I didn't think you even liked jazz all that much."

A smile quirked at the corners of his mouth. "Those aren't for me. They're for you."

"What do you mean?"

His face broke into a grin. He gestured to the machine. "This. This is for you."

She blinked. "I don't understand."

"It's my way of saying thank-you for helping me get the store up and running. I couldn't have done it without you."

"You bought this all for me? Oh, Charlie. I … I don't know what to say." She tried to look at him, but his face went all blurry as unexpected tears formed at the corners of her eyes. Hastily she blinked them away.

"You don't have to say anything." Gently he took the stack of records from her hands and set them on the coffee table. Then he covered her hands with his.

"It's been torture working alongside you all these weeks without being able to say how I feel. A very pleasant torture, but torture nonetheless."

"Charlie."

"*Shh*." Gently he covered her lips with his index finger. Then he shifted, rested his fingertips against the side of her neck. Her skin burned under his touch. "Let me speak. I know you think we're too different, that we have too little in common to become anything more than friends. But I disagree. These weeks have shown me that we have a lot more in common than we have differences. We look at the world the same way. We laugh at the same things. We want the same things. So I'm not accepting that excuse anymore. I want what we had that night in the Bains's parlor."

Her defenses melted like a Milky Way bar left on a sunny windowsill. "I want that too," she whispered hoarsely. "More than anything."

Then her throat tightened, preventing her from saying anything more. Slowly he bent his head, his eyes drifting closed, and kissed her. She resisted for a mere breath, then yielded.

The phonograph hissed, and the song ended. The turntable gradually slowed until it came to a complete halt.

At last Charlie broke their kiss and gently disengaged from Dot's embrace.

"I'd love to stay here with you all day and, uh, listen to songs," he said, "but Pop's expecting us. We should go."

With great reluctance, Dot nodded. She set the tone arm back on its rest and picked up her straw handbag. On the way down the stairs, she slipped her hand into Charlie's. Now that he was hers again, she had no intention of letting him go.

As they drove in contented silence through the Chicago neighborhoods, Charlie rolled over in his mind what had just happened. Did her kiss really mean that she was accepting him back? That she wanted to be more than just friends? Or was she simply expressing her gratitude for the new phonograph?

"Mind if I keep the top down?" he asked as they picked up speed on the highway heading west of the city toward Kerryville.

"Please do. It's a glorious day." She reached into her straw bag, pulled out a red floral headscarf, and tied it around her head to keep her hair in place. She wore a new pair of sun-cheaters over her eyes that she'd picked up at Woolworth's. Although the dark-lensed spectacles took some getting used to, Charlie thought they were quite sensible, and they made her look glamorous, too.

"Quite a change from that snowy ride we took last winter," she continued. "Remember Cal and Ellie Bains and their farm? They were really generous to take us in, a couple of total strangers."

Charlie glanced at her sideways. "That was one memorable night. I couldn't believe you took off without saying good-bye."

"It seemed the right thing to do at the time. We were playing with fire. You weren't ready to start up a romance, and neither was I."

I was so ready, Charlie countered in his mind, but because he couldn't read her expression behind the sun-cheaters and didn't want to spoil the moment, he kept quiet.

She changed the subject. "This is so much fun. I wish I knew how to drive a car."

He shifted gears and said, "Why didn't you say so? I'll be happy to teach you."

"You will?"

"Sure. This afternoon if you want."

When they reached Kerryville, slightly sunburned, their first stop was Pop's store.

"Good afternoon, Miss Corrigan," Charlie said to Helen in a high falsetto voice as they came through the door. "I'd like to buy one million dollars' worth of your most expensive gold-leaf-covered silk. The kind spun by extremely rare silkworms that sleep on feather pillows and are fed exclusively on caviar and champagne."

"You got it, Mrs. Cavendish," Helen teased back, citing one of her snootier customers. "But please don't try to return it in a day or two like you usually do. That's so *common*."

Dot joined their fit of laughter, which lured Pop out of the stockroom.

Charlie's laugh faded. Pop looked thin, and his face had a grayish cast. "You feeling all right, Pop? You look tired."

"Just not sleeping too well in this heat."

"Is this one working you too hard?" Charlie grabbed his sister and rubbed his knuckles on her head. She stuck out her tongue, then broke free and ran to Dot, who gave her a hug.

"No, she's a great help, and I'm glad to have Elvira, too." Pop nodded to a mousy woman who was dusting shelves at the back of the store, ignoring the commotion. "But nobody can take the place of my son." He clasped Charlie's shoulder.

"Aw, Pop."

"Still, I'm pleased as punch that the Oak Park store is doing as well as you said it would. It was a smart business move to open it up. I'm thinking maybe city folk will get more excited about these new wild paisley-patterned fabrics than the Kerryville ladies have." Pop shook his balding head. "I let a salesman talk me into stocking them. I should have known better than to stray from the tried-and-true."

"Hey, you were willing to take a chance on something new, and that's excellent. I'm proud of you," Charlie said. "And, yes, paisley's the hot new thing. It's been selling well in Oak Park."

Pop shrugged. "Maybe I'm catching a little of your innovation bug."

"Wish you'd catch the investment bug, too," Charlie said. "My stock market account has gone sky-high this summer."

"Pie in the sky is more likely," his father grumbled amiably. "I prefer good old Kerryville Bank and Trust."

While Pop helped Charlie load boxes into the roadster, Helen brought Dot up to speed on the latest scoop about the goings-on among the Kerryville High crowd. When all the boxes were loaded, Charlie suggested they all go for lunch at the Tick-Tock Cafe.

Pop begged off. "I have some things to catch up on before I leave for the day. Frances and I have tickets to the symphony over in Dubuque."

"And I have to stay here and study my lines," Helen said. "Don't forget, I'm playing Diana in *Anne of Green Gables* in summer stock. You'll both come, won't you?"

Dot smiled. "Wouldn't miss it. Although I don't see how you can top Helen of Troy."

"If you could fit in a few chores around practicing your lines, that would be most appreciated," Pop grumped to his daughter, but his eyes held a twinkle.

"Well, it looks like it's just you and me, kid." Charlie offered his arm, and Dot slipped her arm through his. Secretly he rejoiced that no one else would come along to interrupt a perfect afternoon with his best girl.

After a hearty lunch of asparagus soup and chicken-salad sandwiches, he wiped his mouth with a napkin, set it by his plate, and pushed back his chair.

"Ready for your first driving lesson?"

Dot's eyes shone. "Am I ever!"

Charlie drove them to some country roads outside of town that were practically deserted, allowing plenty of room to practice. Then he switched places with Dot so she was in the driver's seat. He scanned ahead down the road.

Catching Dot's apprehensive expression, he sought to reassure her.

"It's easy," he said. "Practically nothing to it. Look, there are three pedals on the floor. The right pedal is your brake. The middle pedal is reverse, and the left pedal is the clutch. The parking brake is over here. Now, see this lever here?" He pointed to a knob under the dash. "That's the fuel line. The first thing you do is turn that thing on. Then you've got your throttle up here"—he pointed to a lever on the steering column—"to accelerate."

"Hold on a minute. My head's swimming with all these details."

Charlie patiently went over everything again, then said, "Okay, let's put the car in neutral. Make sure the emergency brake's off. The starter button is down there on the floor. Now turn the key, press down the clutch, and give it gas with this lever here."

The car purred to life on the first try.

"No more cranking!" Dot said in amazement. She loved everything about the car—the comfortable leather seat cushions, the gleaming brass details.

"She's a lot quieter than old Betty."

"And how!"

"Now, let it go. And we're off!"

After a few fumbling tries, the car began moving smoothly. In less time than she ever thought possible, Dot was handling the machine with a minimum of lurches, stalls, and gasps from the passenger seat.

"There! You're getting the hang of it. Now, this switch works your headlights. And this, of course, is the horn." He pressed the bulb, and a startling "ooOOgah" sound echoed across the fields. "Now let's see how Better-than-Betty does on a curve."

By the end of the afternoon, Dot had driving down pretty well. Charlie thought that was great because if they ended up married and living in Kerryville, she'd need to know how to drive to get practically anyplace. There wasn't public transportation like there was in the city. Then he checked himself for letting his thoughts jump ahead to marriage. He was glad he hadn't said anything out loud. Instead he smiled.

"What's so funny?" she asked. "Are you laughing at the way I drive?"

"Not at all. You'll be ready for the Grand Prix in no time."

In high spirits, they returned to the store. As soon as they burst through the door, Charlie called out, "Hey, Helen! Pop! Come on and let Dot take you for a spin."

But there was no reply from Pop or Helen. Instead, Elvira met them, clasping her hands in front of her, face creased with worry.

"Charlie, you need to telephone your stepmother right away. Your father has taken ill."

His pulse pounding in his ears, Charlie called home. Helen picked up.

"Oh, Charlie, it's awful," she wailed. "Pop complained of feeling poorly after lunch, and he looked so pale that I called Frances, and she drove him straight to the hospital. They're over there now. I haven't heard anything more."

"Okay, kid. Stay calm. I'll come get you, and we'll drive over there together." He hung up. *Not again. Not now.*

"What is it? What's happened?" Dot's brow creased with concern.

He rubbed his forehead. "Pop's been taken to the hospital. Sounds like it could be another heart attack. Frances is with him now. I'm going to pick up Helen and head over there right away. Elvira, do you think you can run things here for a while?"

"Sure, sure. Don't you worry about a thing." Elvira made a shooing motion with her hands. "You go on."

"I'll go with you," Dot volunteered.

Charlie turned to her and grasped her hands in his. "I hate to ask this, honey, but would you mind catching the next train back to Chicago and handling the store? We left Bianca there all by herself, and I'm not sure she's up to running the whole show."

"Of course I don't mind. I'm happy to do it."

He squeezed her hands in his. "Good. I'll drop you at the station on my way to pick up Helen."

"Don't be silly. It's just a short walk from here. I'll go right now."

"Thank God for you." He released her hands. "All right. I'll call Marjorie now and fill her in on what's happened. Likely she and Peter will drive out here tonight, but maybe she can close up the shop before they leave. Then you can help Bianca open it in the morning. Ask her to come in early so you make it to Field's on time." He rubbed his face. "Gosh, I'm sorry about all this."

"Don't worry about a thing. I'll take care of everything. You just take care of your family."

Impulsively, he kissed her mouth. Then he whispered, "I really, really appreciate it."

She reached up and gently touched his cheek. "I know. I'll be praying for Pop. And for you."

"Thanks." It took a moment for his brain to register what she'd just said. "You'll pray. You mean—?"

Dot smiled. "I've opened up a line of communication with the Almighty." He enfolded her in his arms, then released her with a kiss.

"Call Marjorie," she said. "You and I will have time to talk later."

As she hurried out the front door, he picked up the telephone again and spoke to the operator. "Long distance, please. Marshall Field and Company in Chicago." When the store operator answered, he asked to speak to Marjorie Bachmann in the display department.

"Hurry, please. This is an emergency."

CHAPTER TWENTY

Pop made it through the crisis with his heart, but it would be many weeks before Charlie would be free to return to Oak Park. In the meantime, Dot would be in charge of keeping things going at Corrigan's Oak Park in addition to performing her job at Field's. A daunting prospect, but Dot was up to the challenge. She'd do anything to help Charlie and the rest of the family that she'd come to love.

A week after Pop's heart attack, while she dressed in a simple navy blue cotton shift and matching cloche—her typical Field's summertime outfit, worn with white cotton gloves for the street—Dot vowed that anyone who worked for Corrigan's Oak Park would be allowed to wear whatever in blazes they wanted. None of this "dark colors only" stuff in *her* store. Then she giggled, realizing that Corrigan's had begun to feel like her store. After the initial panic-driven flurry of activity of figuring out what needed to be done and who'd be responsible for which tasks, now she felt calm and on top of things. Bianca had proved she could handle day-to-day operations of the store on her own, so Dot's workload eased a bit. She was still officially in charge, and she still made frequent visits to check on things, but she was no longer frantic about overseeing every last detail. The previous evening when she'd stopped to lock up the store and accompany Bianca to make the deposit, everything had looked spic and span. The deposit was a healthy one. And now that she wasn't running to Corrigan's umpteen times a day, she felt more relaxed and less distracted at Field's, a fact reflected in fatter figures in her sales book. Although she looked forward eagerly to Charlie's return, she was handling things and doing a fine job of it. In fact, she was beginning to like it.

A little shiver of anticipation ran down her spine.

Maybe it was time to start thinking of opening a shop of her own.

As she rode out to Oak Park on the streetcar, she continued the daydream. What kind of a business should hers be? She decided on a little jewel-box of a shop, small but smart in every detail, with a respectable address in a well-heeled section of town. A hat shop, of course, with the very latest styles, maybe even some she'd designed herself. She'd hire master craftswomen to carry out the designs, perhaps some of the ladies she'd met when she volunteered with Marjorie at the settlement house the previous fall.

The streetcar winced to a stop in front of Marshall Field's, jerking her out of her reverie. She swung off the steps and glanced at her delicate wristwatch. Plenty of time to spare. She'd just whisk down to Corrigan's and check up on things before clocking in. She strode down the sidewalk, the accordion pleats of her skirt brushing against her knees as she walked.

She froze in her tracks. An Oak Park squad car was parked next to the curb directly opposite Corrigan's front door.

A chill ran up her spine in spite of the heat. *Surely it's nothing*, she told herself sternly, but she quickened her step.

The minute she pushed through Corrigan's black-framed door, she knew something was terribly wrong. Shelves had been upended. Drawers had been dumped onto the floor. Merchandise was piled in disarray, and Bianca sat in the middle of the mess, sobbing as if her heart would break. Standing beside her, looking grim, were two policemen.

"Oh, Miss Rodgers," Bianca wailed. "We've been robbed!"

"Are you Miss Rodgers?" The officer looked grim. "She's been trying to reach you. The store was broken into last night."

"I can see that." Dot looked around, rocked by a wave of nausea.

"I tried calling you at Mrs. Moran's, but you'd already left," Bianca sputtered through her tears. "And then I tried Field's, but you hadn't gotten there yet."

"It's all right, Bianca," Dot said, sounding calmer than she felt. She placed a hand on the girl's shoulder. "You did the right thing to call the police." She bit her lower lip as details clicked through her head. "Have you telephoned Mr. Corrigan?"

Bianca's mouth went slack. "Oh, no, miss. I … I couldn't."

"No matter," Dot said, patting her shoulder. "Let me be the one to tell him."

Between the officers and Bianca, Dot began to piece together what had happened. Someone had broken in and ransacked the place. No, it didn't look like much of value had been taken, other than an envelope of petty cash that had been in one of the drawers. Beneath her despair,

Dot felt a flutter of relief that she and Bianca had taken the previous evening's deposit to the bank and no significant money had been stolen.

"Do you have any idea who might have done this?" she asked the officers.

"Not yet," the older one said. "But we'll be keeping an eye out, comparing this to other break-ins in the area."

Dot looked around. The glass hadn't been broken. "How did they get in?"

"That's the strange thing, miss. There's no sign of a break-in. No broken windows or jimmied doors or anything like that. Who all has a key?"

"Charlie Corrigan, of course. He's the owner. And Marjorie Bachmann, his sister. Neither of them is in town at the moment. Bianca has a key, and the only other key is mine."

"Four keys. And all are accounted for?"

"I'm assuming so," Dot said. "I haven't spoken to the Corrigans yet."

The officers continued to gather evidence and asked the women not to disturb anything until they'd finished. Dot telephoned Field's to say she wouldn't be in. Then she walked to the water cooler at the back of the store and filled a paper cup with cold water, which she handed to Bianca.

"Drink this slowly."

The girl took the cup with shaking hands.

"Now, take three deep breaths."

She did as she was told.

"Bianca," Dot said when the girl had regained her composure. "Think hard. Are you *sure* you remembered to make sure the back door was closed all the way last night?"

Bianca's dark eyes were round. "Of course."

"Because if it were open even a crack, or didn't completely latch, the burglars could have gotten in that way."

The girl's voice shook with a note of panic. "But I closed it, miss. Honest. It was shut tight. I'm sure of it."

"All right. I believe you." Dot sighed. She did believe the girl was telling the truth. She'd never known her to tell even the slightest fib. And the officers had confirmed that the door had been locked tight when they'd arrived.

But what other explanation was there?

The officers left around midday. As Bianca began putting the store back to rights, Dot placed the dreaded call to Kerryville.

"I'm sorry," Elvira said over the wire. "Charlie's gone out on an errand. Can I give him a message?"

"Ask him to call here immediately." For a brief moment, she remembered the time she'd called and he'd been unavailable because he was out with Catherine Woodruff. She chased the thought from her mind. There was no time for jealousy today.

They didn't open the store at all that day but spent the entire afternoon cleaning. When Charlie called and Dot gave him the news, after recovering from his initial shock, he said, "Thank God nobody was in the store at the time. Do you need me to come?" Dot could hear anguish in his voice.

"I don't think so," Dot said. "Fortunately, nothing substantial was taken. Just some petty cash. Frankly, I think the robbers must have been pretty disappointed not to find a big, fat bank deposit lying around. Why else would they choose a dry-goods store, for heaven's sake? Why not a jewelry store or something like that?" She paused. "It's almost as if they just wanted to scare us."

"Louie Braccio," he said flatly.

"No. Surely not." But her confidence wavered, remembering that Louie had once tried to extort protection money from Charlie. Although Louie had later denied that he'd meant anything by it. Dot didn't know what to believe.

"I should be there," Charlie said.

"I tell you, there's no need." Dot tried to sound reassuring. "Your family needs you in Kerryville. We've got it handled." She didn't want him to think she wasn't capable of running things in his absence.

"All right. But let me know the minute you find out anything more. And you take care of yourself, you hear?"

Dot promised she would. "Oh, and Charlie, there's one more thing you should know."

"What's that?"

Holding her voice as steady and matter-of-fact as she could, she said, "Speaking of Louie, you'll never guess. As it turns out, Bianca Montalto is Louie Braccio's cousin."

The long thick silence told Dot that Charlie was fighting to keep his composure.

"Tell me again how we came to hire a cousin of Louie Braccio to work in our store," he said, his voice still and unnaturally calm. "Our store that has just been burglarized," he added, as if the matter needed clarification.

Dot sighed. "None of us had the slightest inkling that they were related. Even I didn't find out until Veronica told me."

"And you didn't think I'd want to know?"

"I thought about telling you. Many times. But—"

"But what?"

"But I didn't want you to take it out on Bianca. It's not her fault."

"Well," Charlie said. "I think it's clear enough, then, who broke into the store."

Dot twisted the telephone cord around her finger. "Who?" she asked, knowing full well what he was going to say.

"Louie. Or one of his associates."

She shifted the receiver to her other ear. "But there's no evidence of that. Absolutely none."

"But isn't it obvious? Bianca's his cousin, right? She might have given him her key."

"That's preposterous."

"Or she could have left one of the doors unlocked on purpose so that he could get in."

"Oh, Charlie. Of course she didn't. She swore to me that she checked all the doors before going home."

"I'll admit, she seems sweet enough. But how do we know we can really trust her?" He paused, then said, "I'm afraid we'll have to let her go."

"Oh, no," Dot said. "Charlie, don't do that. It'll be all right. I promise you."

But he remained unconvinced.

"How about this," she said finally. "How about if I ask for a leave of absence from Field's and I work full time with Bianca at Corrigan's until you're able to come back. That way I can keep my eye on her at all times."

"Do you think they'd let you do that?"

"I don't know," she said honestly, "but I could ask."

"It's not the best solution," he said. "But having you on the scene full time would be better than nothing until all this gets straightened out."

As soon as he'd finished his conversation with Dot, Charlie put through a call to the number she'd given him for the Oak Park police headquarters. The officer in charge of the case reassured him that they were doing all they could to solve the crime and that his presence wasn't required in the city.

At least that was under control. But he wasn't reassured about Dot. How could she have kept such a secret from him?

The obvious solution was to fire Bianca, but his conscience nagged. Was it fair to punish her with no evidence that she'd done anything wrong, when her only crime was that the Montaltos happened to be related to the Braccios?

After staring at the silent telephone, lost in thought, Charlie went upstairs to consult his father, who'd been released from the hospital and was resting in bed. He set aside his book as Charlie came into the room.

"I'm afraid I have some bad news, Pop." He seated himself on a wing chair next to the bed. "The Oak Park store was burglarized last night."

"Oh, no. What'd they take?"

"Not much. Some petty cash and merchandise. The store was closed, so nobody got hurt. They sure roughed the place up, though."

"Any idea who's responsible?"

"The police don't know yet, but I think I do." Charlie ran a hand through his hair. "Of all the darn fool things, we've got Louie Braccio's cousin working for us."

"Oh, yeah?" Pop's head tipped. "How'd that happen?"

"Name's Bianca Montalto. Marjie knows her from the settlement house. You met her at the grand opening."

Pop nodded. "Yes, I did. Seemed like a sweet little thing."

Charlie snorted. "Sure, she acts all wide-eyed and innocent, but I suspect she and Louie are in cahoots. And Dot knew about it and didn't tell me. Now she thinks I should keep the girl on. I think I should let her go, to be on the safe side."

"Now you're stretching it," Pop said. "It may have been foolish of Dot not to tell you about Bianca's connection to Braccio, but in this case, she's right." He paused, rested, as though the conversation were exhausting him. "If Bianca has been a hard worker and a loyal employee, she deserves the benefit of the doubt."

Typical Pop, thought Charlie, irritated. *Always looking for the best in people.* He touched his father's arm where it lay on the bed. What would he do without his father's wise advice?

"I'll let you rest now," he said. "I've got everything under control." He went into his own room and lay on his bed, staring at the ceiling.

He loved Dot. But he couldn't help but feel betrayed. What if she'd kept the secret out of some sort of loyalty to Louie? She had admired the man once—why shouldn't she admire him again? He was rich, handsome, powerful—and a crook, it was true, but lately he'd been putting over this saintly reformed act. What if Dot was falling for it—and for him?

The doorbell rang. He paid no attention until Helen called up the stairs.

"Charlie, somebody's here to see you."

Irritated, he swung his legs off the bed and stood. *Dang it all, why can't she just say who it is?*

He went downstairs to find Catherine standing in the entryway.

He stopped at the foot of the stairs. "Hello."

"Hi, there," she said with a sheepish smile. "Sorry to stop by without calling, but I was just on my way to the Orpheum to see *Showboat*. I couldn't talk Mother into coming with me, so I thought you might like to come along. And Helen, of course," she added quickly, evidently observing the eager glow on the younger girl's face.

"Would we ever!" Helen breathed. "Wouldn't we, Charlie?"

"I don't think so. It's a musical, isn't it?"

Catherine spoke quickly and crisply, lifting her chin a little. "Well, of course, if you don't like musicals …"

"He loves musicals," Helen broke in.

"I don't—"

"Come on, Charlie. Don't be a flat tire." His sister grabbed his arm.

He gave in to the eager look in his sister's eyes, if not Catherine's.

"All right, I'll come." He heard the amusement in his own voice. Well, and why not?

After all, a movie might be a good way to take his mind off his troubles. Especially off of Trouble Number One: Miss Dorothy Rodgers.

At the theater, he carefully maneuvered to make sure Helen was seated between himself and Catherine. But when he got up to fetch popcorn, he returned to find the order had been switched and he was now sitting in the middle. In response to his questioning look, Helen pointed subtly to a man seated in front of them.

"He's tall. You're tall. I'm not," she whispered, grabbing a handful of popcorn. "I'd like to see something more interesting than the back of someone's head, thank you very much."

When the room darkened and the first reel flickered, he kept his eyes firmly glued to the screen. The story wasn't bad, but it was the kind of production he hated, where people stopped and sang what seemed like every five minutes, interrupting the action. His arm cramped from holding it close to his side so as not to brush against Catherine's on the shared armrest. Nonetheless, every time she reached for popcorn, she leaned a little closer to him.

When the movie ended, she suggested getting ice cream. Helen's face lit up at the prospect, but Charlie begged off. "It's been an exhausting day," he said. "I'm going to have to call it a night."

When they got home, Pop had gone to bed, but Frances was still up, knitting in the front room.

"Back already?" she said. "How was it?"

Charlie said "Boring" and Helen said "Dreamy" at the same time.

"That's nice," Frances said, not seeming terribly interested. "Oh, by the way, Charlie, Miss Rodgers called." Her tone carried a note of distaste.

Charlie's adrenaline surged. "Oh, yeah? What'd she say?"

"She said she wanted to talk further about what happened at the store today."

"What'd you tell her?"

"Why, the truth, of course." Frances didn't lift her eyes from her knitting. "That you were at the movies with Catherine."

So the store gets robbed, and he goes to the movies with Catherine. Dot scrubbed at her face with a washcloth, making her cheeks alarmingly red when she glanced at the bathroom mirror. *Well, that's just dandy. Don't worry about me. I'll take care of everything while he's off gallivanting with whatsername.* She picked up her hairbrush and attacked her cap of dark hair with vicious strokes. *I know I told him he didn't need to drive all the way out here, but what I meant was—*

Thump. Thump. The insistent rapping of Mrs. Moran's broom handle through the floor interrupted Dot's thoughts. She dropped her hairbrush in the sink and hurried downstairs in her robe and slippers.

The landlady was similarly attired when she opened the door. "Do you have any idea what time it is?" she grumped. "Good thing I was still up listening to *The Voice of Firestone*."

Dot apologized and lifted the receiver to her ear. "Yes?"

"Whatever you're thinking, it wasn't how Frances made it sound," Charlie's voice burst over the wire.

"I have no idea what you're talking about," Dot replied coolly. "I was just on my way to bed to get a good night's rest after this most harrowing day."

"I'm sorry for calling so late," he said. "Tell Mrs. Moran I'm sorry, too. It's just that Frances said she told you I was at the movies with Catherine."

"Well, weren't you?"

"Yes, but Helen was with us, too." He paused. "I just didn't want you to get the wrong idea. About Catherine, I mean. Not that you would. But I didn't know … I thought maybe …"

As he fumbled for words, Dot's insides relaxed a little. He cared what she thought. "Goodness. You have every right to kick back and enjoy yourself at the movies after such a terrible day as we've had. Was the picture good?"

"I've seen better. I would have enjoyed it more if I'd been there with you." She heard him inhale deeply and pictured him running a hand through his sandy hair. "You're sure you're all right? You don't need me to come there? Because I will. I'll leave right now."

"Don't be silly," she crooned in her most soothing voice. "I've told you I've got everything handled, and I do." Relief that he no longer sounded angry about the Bianca incident poured through her. "We'll talk again in the morning. All right?"

"Okay, honey. I love you. Sweet dreams."

"Love you, too." She hung up the receiver, thanked Mrs. Moran with a smile, and hummed a nonsense tune as she climbed the stairs.

He was adorable when he was nervous.

Later that week, Dot's supervisor pulled her aside to respond to her request.

"A leave to get married, perhaps," Mrs. Peterson said. "A leave to visit your dying elderly relative, maybe. But a leave to go and work at a competing retail store? Not on your life."

So it was with a thumping heart—not to mention a quaking pair of knees at the risk she was about to undertake—that Dot handed in her official resignation to Marshall Field & Company and placed her future squarely in the hands of Charles Corrigan of Corrigan's Dry Goods and Sundries, Oak Park Branch.

CHAPTER TWENTY-ONE

In spite of the occasional quiet telephone conversation or letter, falling back on a long-distance relationship after declaring her love was proving difficult for Dot. While absence was definitely making Dot's heart grow fonder, she wasn't too sure about Charlie's.

"I don't know why," Dot confided to Veronica over plates of German food in the crowded Berghoff restaurant, "but he's seemed distant these last few weeks. Ever since the break-in."

Conversation was challenging over the clatter of dishes and the buzzing hum of voices in the popular German bistro. She poked listlessly with her fork at a piece of wiener schnitzel. Chicago had been experiencing a particularly oppressive heat wave that summer, which had taken her appetite for heavy fare clean away. But she admired the restaurant's electric chandeliers overhead and the checkerboard tiled floor below. Dark polished wood paneling against white stucco walls gave the place an old-world European feel. And Veronica seemed to be enjoying her sauerbraten.

"He *is* distant," Veronica reminded her. "He's in Kookooville, you're here."

"Kerryville," Dot said, even though she thought Kookooville sounded more apt.

"Does he blame you?" Veronica asked between bites. "For the burglary?"

"I'm sure that's not it." Dot sipped her water. "He would have said something if it was. And he doesn't blame Bianca anymore, either, now that the police have found the culprits."

"They did? You didn't tell me. Who was it?"

"Kids from outside the neighborhood, doing mischief. They got hold of a key that had been dropped on the ground in the alley, right outside the back door. Apparently, they tried it and it fit, so they came back at night to see what damage they could do. The police found it in the possession of the ringleader."

"Whose key was it?"

"Marjorie's. The poor thing didn't even realize she'd lost it until she returned from Kerryville after her dad's heart attack."

"How's the old man doing?"

"Better than expected, I think. He's recovering at home, but he can't go back to the store for a while, so Charlie will have to run things out there for the foreseeable future. At least, that's what Marjorie told me. As I said, Charlie hasn't been in touch with me much, except about business matters concerning the store."

"As far as I'm concerned, he should be kissing the ground you walk on after you gave up your great job at Field's to run his mangy little store." Veronica drummed her fingers on the table, her long painted nails clicking against the polished wood. She spotted something behind Dot, and her face lit up. "Well, will you look who's here." She smiled and waved across the restaurant in what even Dot could see was feigned surprise.

She turned to see Louie sauntering up to their table, wearing a white summer suit and a straw boater. A ring with a large jade stone adorned his little finger. He had a matching stone in the clip on his tie.

"Well, if it isn't my two favorite girls. Mind if I join you?"

Dot started to say they were having a private discussion, but Veronica spoke first. "Sure, Louie, have a seat." He pulled up a chair and sat between them.

"A thorn between two roses. Speaking of roses, Dottie, have you been getting mine?"

Dot didn't answer. Louie signaled to the waiter and asked for a glass of iced tea.

"I get absolutely parched in this hot weather. Don't you agree?"

He and Veronica chatted for a few minutes while Dot fumed silently. Eventually, Veronica excused herself to go to the ladies' room, leaving Dot and Louie alone at the table.

"She's not coming back, is she?" Dot said when Veronica hadn't returned after several minutes.

"I was hoping to see you alone. You've been avoiding me."

When Dot didn't answer, Louie shifted closer, "Did you like the flowers? Red roses were always your favorites."

"Red roses were never my favorites, Louie." Dot moved to pick up her handbag. "Orchids are my favorites. You must have me mixed up with some other girl."

"Wait a minute, Dottie." He covered her hand with his.

She sat back down, reluctant to make a scene.

"I wanted to ask you to sing again. To sing in my new restaurant. You'd like that, wouldn't you?"

Dot sighed. "I love to sing. You know that. But not in one of your speakeasies. I don't want anything to do with that life anymore."

"It's not, Dottie. I promise you, it's a nice family restaurant. I told you, I've gone clean." He cocked his head and gave her his most ingratiating smile—the smile that had once made her heart beat fast, so long ago. "Come on, Dottie. I need you."

She pulled her hand away.

"But I don't need you." She stood.

His smile hardened.

"You think you've got your future all sewn up with that yard-goods fellow. Sewn up. Yard goods. Get it?" He laughed at his own joke. She didn't.

He locked his gaze on hers. "You might not think you need me now, Dottie. But you will. One of these days, you will."

She left the restaurant without a backward glance. At the streetcar stop, the sun beat on the pavement. The air was suffocating, almost asphyxiating. She fumed, furious with Veronica for setting her up to meet with Louie, furious with Louie for—well, for being Louie.

But most of all, she missed Charlie. She missed his friendship and his joking. She missed the conversations they'd shared, their easy camaraderie as they worked together around the store.

And—darn it all!—she missed his kiss.

Her heart ached for him. She understood why, despite her attraction, she and Charlie hadn't made a good love match. They were too different, wanted entirely different things out of life. But still, next to Marjorie, he was her closest friend. At least, she'd thought he was her friend. But now that he was acting so distant and cold, she wasn't sure of anything anymore.

The streetcar lurched to a stop at the end of her street. She stepped off and dabbed her forehead with a hankie. She'd be glad to get home and into a cool bath.

As she approached the two-flat, however, she saw someone sitting on the concrete steps at the front. It was a girl—a tall, leggy girl wearing a yellow cotton skirt and a brimmed hat pulled so low that Dot couldn't see her face. She squinted. Surely it wasn't Helen. Why would Helen be sitting on her doorstep?

As she approached, the girl stood. Dot stopped on the sidewalk, her mouth open in surprise.

It wasn't Helen.

It was her own sister, Rose. The girl smiled uncertainly.

"Hello, Doro. I've come for a visit."

CHAPTER TWENTY-TWO

"Rosie!" Dot clasped her younger sister in her arms, her blouse sticky with perspiration. Then she held her at arm's length. "Let me look at you in your stylish clothes. Why, you're all grown up."

"Seventeen," Rose said with a shy smile. She'd lost much of her early teenage awkwardness. Her hair, cut in becoming waves around her face, was dark like Dot's, but her eyes were blue, and her cheeks were quite pink—from the heat, Dot surmised on closer examination, not rouge.

"Seventeen," Dot marveled. "When did you get to be seventeen?"

"I'm almost finished with school, and I have a job in Gaylene's Dress Shop in town."

"Is that where you got the swell outfit you're wearing?"

"Yes." She gave Dot's arm a squeeze. "Oh, Doro, I've missed you so much."

Dot cringed at the childhood nickname. Doro had been abandoned in favor of Dot when she'd moved to the city, along with the Barker surname. But nothing could diminish her thrill at reuniting with her sister.

As they walked up the steps arm in arm, Dot peppered her with questions.

"What are you doing here? Did you take the train? How long were you waiting? You should have told me you were coming. Is everything all right at home?"

"If you give me a chance, I'll answer," Rose said, laughing. Then her face clouded. "I'm afraid it's not all good news, though."

"Let's get inside and pour ourselves a cool drink, and then we'll settle in for a chat."

They sat at the kitchen table. As Dot filled tall glasses with cold tea from the icebox, Rose unpinned her hat and eyed the apartment with evident approval.

"It's nice here," she said, tugging off her white cotton gloves. "I wasn't sure what to expect, after you ... I mean, well, we weren't sure where you were living, that's all. I got your address off of your latest letter to Mother."

"How is Mother? And little Trudy?"

"They're both fine." She took a grateful sip of tea. "Trudy's fourteen now."

"Hard to believe so much time has passed." Dot shook her head. "Does Mother know you're here?"

Rose shook her head. "I told her I was coming to the city with Janie Penzler to shop. I did ride up on the train with Janie, but she's visiting a friend up at Northwestern."

"Does Father know you're here?" Dot had to ask the question, even though she knew the answer. Reverend Oliver Barker had long ago forbidden his two younger daughters to have any contact with their older sister.

"No."

They were both silent for a moment. Rose bit her bottom lip as if holding back the words. Dot sensed her sister had something important to tell her, but she didn't want to pry. Rose would come out with it in her own time. In the meantime, she'd treat this as an ordinary sisterly visit.

"Cookie?" She reached for the jar, which held a few slightly stale sugar cookies left over from Marjorie's last visit.

"No, thank you." Rose gazed down at her hands, then lifted her head and met her sister's gaze. "Doro, Father's been arrested."

Dot nearly choked on her tea. "He's been what?"

"He's been accused of fraud, of cheating people out of money, and worse. Apparently, they've been investigating him for quite some time."

"Mercy. Who is 'they'?"

Rose shrugged. "Whoever it is that investigates these things."

A thousand thoughts and feelings swirled through Dot's head. But the most prominent thought was, *He got what he deserved*, accompanied by an odd feeling of relief.

"How's Mother taking it?"

"She's ashamed, of course. Ashamed and embarrassed. But I think she's relieved, too, in some ways, to have it out in the open." Rose swallowed a sip of tea. "I think we all are. Maybe now he'll change his ways."

Dot understood that. Oliver Barker was far from the ideal husband and father. But he was still her father.

"Where is he?"

"He's being held in the county jail at Valparaiso."

"I see."

They sipped their tea silently. Dot was lost in her thoughts, imagining how her mother and sisters were taking this, wondering how this would affect them, their finances, their home.

Then Rose spoke again. "Doro, we're in a bad way." Tears that had glistened at the corners of her eyes all evening coursed down her cheeks. "We hardly have any money left. Father's assets are frozen, whatever that means, and most people at the church are mad at Father and think Mother must have had something to do with it, or had to have known somehow what was going on. And she didn't, Doro. She didn't know a thing."

"I think she did know, sweetie, at some level," Dot said slowly while her mind raced. "I tried to talk to her a few times about all the fakery, but she didn't want to hear it. I'm sure it was easier on her to look the other way. Not that she's to blame for his misdeeds, mind you, but her silence didn't help matters, either." Dot understood. She'd been disappointed at her mother's lack of backbone, too, but after all, she'd done the same thing with Louie—looked past his illegal activities and shabby treatment in exchange for a false sense of security. It was wrong, but she could see how it happened.

Rose gave a hearty sniff. "Mother's willing to clean people's houses or take in ironing or anything at all, really, but people who know about Father don't want to hire her. And I earn so little at Gaylene's, and Trudy's too young. Oh, Doro, we don't know what to do."

Dot reached into her pocket and handed her sister a handkerchief. "Why, you'll come here, of course, all of you." She had no idea where this strong, assured version of herself was coming from, but she meant every word. "You'll move in right here with me. Nobody in Chicago will care about Father's reputation. Mother will be able to find work here, if she wants—pleasant work, not scrubbing floors—and when September comes, you and Trudy can start school."

A smile of relief broke through Rose's tear-stained face. "Oh, Doro, do you think so? Do you really, truly want us?"

Dot's heart practically cracked in two. "Of course I really, truly want you. I'll telephone Mother right away." She stood and paced with the energy of a thousand plans to be made. "You'll stay with me tonight, and then tomorrow you'll scurry back to Indiana to help Mother pack. We'll either sell the house or rent it out—Mother and I will discuss that—and I'll send you all money for train tickets. In the meantime, I have some money in the bank, and I'll send it to Mother for expenses. You and Trudy can share my bed because it's the biggest, and Mother can have the spare room. I'll sleep on the sofa." Pausing for breath, she grasped Rose firmly by the shoulders and gazed directly into her red-rimmed blue eyes. "Do not worry yourself over this. We will make it work."

Late into the evening, the sisters sat in the kitchen and caught up on all that the intervening years had brought. Being a more docile, obedient type of personality by nature, Rose had not chafed under their father's rule the way Dot had. But she still suffered from his cold, callous treatment. He'd not treated her, Mother, or any of them with any kindness or tenderness whatsoever.

"I was still so young when you left," she said to Dot. "I never understood exactly what happened. And Mother and Father never talked about it. They hardly mention you at all, ever."

Even though that news didn't come as a surprise, it stung and she winced.

"Well, there's no reason you shouldn't know the truth," she said. "As a kid, there was nothing I loved more than singing."

"I remember," Rose said. "We used to sing hymns at church all the time."

"And Father had all us sisters sing together at his healing services. Remember?"

"Yeah. He still makes Trudy and me sing duets sometimes. Although now that we're older, we aren't quite as cute and winsome, so ..." Her voice trailed off.

"You're still plenty cute." Dot tapped her little sister on the nose like she'd done when the girl was a tiny thing.

Rose leaned away, stifled a giggle. Dot giggled, too, then turned serious.

"Did he ask you to let him heal you in public?"

Rose nodded. "Yes. I did it once. I pretended to limp and then be healed of limping. I wasn't very convincing, though. He never asked me again." Her brows lifted in a hopeful expression. "But another time, I had a cold, a real bad one. And he had me come up on stage and told the people I could barely breathe. And he put his hands on me, and by the next week, I was better, and he got me back up on stage to say so. So maybe it does work, sometimes."

Dot sighed. "Don't you see, Rose? You had a cold. You would have gotten better anyway."

"You're probably right." She hung her head. "That time I limped ... I was sorry I did it. It felt wrong, no matter how he justified it."

Dot folded her arms. "Let me guess. He told you some applesauce about people needing to see the power of God, and it would be all right to fudge it a little bit to make that happen."

Rose's eyes widened. "How did you know?"

"Because when I was around your age, he told me the same thing. I had laryngitis, and he wanted me to come up on stage so he could tell people I had throat cancer and pretend to cure me."

"That's terrible. What did you do?"

"I refused. He screamed at me, called me selfish and ungrateful, forbid me to see my friends. But I refused to budge. I wanted no part of his charade." Dot stood and stretched. "I'm famished. Want a sandwich?"

Rose nodded. Dot opened the bread box, pulled out half a loaf of pumpernickel, set it on a cutting board, pulled out a knife, and began slicing.

"What did he do then?" Rose asked. "Did he punish you?"

"Not right then, but eventually he got his revenge. Later that year, my beloved music teacher, Miss Swanberg, asked me to try out for the school musical. I won the leading role, but Father refused to let me participate. Said it was a disgrace for a preacher's daughter to act on stage. Which struck me funny because what did he do all the time but get up on stage and put on a show?" Dot set the breadboard on the table, along with sliced ham, cheese, tomato, and mustard from the icebox, and assembled a couple of sandwiches. "Anyway, I had to tell Miss Swanberg no, with great regret. The runner up, Mary Lou Spratt, would be the star. And that would have been the end of it, except Mary Lou got pneumonia two weeks before the performance."

"What did Miss Swanberg do?" Rose delicately tore the crust from the edge of her sandwich and set it on her plate. Dot's heart warmed at this ritual left over from her sister's childhood.

"I forgot about you and crusts. Well, Miss Swanberg begged me to fill the part. She even came over to the house to reason with Father, but he was traveling at the time. She spoke to Mother, though, who became my ally. She helped me get together my costume and promised to smooth things over with Father. I was sure he'd come to the show, see how wholesome the production was. I had this idea that maybe, then, he'd be proud of me.

"But on the night of the performance, the seats I'd saved for him and Mother—for all of you—remained empty."

"I would love to have seen it," Rose said.

Dot chewed thoughtfully and swallowed a bite of her sandwich, remembering. "After the show, I skipped the cast party and went home, bracing myself to be yelled at. But what happened was worse. My suitcase was packed, and Father was icily cold."

"No!"

"He said, 'You have shamed me and shamed this family. You are eighteen and no longer my legal burden to bear. You are no longer welcome in this house.'"

"I remember that part," Rose admitted.

"You and Trudy and Mother were all cowering in a bedroom."

"But my memory's hazy on the details." Rose paused, then said, "We should have stood up for you."

"What could you have done? You were children."

"Well, Mother should have."

"She was frightened, too. She grew up in a world where you didn't question your husband."

"But still."

Dot set her teacup on the end table. "That's when I moved to Chicago. I didn't have my diploma, and at first, I had trouble finding work. I answered an ad to wash dishes at a place called the Villa Italiana, and they took me on. Every night, I tiptoed back in after everybody thought I'd left, slept in a supply closet. Then, they caught on, and a friend of the owner's, a woman named Veronica, let me live with her until I got a daytime job selling hats at the department store where she works. Marshall Field's."

"I've heard of that place," Rose said.

"Maybe you can work there, too, if you move here," Dot said. "Your experience at Gaylene's will make you a good candidate. Anyway, I did both jobs for a while, at Field's during the day and the Villa Italiana at night. Then I learned I could get paid for modeling for classes at the Art Institute, so I did that, too, on my nights off from the restaurant."

"You worked three jobs?" Rose's mouth formed an O.

"I did. That's what it took to afford an apartment of my own. And even then I shared it with another girl to share expenses."

"Then what happened?" Rose stood and carried her plate to the sink.

"One day, I was singing in the restaurant kitchen to make the work go faster, and the owner came through and said I ought to be on the stage. And the next thing I knew, I was no longer washing dishes but out in the dining room, singing for the customers. I loved that part."

"Why'd you quit?"

Dot didn't want to share this with her little sister, but she'd started the story, and her sister deserved to know the whole truth. She deserved to know what had become of her in the missing years. "I didn't quit. The place wasn't just an Italian restaurant; it was a speakeasy. One night, it was raided by the police."

"Oh, my." Rose's eyes grew wide as boater brims. "Did you get put in jail?"

"My friend and I escaped. But from then on, that kind of life started to seem less glamorous than I'd thought. Once in a while, I'd get together with the old gang, but the experience never turned out as fun as I'd hoped." She shrugged. "I haven't been to a party like that since New Year's Eve. Don't miss it, either."

"But what about your singing career?"

"That will have to wait. I have other priorities right now. If God ever decides he wants me to use my voice again, he'll make a way."

As her words rang in her ears, Dot nearly slapped her hand over her mouth in surprise. Where had that come from? She wasn't in the habit of going around saying God this, God that. But deep inside, she knew it was true. There was a God. He cared about her. If He ever wanted her to sing again, He would make a way.

"Doro? Are you listening?" Dot realized Rose was still talking to her.

"Sorry. What?"

"I said, what did you do after that?"

Dot stood, reached into the icebox, and pulled out a pitcher. "Well, there's not much more to tell. As I said, to make ends meet, I'd pieced together different jobs, my favorite job being the one I have now—selling fabric at a place called Corrigan's. I'm finding that I really like working in a small, family-run business." She shrugged. "Who knows? I might open a business of my own someday. Maybe a hat shop."

Rose blinked. "I think you should. I can just see the sign over your shop. 'Dorothy Barker, Milliner.'"

"I don't call myself Barker anymore," Dot said. "Not after the way Father treated me. I use Rodgers. Mother's maiden name."

Rose was silent a moment as she absorbed that information. Then her face lit up, and she said, "I know. The sign will say, 'Dorothy Rodgers: The Singing Hatmaker.'"

Dot laughed. "Now you're cooking with gas."

By the first week of August, Amanda Barker and her two younger daughters, Rose and Trudy, had moved from Indiana to Chicago and crowded into Dot's small apartment. When Dot had first cleared this plan with the landlady, Mrs. Moran had invited Dot to sleep in her spare room at no extra charge.

"We'll at least try out the arrangement," she said graciously. "And frankly, as a widow living alone, I would welcome the company. You're down here half the time anyway, using my telephone," she added with a wink.

With all the commotion of her family moving in, plus keeping up with her full-time job at Corrigan's, Dot hadn't had a lot of time to stew over the cooling-off of her friendship with Charlie. But, late at night as she lay in Mrs. Moran's spare bedroom—a virtual broom closet like her own—her distance from Charlie nagged at her. What had she done? Why had he become so distant? Perhaps he did find another woman, after all. The unwelcome memory of a head of auburn curls floated through her mind.

But during the day the shop was thriving. Dot percolated at top speed. Underneath her daring, modish exterior beat the heart of a level-headed businesswoman who could read a balance sheet as easily as she read a fashion magazine.

September came. Mrs. Barker enrolled Trudy in the local public school. Rose decided to return to Indiana to finish her senior year of high school among her friends. It was arranged that she'd stay with her friend Janie Penzler's family and visit Chicago on the weekends and school holidays.

Later that month, Pop was finally cleared by the doctor to return to work full time in the Kerryville store, freeing Charlie to return to Oak Park. He'd promised that one of the first items on his agenda after his return was to take Dot out to dinner, where they could finally clear the air.

The Saturday before he was due back, Rose took Trudy out to see a show. Dot welcomed the opportunity to have some time alone with her mother.

Through Dot's influence with Mrs. Carlson, Amanda Barker had landed a job doing alterations at the downtown Field's. She looked tired but also calmer and more relaxed than her daughters remembered ever seeing her. She was gradually losing the pinched, worried look she always wore when living under the thumb of their father. Now, as she and Amanda sat listening to recordings on the new phonograph after supper, Dot encouraged Amanda to open up about Oliver's case.

"It's crawling through the courts," she told her daughter. "The whole mess is turning out to be more complex than anyone expected. Fraud, malfeasance …" She sighed. "Although it's good that it's all coming to light. It's a relief. There's nothing to be gained by hiding in the darkness."

"I think you're very brave," Dot said.

Amanda smiled sadly. "Not brave enough, soon enough, to save my daughters."

Dot reached across the sofa and patted her mother's hand. "We turned out well enough. You know, Mother, it's the twentieth century. No one would blame you if you divorced him. After all, he broke his promises to you."

Amanda shook her head firmly. "I didn't make vows only to Oliver. I made them to God. For better, for worse. Even for *really* worse. Things look bleak now, but they could turn around. In any case, the secrets are over." She turned to her daughter and smiled brightly—a little *too* brightly, Dot thought, a little too forced. But she let it go.

"And you," her mother continued. "Tell me about this young man you're so keen on."

Dot filled her mother in on Charlie, how they'd met through Marjorie, how he'd opened the store, the ups and downs of their courtship.

"It's been hard," she confessed. "He's so wonderful. And so darn *good*. I just feel I can never measure up to be the kind of woman he deserves."

"You're wrong," Amanda assured her. "No matter what your father ever said to you, you are worth the love of a good man. Never forget that."

Could it be true? Her father had proved to be a liar in every sense of the word. Why did she still let his judgments of her taint the way she saw herself?

"He'll be back tomorrow night," Dot said. "And I must admit, I'm nervous as a squirrel."

She'd invited Charlie to have Sunday-night supper at her place so he could meet her mother and sisters. He was supposed to arrive at six, but it couldn't have been later than four when she started to dress.

"What do you think?" she asked Rose, holding two different dresses and swapping them out in front of the mirror. "Yellow? Green?"

"Definitely yellow," Rose said. "It makes you look all sunshiny." So Dot put on the same dress she'd worn to the grand opening. She hoped it would spark good memories for Charlie and not bad memories of meeting Louie Braccio.

She had never spent much time in the kitchen, so she welcomed Amanda's help in pulling together the simple dinner of roast chicken, green beans, and apple pie. At precisely six o'clock, the buzzer sounded, and Charlie walked in carrying flowers and looking more handsome than Dot had ever seen him.

She made introductions all around. Her mother seemed shy at first, but she warmed up as Charlie put her at ease. As for her sisters, she could tell by the way they giggled and glowed that they admired him.

"Next time I'll have to bring my sister Helen," Charlie told them. "She's sixteen and a pistol. She'd like nothing better than to compare favorite movie stars with you."

After dinner, the girls cleaned the kitchen while Amanda wrapped up the extra food and stored it in the icebox for later in the week.

"Go for a walk?" Charlie suggested to Dot. She nodded, eager to spend some time alone with him.

He swung her hand as they strolled down the sidewalk. The leaves had a tinge of gold, and there was a slight nip in the air, cool and refreshing after the stuffy apartment.

"I'm sorry I've seemed so preoccupied lately," he said. "Pop's health and the Kerryville store have been absorbing all my available time and energy."

"I'm so relieved," she said. "I thought you were still angry with me about the burglary. Or taking another gander at Catherine Woodruff," she teased.

He smiled and shook his head. "Not at all. Catherine and I are friends, that's all. As for the burglary, you were absolutely right to stand up for Bianca. It would have been a serious mistake to let her go."

Dot struggled to find the right words. "It just seemed so unfair to hold her responsible for something someone else did. We should judge people on their own merits and not on the family they come from."

Charlie smiled. "Are you listening to yourself, Dot?"

She tilted her head to look up at him. "What?"

He lifted the hand he was holding and kissed the back of it. "You don't want to judge Bianca by her family. In the same way, you shouldn't judge your own worth by the behavior of your father. Whatever he's done or not done has nothing to do with you." He was right, of course. She no longer needed to order her life according to what Oliver Barker did or didn't do—either following his rules or rebelling against them with all her might. She was free to walk her own path. And since seeing her father in the character of Elmer Gantry, she understood that he was no reliable spokesman for Jesus.

"I've done as you suggested. I've been reading my Bible and praying."

"And?"

"And the lines of communication remain open."

They'd completed their walk around the block and were back on the sidewalk in front of her building. He stood quiet, looking down into her eyes. She held her breath, feeling pulled toward him as if by magnetic force.

"I'm awfully glad you're back," she whispered.

He didn't say anything. But his kiss told her everything she needed to know.

CHAPTER TWENTY-THREE

With Pop in stable health and business taken care of in Kerryville, Charlie resumed living in the space above the Oak Park store. Dot enjoyed helping him fix it up. They added new furniture, rugs, and paintings he could easily afford, thanks to his thriving investments and the success of the store. She secretly enjoyed thinking about how these things would look in the home they would share after they were married—*if* they were married.

After taking a leave of absence to care for Pop, Marjorie had resumed her job dressing windows at Marshall Field's, and she and Peter frequently joined Dot and Charlie for dinner. One person Dot did *not* see as much of was Veronica, who evidently had a new man in her life who was absorbing all her time. Happily, it appeared that Carlo was out of the picture. And Louie, bless his dark little heart, stayed away.

Later, Dot would remember the rich and golden autumn of 1929 as a productive and happy time. Radio announcers crowed about the flourishing stock market. Ladies scooped up yards of the most expensive fabrics that Corrigan's offered without a glance at the price tags. Theaters and restaurants were packed whenever Dot and Charlie went out together, which was often.

On nights when Rose was away at school in Indiana, Dot slept in her own apartment to give Mrs. Moran a break. So that's where she was one October night, lying awake with Trudy snoring gently beside her. A bright autumn moon shone through the window. She stared at it and thought about what Charlie had said.

You don't want to judge Bianca by her family. In the same way, you shouldn't judge your own worth by the behavior of your father. Whatever he's done or not done has nothing to do with you.

On a brisk October Sunday, without telling anyone, Dot rose before dawn and caught an early train to Valparaiso. She took a taxi to the jail, a grim limestone structure that squatted next to the stately county courthouse. The air was crisp and scented with burning leaves, a smell Dot had loved since childhood. But once inside the heavy doors, she held her handkerchief to her nose at the dank, unpleasant smell that greeted her. She checked in at the reception area and waited for someone to tell her where to go.

At last an attendant said, "This way," and led her down a narrow, dimly lit hallway to the visiting room, a dusty, cheerless place with cinder-block walls, a concrete floor, and a long table running down the center. A heavy wire screen separated the two sides of the table. No other visitors were in the room at the moment. The uniformed attendant pulled out a cold metal chair and invited her, or rather told her, to sit. Then he moved to the doorway, where his vantage point would allow him to keep an eye on everything that went on in the room.

Oliver Barker shuffled in through a doorway that Dot presumed led to the cell block. He looked thinner, paler, and older than Dot remembered. Weak, she thought, and tremulous, quite different from how he looked up on stage in front of a packed house, dangling false hope of miraculous healing in front of their eyes. On stage, he was meticulously groomed, dressed in finely tailored suits. Here, he wore a prison uniform, his hair a tousled mess. His unshaven face was expressionless, but she thought she saw a slight flicker in his eyes as he recognized her.

"Hello, Father," she said in a low-pitched voice. She bit her lip and held her breath to keep her emotions in check.

He didn't reply immediately, but as she watched, his expression hardened into defiance. After a moment, he said in a gravelly voice, "What are you doing here, Dorothy?"

Not even a hello. She swallowed her disgust. This man was her father, but she scarcely knew him.

"How are you?" She found herself barely able to look at him, so revolted was she by his mocking, sneering expression.

He sat on the metal chair on the opposite side of the heavy screen. He placed his folded hands on the scarred wooden table.

"I'm going to beat this accusation. They won't be able to prove anything."

Not a word asking after her mother or sisters. Or herself. Dot just nodded. There were no words. Silently she prayed to know what to say to this man, this stranger.

Finally she sorted out her words.

"I've come to tell you I forgive you, Father."

A spark of surprise crossed his dull-eyed face. "What did you say to me?" She could hear the anger simmering under the words.

"I forgive you," she repeated. "You threw me out of the house, told me I was a disgrace, but I did all right. I found my way."

He sneered. "Singing in a speakeasy. Dressing like a harlot. Always doing as you please. You're a selfish and ungrateful girl, always will be."

She drew herself up. "I don't think you're in a position to judge." She gave herself a moment to calm down, then continued. "It's not only for myself that I'm here. For years, you've told lies and misrepresented God and misled people into thinking you had the power to heal them. And you've treated Mother and the girls terribly. I'm glad you were caught, and I hope you receive the appropriate punishment."

He said nothing.

"But I forgive you. I sincerely hope that the Lord will touch your heart and give you genuine faith. It's not too late. As long as you're still breathing, it's not too late."

His voice was low and menacing. "I don't want you coming here again."

She returned his gaze. Then she reached into her handbag, pulled out a small Bible, and pushed it through the opening at the bottom of the screen.

"I'll pray for you. Good-bye."

She stood and nodded to the attendant, who opened the door for her. She returned down the dank hallway the way she'd come. When at last she burst out of the terrible building, she steadied herself against a railing and inhaled great lungfuls of fresh, cool, autumn-tinged air. Finally, her pulse slowed and her heartbeat returned to normal.

Then she straightened, hailed a taxi, directed the driver to take her to the train station, and moved forward into the rest of her life. She would not go back again.

CHAPTER TWENTY-FOUR

Toward the end of October, the crisp, beautiful weather had turned into a soggy chill that dampened spirits along with coats and hats. For at least a week, Charlie had been restless and ill at ease. There was a certain charge to the air, a jittery feeling that was palpable whenever he found himself out among other businessmen, at a coffee shop or on a streetcar. Words like "stock market," "margins," and "broker" seemed to be on everyone's lips. He reminded himself he had nothing to feel skittish about. The store was showing a healthy profit. He'd been able to raise both Dot's and Bianca's salaries. His most recent brokerage and bank statements showed only meteoric growth over the summer and early fall. But maybe that was the problem—the unprecedented growth, which should have made him ecstatic but instead gave him a sort of vertigo, like teetering on the highest step of a ladder. He felt constantly on edge. In the shop, he had to remind himself not to snap at Dot or Bianca out of sheer brittleness.

"Maybe it's this weather," Dot said one afternoon when he confided his anxious mood. She gazed out the display window. "Look at it out there. It's getting so dark and gloomy outside. Maybe a nice dinner at the Orange Garden will cheer you up. Let's go after work."

She slipped her hand into his. He felt soothed by her warmth and caring. But even her loving support and the prospect of a good meal at his favorite restaurant failed to dispel the sense of disquiet that reached down to his soul.

On the morning of October twenty-ninth, he drove into the Loop, rain spattering against the roadster's windshield, for a meeting with a representative of a fabric supply house. As long as he was in the city, he thought he might arrange to casually drop in at his stockbroker's office and receive some reassurance that his investments were indeed as sound as they seemed. Then he'd be able to rest easier. He tried to laugh at himself. *Good grief, I'm starting to turn all conservative and tight-*

fisted about money, like Pop.

His car was stopped at a red light when he saw, or rather heard, the shouts of the newsboy on the corner. "Get your paper here! Stock market plummets! Banks run out of money! Get your paper here!"

His meeting with the fabric supplier would have to wait. He hurried straight to the brokerage house.

Palms sweating in his fine leather driving gloves, Charlie maneuvered the roadster into a parking spot on a side street and stepped out. The atmosphere in Chicago's financial district was unusually electrified, like the moments before a lightning storm, and strangely muted. Men from all walks of life, from well-dressed executives to pushcart peddlers—gathered in clumps up and down LaSalle Street and spoke in fervent murmurs to one another. Some walked unseeing down the street as if their minds were miles away. Some faces bore angry expressions, others looked tight-lipped and scared, still others pale and confused. Crumpled bits of newspaper and ticker tape littered the street and clung damply to the gutters.

By the time he reached the skyscraper that housed his brokerage firm's offices, a crowd had gathered on the sidewalk outside the building. Two guards flanked the doors, forbidding anyone to enter. Angry shouts were building to a crescendo.

"I want my money!"

"Crooks!"

"Is it all gone?"

But the guards stood frozen like statues and refused to make eye contact with anyone.

It would be another day or two before Charlie understood the full extent of his losses, and another month before the bank called his loan.

But at that moment, somewhere deep in his gut, he knew.

His investments weren't worth the paper the statements were printed on. Financially, he was finished.

CHAPTER TWENTY-FIVE

In early December, while Bianca busied herself hanging holly and evergreens around the store, Dot stared at a ledger book and chewed the end of her pencil. Business at Corrigan's Oak Park store had fallen off. Knowing Charlie had suffered a severe financial loss in October's stock-market crash—but not knowing exactly how much—she was reluctant to burden him with more worries. Still, she was concerned. She had no desire to pry into his personal finances, but the store's well-being was a different matter. She would have to talk to him about it. For now, as it was payday, she wrote out a paycheck for Bianca, then quietly wrote her own out—for exactly half of its usual amount.

Not that she could get by on half her salary. Not for long, anyway. Not with three extra mouths to feed and certainly not after having given all her savings to her mother to help with her father's legal expenses and other burdens. These days, she needed every penny. But this was only temporary, that she was making a loan to the store that the store would pay back when business picked up.

But if it hadn't picked up by now, with the Christmas shopping season upon them, when would it?

Not for the first time, Dot thought of her safe, secure job at Marshall Field's. She closed the ledger with a decisive slam. No sense thinking about that now. Charlie needed her, and that was that.

A few days later when Charlie reviewed the books, he came to her, frowning and pointing to the entry for her paycheck.

"You can't do this, Dot."

She sighed. "How else are we going to balance the books?"

He ran a hand through his sandy hair, which she noticed was in need of a trim. "I'll figure something out."

Not knowing what to say, she placed her hand on his shoulder. He reached up, gave her hand an absent-minded pat, but the haunted look in his eyes told her his mind was elsewhere.

"I have to do something," she confided to Veronica later that week when they met for coffee. "We've hardly had any customers, even though it's the Christmas season. And those who do come in are buying necessities like thread, not the costly fabrics we really need to sell. It's my fault. I talked him into bringing in lots of silks and brocades. But nobody's going to balls. Or if they are, they're making over last year's gowns.

"Charlie still owes on the bank loan. If we don't come up with a chunk of money soon, we won't be able to make both the loan payment and the rent payment. The landlord is not prone to acts of charity. I'm afraid we're going to lose the store."

"Why doesn't he ask his father for the money?"

Dot shook her head. "I know Charlie. He'd rather chew tinfoil than ask his father for money," she said. "He'd close down the store first."

"I'd love to help you out, doll," Veronica said, "but I don't have that kind of dough. I don't know anybody who does. Except for Louie, of course. Why don't you ask him for a loan?" Veronica's dark eyes regarded her intently. "I'm sure he'd give it to you."

Was this a test? From Veronica, or from God? Either way, Dot wouldn't fail. She changed the subject.

"Tell me about this new man of yours," Dot said. "He's sure been keeping you busy. You're hardly ever available to go out with little old me."

Veronica stirred her coffee. "Oh, he's nice. A big spender and all that. But he's very busy. I have to spend time with him whenever he's available because I don't always know when the next time will be."

Dot frowned. "He's not married, is he?"

"No, but so what if he was?"

Dot opened her mouth, then shut it. It would be just like Veronica to do something wrong, just for the sake of doing it.

"You can meet him if you come to New Year's. He'll be there."

Dot shuddered. The last thing she wanted to do was go to another New Year's Eve party. Last year she'd thought Veronica's parties were the height of sophistication. Now they just seemed sad and ... well, kind of tacky. She looked forward to a quiet holiday spent somewhere warm and toasty with the man she loved.

When another week had passed with no improvement in either customer traffic or finances, Dot's concern deepened. Laboring over the ledger books in the quiet store, Charlie looked gaunt, gray shadows ringing his eyes. Obviously he wasn't sleeping well. Probably not eating well, either.

She walked up next to him and rubbed the back of his neck. He tensed.

"Can I get you anything?"

"A few hundred dollars would come in handy," he snapped.

She stepped back. "I meant a sandwich or something."

He dropped his pencil and rubbed his eyes. "I know. Sorry."

"I wish there were some way I could help."

He turned and slid his arms around her waist, drawing her close, his breath hot against her hair. "You do help. Just your being here helps."

But Dot knew it wasn't nearly enough. Veronica's suggestion rang in her head. The only person she knew with the kind of dough Charlie needed to keep his business running was Louie.

She knew Louie wouldn't deny her anything. Not if she really needed it, if she pleaded. Not if she promised ... promised what? Surely he would exact some price. The idea of owing Louie one single cent made her stomach churn.

Besides, Charlie would throw a fit if she tried to borrow money from her former beau. He'd never in a million years accept it.

But where else would the money come from?

But if he didn't know ... If she didn't tell him where the money came from ... just made up a story.

A *lie*, her conscience hissed.

A *story*, her brain hissed back.

She formulated a plan. It was risky, and frankly, made her a little dizzy with self-disgust. But this was no time to stand on ceremony. Charlie needed money, and there was no time to waste.

"I'm going to take off a little early tonight if it's okay with you," she said lightly.

From his perch over the ledger books, he grunted. "See you tomorrow."

She caught the streetcar to her flat, all the while questioning her sanity. But try as she might, she couldn't think of another way. In her apartment, she was relieved that nobody was around to ask uncomfortable questions. Her mother hadn't yet returned from work, and Trudy had gone to a school basketball game. She swallowed her pride, put on her prettiest dress, a cobalt-blue velvet with a pleated skirt and satin sash, and added the gold earrings Louie had given her.

He'd mentioned once that he especially liked them. Maybe seeing them would bring to mind his past generosity. She splurged on a taxi to take her to his new restaurant, the Trattoria Fiorenza. The doorman scrutinized her closely and let her pass. She descended a set of stairs. At the bottom, she heard the throbbing rhythm of a jazz band, smelled the familiar scents of garlic, cigarette smoke, perfume, and gin.

Family restaurant, my eye. It was another speakeasy, looking for all the world like the Villa Italiana, only even more elegant and expensive.

She shouldn't have been surprised.

Arranging her features into a brilliant smile, she scanned the room for Louie and spotted him next to the stage talking to a pretty girl in a skintight evening gown. The girl smiled down at him from the stage, then took her place before the microphone and began to croon a hit song.

A year and a half ago, that girl was me. Who knew so much could happen in so short a time?

She caught Louie's gaze. His black eyes lit up when he saw her, then his handsome face broke into a grin. He made his way toward her across the crowded dance floor.

"Dottie! What a swell surprise." He lifted her hand in his own and kissed it. She cringed but outwardly only deepened her dimples in a coquettish smile.

"Come on back where we can talk." He led the way to a small office under the stairs. Passing a waiter, he barked, Two Scotch and waters."

"Oh, nothing for me, thanks," Dot said quickly. She had to stay alert, keep her wits about her. Louie shrugged. "Just one, then." The waiter scurried off.

Louie ushered her into the office and shut the door behind them, muting the clamor. She took a seat in a leather chair across from his polished-walnut desk. "To what do I owe the pleasure of your company?" Louie asked, half sitting on the edge of the desk.

Dot twisted the handle of her beaded bag in her hands and tried to sound lighthearted.

"Oh, I thought it was time I finally got a look at your new place."

He quirked an eyebrow. "And?"

"And ... and to ask if you can lend me some money. I'm in kind of a jam."

He folded his arms. "What kind of a jam?"

The waiter brought in the drink and set it on a side table, then exited.

Dot used the interruption to collect her thoughts. Charlie would be deeply ashamed if he knew she were here, begging for money to save his store. He would never accept Louie's money, not in a million years. And Louie might not even give it if he knew she'd use it to help Charlie.

"I ... I'd rather not say." She looked down at her lap.

"Hey." Louie gently lifted her chin so her gaze was level with his. "Don't be like that. I heard all about the trouble with your father being put in the slammer and all."

She blinked at him but said nothing.

"And I know you got your mother and sisters living with you now. I find that very admirable. Family is very important to me, you know." He lowered his hand. His eyes lit up as if he'd just remembered something. "In fact, at this very moment, my mother and aunts are in the restaurant kitchen, preparing cannoli for Christmas dinner. They said they wanted more elbow room, but it hasn't stopped them from squabbling. Want I should introduce you?"

Dot shook her head. The idea of someone as ruthless as Louie Braccio having a mother seemed incongruous. But then, she supposed that even Al Capone had a mother.

She exhaled sharply. She mustn't forget what she came for. She blinked again, allowing a small tear to form in the corner of her right eye.

Louie's eyes softened. "So you got expenses," he said. "That ain't nothing to be ashamed of."

He looked at her for a long moment, then walked around the desk, opened a drawer, and pulled out a leather-bound check register. He picked up a fountain pen and uncapped it.

"You must never be ashamed to come to me for money, Dottie," he said. "You know I'd do anything for you."

She swallowed hard. "Thank you, Louie. I'll pay you back just as soon as I can. Every penny. With interest."

"You don't owe me nothing, baby." His pen scratched across the paper. Then his gaze locked on hers. "Consider it a gift."

Deep inside, Dot knew that with Louie Braccio, there was no such thing as a gift. There'd be a price for this, sooner or later. But she couldn't worry about that now. She had to help Charlie save the store. His livelihood and hers and Bianca's depended on it.

With a flourish, Louie ripped the check out of the register and handed it to Dot. She glanced at the amount, pressed her lips together to suppress a cry at the high figure. It would solve all Charlie's problems, at least temporarily. As for how they'd pay it back ... well, business would pick up soon. She was sure it would.

Suddenly, the numbers on the check blurred. The room seemed to tilt. She laid a hand on the mahogany desk to steady herself. The thought of Charlie made her stomach roil. What would he think if he knew what she was doing? What *was* she doing? Had she finally sunk this low as to accept Louie's dirty money? No amount was worth the price it would ultimately cost.

Louie stood and walked toward her with a look of concern. "You all right, Dottie? You need a drink?"

She let the check flutter to the desk and fought to keep her voice steady.

"I ... I've made a big mistake coming here. Thank you for your generosity, but ... I'm sorry."

She turned and fled the office. Louie's voice called after her but was drowned out by the jazz music from the stage. She ran past the bouncer, who gave her a puzzled look but thankfully didn't try to stop her.

When she reached the street, she took great, gulping gasps. "Thank you, Lord," she breathed as she hailed the first cab she saw. "Thank you."

As the cab crawled through rush-hour traffic on the long ride to her neighborhood, she leaned her head against the window and sifted through her options. She could try to get her old job back at Field's. Then she wouldn't need to draw a salary from Charlie. But that still wouldn't be enough to help him save the store.

From the front seat, she heard a crackling sound. She looked up to see the driver fiddling with a knob on the dashboard.

"Is there something wrong with the cab?" she asked with concern.

"No, ma'am." The cabbie smiled at her over his shoulder. "This here's a radio. Listen." He turned the knob. Dot leaned forward and, through the crackling, she could make out the tune of a Christmas carol, sounding tinny and far away.

"A radio in an automobile," she said. "That's amazing."

"Ain't coming out for a few months yet," the cabbie said, "but I got to test out this one and let 'em know how I like it. My brother-in-law works at the company that makes it, see?" He sounded quite proud. "It's like a Victrola that goes in a motor car, so they call it a Motorola. Get it?"

"It's really something," Dot agreed. Charlie would love a radio to put in Better-than-Betty. But there'd be no money for Christmas presents this year.

Charlie. How could she help him? She'd never been any help to anybody. *You selfish girl.* She had come so close to making a huge mistake. She felt as if she had nothing left.

The Christmas carol crackling over the radio drew to a close, and another song began. Half consciously, she found herself breathing the familiar lyrics.

She gazed out the window as the cab slowly passed a downtown church, its great wooden doors decorated with evergreen boughs, cheery red ribbons glowing in the setting sun. Through the gathering dusk, a lighted sign advertised an evening carol sing. She'd never felt less Christmassy. And yet she envied the people passing through the doors. They seemed so assured. So comforted.

Forget what Oliver Barker had taught her about faith and the people who had it. They weren't weak. They weren't easily duped. They weren't hypocrites.

They were right.

Oh, Lord," she silently prayed. *"I'm a mess. I can't even begin to put things right. But You can. I want to follow You. Help me understand You. Show Charlie and me which way to go."*

She prayed until the taxi turned onto her street. As she gathered up her handbag, something fell onto her lap. It was a gold earring, the same one that had fallen off and gotten misplaced months earlier in Charlie's car. The clasp must have been loose. She'd have to try to fix it, or it would keep falling off. And a single earring without its mate was useless. Come to think of it, the complete pair was pretty useless too. While she loved them, and she sensed they were valuable, they only reminded her of bad things. Of Louie, and of speakeasies, and of the kind of life she wanted to leave behind. She ought to get rid of them.

Something hitched within her chest.

Get rid of them.

Turning the earring over in her hand, she had a sudden inspiration. The cab pulled up in front of her building. She opened the door.

"Can you wait here a few minutes, please? There's somewhere else I need to go."

The cabbie nodded and put the vehicle in park. She slid out and scurried into the building and up the stairs to her apartment. She yanked open the top drawer of her dresser and grabbed her jewelry box, then ran downstairs again. Out of breath, she gasped instructions to the cabbie.

"Hurry, please. We don't have much time."

Indeed, the cab pulled up in front of the pawn shop just as the proprietor was covering the display window for the night.

Dot thrust some bills at the driver. "Keep the change." Clutching her jewelry box, she slid out of the cab, ran to the door of the shop, and pulled. It was locked. She caught the eye of the proprietor within. He pointed to his wristwatch and shook his head.

"Please. Oh, please," Dot said. "It's an emergency." She turned on her most beseeching smile.

The proprietor glanced upward, then unlocked the door and muttered, "It's always an emergency. You might as well come in."

"Bless you," she said as she slid past him. He grimaced as he locked the door behind her, then lumbered to the counter.

"Whatcha got?" he said, sounding bored. Dot set the box on the counter and opened it. The man's face brightened a bit when he saw its contents.

"Say, this is some good stuff." He picked up a necklace and squinted at it under the lamp on the counter. Then he glanced at her sharply.

"Hot?"

"What? No." Dot shook her head, her face heating with embarrassment as she grasped his meaning. "These are certainly not stolen goods," she said, her dignity wounded. Although with a fellow like Louie, how could one be sure? She swallowed her pride and smiled at the man. Too late to worry about that now.

He continued sifting through the box, then named a price Dot thought was too low. They debated for several minutes, then he landed on a figure that pleased her.

"My final offer," he said.

"Deal," she said.

As she left the shop with money fattening her purse, she smiled with satisfaction. Louie had helped her and Charlie out of a jam after all, but not in the way anyone would suspect. And by selling every bit of jewelry he'd given her, she'd removed the last traces of him from her life.

※

The next day, Charlie stared in amazement at the check Dot handed him.

"This is more than generous," he said, his voice thick with emotion. "This is … out of this world." To his horror, tears stung the backs of his eyelids. "Are you sure you can afford this?"

"Sure, I'm sure." Dot perched on the arm of his chair and smoothed the back of his hair. "I happened to come into a little money, and I thought that investing in the store was as good a way to spend it as any." No need to tell Charlie she'd sold her fine jewelry. She still had her costume stuff, and frankly, she didn't think he'd know the difference.

"This is much more than just 'a little money.' I … I don't know what to say."

She pressed her cheek against his.

"Say you love me."

"I do. You know I do."

The money paid off the loan and bought him some time, but business continued to be slow. It seemed that no one, from the fanciest seamstress to the humblest housewife, was feeling much like spending these days.

CHAPTER TWENTY-SIX

On Christmas Eve, Charlie and Bianca were the only ones left in the store. With dismayingly few customers to serve, considering it was ordinarily a busy shopping day, he let Dot leave early so she could help Marjorie prepare for the evening's festivities. The Corrigans and Barkers, including Amanda, Rose, and Trudy, were to celebrate the holiday at the Bachmanns'. Since Charlie, Dot, and Marjorie all had to work the day after Christmas, it seemed more prudent for the rest of the Corrigans to drive in from Kerryville for the holiday, rather than the other way around. Charlie knew that, right after the holidays, he and Pop would have to have a serious conversation about the future of the store. But first, he would enjoy celebrating the birth of Jesus with all the family together.

Bianca was dusting a shelf that she'd already dusted earlier in the afternoon while Charlie swept the floor. With no customers present, they chitchatted about their respective plans for the holiday. Then the girl said, "I think it's wonderful that Miss Rodgers is going to start singing again. She has such a pretty voice. I loved it when she sang with the choir at the settlement house."

Charlie glanced up from the broom. "Singing? Like at church?" He was pleased that Dot had started attending Sunday services with him.

"No, I mean, at my cousin's restaurant."

It took him a moment to grasp her meaning. His blood ran cold.

"What are you talking about? She's not singing at any restaurant."

Bianca shrugged. "It's just that I was over there the other day, making cannoli with my mother and aunts, and she was there. I saw her."

"Dot—Miss Rodgers was there?"

Bianca nodded. "Yeah, but she left before I could speak to her. She seemed in kind of a hurry. I asked my cousin about it later, and he said she'd come to ask him about singing."

"I see." Charlie's mind whirled as everything clicked into place.

So that's where she'd gotten the extra money she'd given him to make the loan payment. She'd gone begging to Louie for it. And he'd given it to her, agreed to hire her back on as a singer. She'd gone behind his back, and now Louie knew all about the store being in trouble. He was probably gloating. There was no way Charlie could use Louie's dirty money to save the store, or he'd never be rid of the creep.

Except he'd already made the loan payment. The money was gone. Well, he'd just have to figure out a way to pay it back. Every cent.

And as for Dot ... well, if she was still comfortable taking money from Louie Braccio, however well intentioned, and then lie about it, then she was not the girl for him.

Inwardly distraught but outwardly calm, Charlie wished Bianca a merry Christmas and let her go home. He fumbled with the locks, then stood shaking for several minutes, trying to think. He needed to find a way to pay Louie back, the quicker, the better. But how?

Worst of all, the cause of all the trouble was Dot.

Somehow, he managed to finish up at the store. On the silent drive to the Bachmanns' apartment, he played through possible scenarios in his mind. How he'd talk to her about it. What he'd say. What she'd say.

But the only thing he managed when she greeted him with a cheerful "There you are!" and tried to kiss him, was "How could you?"

Her eyes looked huge. He'd frightened her, and it broke his heart. He hated talking to her this way, but when he thought of her begging for money from that dirty scoundrel ...

He grabbed Dot's arm. "Get your coat. We're going for a walk."

They ended up standing in the freezing vestibule of the apartment building, their breath steaming up the windows, so as not to argue in front of the rest of the family.

"You went to see Louie. You asked him for money."

Her eyes grew huge. "How did you—?"

He didn't let her finish. "Now I need to pay him back every red cent. Where am I going to get that kind of money?" he hissed.

Dot reached for him. "You don't understand—"

He pulled away. "No, *you* don't understand. How could you go to him for help, after all he's done?"

Her face looked stricken. "If you'd just let me explain."

His eyes locked with hers. "I don't want to hear it. You sold out to Louie."

Something changed in her face. She was no longer pleading, but angry. Her voice was cold.

"I didn't."

"What were you doing over at his place, then?"

"I did go to Louie."

Charlie snorted in disgust.

Dot continued. "I'm sorry I didn't tell you the truth. I was afraid that if I did, you'd talk me out of it."

"You're darn right."

"I had every intention of asking him for money. He was the only person I could think of who had any. I thought if we could just get enough for the loan payment, we'd be able to keep the doors open longer. Then business would pick up, and we'd get back to normal."

"And now we owe hundreds of dollars to an ex-con."

"We owe him nothing because I didn't end up taking the money."

"What?"

"I knew it was wrong. Felt it in my bones. So I got out of there quick."

"So then where'd you get the money?"

"I pawned all my jewelry."

His heart melted. "You did what?"

"Pawned my jewelry." She sighed, looked away. "So now you know."

He reached for her, but this time, she was the one who backed away.

"I'm sorry, honey. I didn't know."

"I should never have gone to Louie's without letting you know. That was wrong. But you were wrong, too, to think the worst of me before bothering to find out the truth."

"I'm sorry," he repeated. "But when it sounded like you were tied up with him again, I lost my head."

"Because that's the kind of woman you think I am."

"No! That's not it at all. I just ..." Words failed him.

She said nothing, just looked small and tired and cold. He longed to wrap her in his arms, to make her understand how truly sorry he was, but her weary gaze held him at bay.

"I'll pay you back every cent," he vowed.

"You don't have to do that," she said. "I'll continue to work for you until you can afford a replacement. Then after that ..." She drew a deep breath. "After that, I think it would be a good idea if you live your life and I live mine."

CHAPTER TWENTY-SEVEN

It had been a hard winter and spring—harder than it had to be. Dot knew that Charlie regretted accusing her of asking Louie for money. But the truth was, he hadn't been wrong to make that assumption. She had planned to do exactly that and would have if she hadn't changed her mind at the last minute. Chickened out, more likely. And if it weren't that screw-up, it would be another, eventually. Charlie needed a good woman in his life, someone with strength of character, and she wasn't that woman. She wasn't good, and she wasn't strong. She'd never be anything but what she was, what her father always said she was. *You stupid, selfish girl.* She'd tried to be unselfish, tried to be useful to someone for once in her life. But even her attempt to help turned sour. Everyone would be better off if she minded her own business.

Day after day, Dot and Charlie and Bianca worked hard to keep the store going. If Bianca noticed a certain coolness between her coworkers, a brisk and businesslike attitude brushed with a thin layer of disappointment and a spattering of anger, she didn't let on.

In January, Dot had started attending a Bible study at the Chicago church the Bachmanns attended. The class was the first step in unlearning the false religion of her father and soaking in the truth. She made friends in the class, and soon, her calendar was peppered with invitations to join them on toboggan runs and automobile rides, helping somewhat, but never completely, to ease the loneliness of losing Charlie. Most important, they encouraged her to follow Jesus, the One who accepted her, failings and all. Her soul was healing.

Easter Sunday, she was seated in a pew beside Marjorie, Peter, and her mother and sisters in the stately, lily-festooned sanctuary, thinking of Charlie, as she often did. She knew he was heartsore that she wouldn't give their relationship another chance. She didn't know whether he'd ever forgive her for hurting him, even though it was for his own good. But she knew for certain that Somebody had. As the pipe organ pealed the opening notes of a hymn, she stood, along with the rest of the congregation, and began to sing, glancing at the words in the blue leather-bound hymnal.

"Christ the Lord is risen today, Alleluia."

Her spirit soared along with her voice. As warmth spread in her chest, the truth settled in her heart. She belonged here. These were her people.

And this was exactly the place where God wanted her to sing.

In the end, in spite of the cash from the pawned jewelry that helped keep the business going through the winter and early spring, the store could not be saved. Customer traffic simply didn't pick up enough in the new year to make enough of a profit to meet the loan payments and keep up with the rent. They were bringing in less than it cost to keep the doors open. Charlie made the hard decision to close the store at the end of April, almost exactly one year after its grand opening. A large fabric dealer in the garment district snapped most of the inventory and fixtures, at a considerable loss. The landlord hired a rental agent to look for a replacement tenant.

In late April, the sun-dappled streets of Kerryville, fragrant with the moist, earthy scent of spring, belied the discouragement that was in Charlie's heart as he puttered up Maple Street in old Betty. His hometown looked the same as it always had, as long as he could remember—the Victorian houses with their cupolas and wide porches, their green lawns and stately elm trees, the brilliant yellow forsythia and lacy canopy of budding leaves arching overhead. Soon, the lilacs would burst into bloom. He felt as if the calendar had fluttered back two years, before he'd ever thought of opening a branch store or bought a slick automobile or a new suit of clothes. When he was just old Charlie Corrigan, working in his family's store, living under his father's roof. But no matter how hard he wished, there was no turning back the clock. What was done could not be undone. He'd sold the roadster, the swanky suits, practically everything he owned—at least, everything he could find a buyer for—in order to pay his debt. And now he felt as old as Father Time whose youthful dreams had soured.

The one bright spot was his longtime friend Riley, who'd been willing to sell Charlie's old car back to him for a song. Good old Betty was as loyal and sturdy as ever, and sitting in her driver's seat felt, in a strange sort of way, like coming home.

He parked her on the street in front of the Corrigan house. Pop was sitting on the porch, enjoying the warm evening, reading the paper and puffing on his pipe. The spicy tobacco scent on the evening breeze carried Charlie back to his boyhood when things had seemed so much simpler. Even through the war, even through his years of pain and rehabilitation, discouragement had never weighed as heavily on his heart as it did this night.

He trudged up the steps and sat on a wicker chair that creaked loudly under his weight.

"Sounds like this old porch furniture's on its last legs," he commented idly.

Pop set aside the paper and tapped the bowl of his pipe. "This furniture's been around for a generation. It's a lot more resilient than it seems. Nothing a fresh coat of paint can't cure. I expect my grandkids will sit on it. "

Charlie wished with all his heart that that were true. But some things couldn't be fixed, no matter how pretty you made them look.

They sat in silence for a while, listening to the crickets. Then Charlie cleared his throat.

"I just dropped off some leftover inventory at the store. Stuff the buyer didn't want. The rental agent says he's found a potential renter to take over the lease." He grimaced. "It's been hard to see everything go."

Pop's eyes held genuine sympathy. "I'm sorry, son."

"I feel like I've lost everything."

"It's not as bad as all that. We still have our store here in Kerryville. And we'll be here as long as ladies need yard goods and needles and thread. You've got a roof over your head, and you've got old Betty back. You'll start again. You'll find your way."

"You've every right to say, 'I told you so.' You tried to warn me, but I wouldn't listen."

Pop was silent for a few minutes. "When I was your age—younger than you, even—I had an idea to open a store of my own."

Charlie shifted in his chair, making it squeak. "I know. You opened Corrigan's."

"No, this was before that. A different Corrigan's." Pop smiled, and a dreamy look came into his eyes. "Corrigan's Bicycle Shop."

Charlie perked up in surprise. "I didn't know you had a business before the dry goods store."

"It's not something I talk about much," Pop said ruefully. "Oh, I was crazy about athletics back then—too scrawny to qualify for any teams, but an avid fan. The one thing I did do well was ride my bicycle. I tooled all over town on that thing, the first in town, one of those old contraptions with the great big wheel in front and a tiny one in back." He shook his head, smiling. "I was something. Kids used to pay me a penny to let them ride it.

"When I graduated from high school, I thought that what this town needed was a shop devoted to selling bicycles. I had a little retail experience, bagging groceries after school. But I was dumber than a post." He laughed and shook his head. "My father tried to talk me out of it. He said, 'Son, if you want to build a business that will last, don't sell bicycles. Carry something that people will need to buy over and over again, come hell or high water.'"

"But you didn't listen."

"Of course not. I took some money my grandparents had sent me for graduation, and I rented that little space next to the train station, where the newsstand is now. Turned a tidy profit for about four, six months. Learned the retailing business from the ground up. A trial by fire, let me tell you."

"What happened?"

Pop took a puff on his pipe. "Two things. First, winter happened. People wanted bicycles in the summertime, and a few people bought them as Christmas presents. But then the snow flew, and people stopped thinking about bicycles. And then Meyer's Department Store happened. They opened up on Main Street the spring after I did. Bought up bicycles in quantity and sold them for a fraction of what I was able to sell them for. I limped through that second summer, but by August, I was through."

"Why didn't you ever tell me this before?"

Pop shrugged. "Felt foolish, I guess. I wanted my son to have it easier than I did. But experience is the best teacher. You gave it your all. And the fact that the new store failed wasn't your fault. Seems the whole country's headed for some hard times." He sat forward. "None of us knows what the future will bring. But we've made it through lean times before, and we'll do it again. Some things are certain, no matter what. You'll always have the Lord, and you'll always have me." He placed his hand on his chest. "At least as long as this old ticker keeps going."

"You'll be here a long time, Pop."

"Your God, your family, and your friends will see you through." Then he glanced at Charlie and added nonchalantly, "And the love of a good woman never hurts."

The words hit their mark. Charlie stood, walked to the edge of the porch, and leaned against a pillar.

"I really thought she went to her old boyfriend—a gangster, mind you, a convicted criminal—to get money to bail out the business. When all she did was sell the jewelry he'd given her to get me out of a jam. I was so wrong."

"From where I sit, she risked everything to help you. Sounds like true love to me. That's not the sort of thing a man should take lightly."

The breeze picked up and fluttered the budding branches as twilight fell over the quiet street. From inside the house, Frances called, "Supper." Pop folded his newspaper and stood.

"Think about what I've said."

"I will."

Charlie stood for another few minutes on the porch. He had a word with God—about his future, about his finances, and about a certain girl with smooth dark hair and big brown eyes.

The warm breeze ruffled his hair. And when he finally turned to go inside, his step wasn't quite so heavy.

In the quiet of the store, stripped bare of everything but the fixtures, Dot lovingly swept the wooden floor with a long-handled broom. She felt as if she were sweeping up shards of her broken heart along with the lint and bits of thread, the only reminders that the magnificent Corrigan's branch store had ever existed. It had been a fantastic dream, a marvelous adventure. But now it was over.

She'd gotten her old job back, at Field's in the Loop. Mrs. Carlson had been gracious about letting her reapply, and although quitting had cost her seniority, she was confident that her knack for selling hats would help her move quickly back up the ranks. As for opening a shop of her own someday ... well, that dream could wait. Lord willing, there'd be time enough for that later. She'd learned a lot about the retail business from working at Corrigan's, as well as at Field's, and the lessons wouldn't go to waste. In time, God would work everything out for good.

Her heart was heavy, but her faith was strong.

She rested an elbow on the broom handle and looked out the wide display window, where a Space-For-Rent sign now hung. Outside, traffic rolled up and down Lake Street as if it were an ordinary Sunday, as if nothing unusual had happened. As if a man's dream—and, yes, a woman's—hadn't gone up in a puff of smoke.

As she watched, an old black Model T chugged up the street and parked next to the curb. Dot smiled in spite of herself. The jalopy looked for all the world like old Betty. Then the driver got out, and she gasped. It *was* old Betty, and that was Charlie, coming to the door. Hastily Dot smoothed her hair and hoped she didn't look too frightful in her cleaning clothes.

The passenger door opened. Who was that? She hoped it was Helen or Marjorie. Her heart sank as she saw the auburn curls. It was Catherine.

He'd brought Catherine to the store.

It was too late to run out the back door, to pretend she hadn't been there. She leaned the broom against a wall and pasted on a brave smile as the couple walked in.

"Hello," Dot said. "I was just taking care of a few last-minute details. The rental agent will be picking up the keys this afternoon." She heard herself babbling and forced a smile.

"Thanks for taking care of that," Charlie said. "Dot, you remember Catherine Woodruff? Catherine, Dot Rodgers."

"I remember you from Marjorie's wedding," Catherine said. "You're a wonderful dancer."

"Thank you." Dot's face heated at the unexpected compliment. At least Charlie had chosen someone kind to spend the rest of his life with. Maybe Marjorie's worries about Catherine's character were unfounded. Still, seeing the two of them together made her jaw ache from clenching. She reached for the broom and attacked the already clean floor with unnecessary vigor.

Charlie spoke up. "The agent asked to do a final walk-through with me. He'll be glad to see we're leaving the place in ace condition."

Out of the corner of her eye, she watched him step into the middle of the room and look around with a wistful expression. Catherine joined him, standing close.

"I wish I'd seen the store when it was thriving," her low voice murmured. "I'll bet it was something else. But Corrigan's Kerryville is a fine store, too."

Dot swept harder, the bristles whisking violently across the wooden floor.

Charlie nodded. Her heart cracked open afresh, sensing his disappointment and dashed hopes that lay behind his silence. She tried to think of something encouraging to say, something to outdo Catherine in sympathetic allure, but she had few words.

"I see you got old Betty back."

"The guy I sold her to was willing to sell her back to me. I unloaded the Packard at a loss."

"I'm so sorry."

He shrugged. "Good riddance, if you ask me. She turned out to be more trouble than she was worth."

Dot swallowed hard. *Like me*. She caught Charlie's gaze. They looked at each other for a long moment.

Catherine cleared her throat, "Well, I'll be off to Aunt Sylvie's then. I'll just get my bag out of the car. Thank you so much for the lift." With a little wave, she turned and walked out the door, which still tinkled cheerfully in spite of the circumstances.

Dot frowned. "Who is Aunt Sylvie?"

"A relative who lives here in Oak Park. Catherine's going to stay with her for a bit while she figures out what to do next with her life."

Dot turned to Charlie, tilted her head. "You mean she's not with you?"

He rubbed his chin and gave her a quizzical look. "I gave her a ride since I was coming this way anyway. But no, we're not together. Whatever gave you that idea?"

"It's just that you and she …" Dot faltered. "Never mind."

"Speaking of living with relatives, I'm back living with Pop and Frances. Just like it was before … before everything."

"I got my old job back at the downtown Field's," Dot said. "It's almost as if none of this ever happened." She wrung her hands, swallowed her pain. "Except it did happen."

"And we tried so hard to save it. You sacrificed so much. And it wasn't even your store."

She focused her gaze on the broom handle. "Made no difference. It felt like mine. I wanted what you wanted."

She sensed his strong gaze on her face, willing her to look at him. "I'm so sorry I doubted you about where you got the money," he said.

"You don't know how often I've wished I could take back my words."

Dot waved his words away. "Water under the bridge. I might have thought the same as you if I didn't have all the facts. If the economy had turned around, it would have worked, too. If business had picked up … If, if, if. Seems we were going to lose the store no matter what we did." She looked around at the bare walls. "We had some good times, didn't we?"

"Sure." He scrubbed a hand over his face, his smile tinged with bitterness. "I had a ring for you, you know."

Her breath hitched. "I didn't know."

"It's gone now. Gone to pay the bank, along with practically everything else I owned."

Her vision blurred. She reached out and gently touched his arm. Her voice was quiet, her words carefully chosen.

"I would have cherished a ring from you."

"Would you have?" He shook his head. "Who did I think I was to try to be a hotshot dry-goods dealer? Some dream."

"It was a great dream, Charlie. It still is. It's just that now is not the time. God knows. He's got a plan."

"I know. I know He's in control. But sometimes …" His voice trailed off.

She set aside the broom, stepped closer, and put a hand on his shoulder. "You're still a hotshot to me, you know."

He took her hands. "I was going to make it rich, Dot. I was going to be the guy with the goods, the guy who would win your heart. But I failed."

"What made you think I wanted a rich big shot?" Her voice wavered. "I don't care about being rich or having jewelry or a nice car, or any of that." She glanced out the front window. "Old Betty looks as fine as Cinderella's coach to me."

He looked doubtful. "I live in Kerryville. Probably always will. And you love the city."

"I don't love the city more than I love you."

He dropped her hands, looked at the floor. "You shouldn't have to work multiple jobs just to stay afloat. I want to take care of you. But I can't do that now."

"You do take care of me, silly." She moved still closer and caressed his lapel. "You take care of my heart. That's the one thing I *do* want."

"Even now?"

"Even now."

His crystal-blue eyes were soft, glowing as if through a sheen of tears. He took her in his arms. Her tummy fluttered as she slid her arms around his neck and dropped her head to his shoulder, where it belonged. The flannel of his jacket pressed warm and comforting under her cheek.

She was still locked in the intoxicating strength of his embrace when the rental agent arrived, clearing his throat. Laughing, Charlie walked through the store with him, making notes, while Dot finished sweeping. Then together they climbed into old Betty and chugged away to their future. Whatever God had in store for them, they would face it together.

THE END

AUTHOR'S NOTE

Readers have asked me how much of *Ain't Misbehavin'* is true. It is a work of fiction, with invented characters, settings, and details. All of the primary characters and the entire plot are fictional.

Marshall Field & Co. was a real department store, one of the most elegant of its day. Today it is a Macy's, but the old "Field's," as the locals call it, is still missed by many longtime Chicagoans. The Oak Park branch store, where Dot works, opened in 1929 and closed in 1986. The Field's employees mentioned in the book are fictional except for Marcella Hahner, who established Field's book department in 1914 and headed it until her retirement in 1941. A skilled marketer, Mrs. Hahner is credited with such bookselling innovations as the book fair and the author book signing. Other businesses mentioned in the story—Peterson's ice cream shop (opened 1925) and The Berghoff restaurant (opened 1898)—are both still operating in 2017.

The St. Valentine's Day Massacre took place on February 14, 1929, when seven men were gunned down in a garage by rival gang members posing as police officers. While notorious gangster Al Capone is widely suspected of ordering the hit, he was in Florida at the time and never formally charged. The case remains unsolved and crime historians are divided as to who was ultimately responsible. The garage was later torn down and is now a parking lot.

Another real-life event referenced in *Ain't Misbehavin'* was "Black Tuesday," the stock-market crash of October 29, 1929, which ushered in the Great Depression.

ACKNOWLEDGMENTS

To God be the glory.
I offer my deepest thanks to:

Pegg Thomas, Robin Patchen, and the hardworking team at Smitten Historical Romance and Lighthouse Publishing of the Carolinas, experts at turning straw into gold;

Anita Aurit, Cassandra Cridland, Terese Luikens, Grace Robinson, and Melissa Bilyeu, cherished writer friends who temper their honest feedback with kindness and general hilarity;

The staffs of the Newbery Library, Chicago Historical Society, and Chicago Public Library for research help and serious answers to oddball questions;

The Lamont and Leo families for their unwavering support of my writing endeavors;

My husband, Thomas Leo, without whom none of this would be possible;

And thanks to you, dear reader. As Dot would say, you're the bee's knees. Please visit my website at http://jenniferlamontleo.com to join the reader community or drop me a line. I'd love to hear from you.

Made in the USA
San Bernardino, CA
16 March 2018